THE WICKED
LORD RASENBY

For J always. Just love

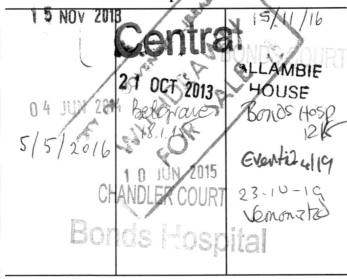

Kit stood and raised a hand to help Clarissa out of her seat.

Taking her by surprise, he pulled her close, one arm around her slim waist, cool on her skin through the thin fabric of her dress, the other tilting her chin upwards.

'No women other than you? You ask a lot of me. I think a sample of the merchandise would be appropriate, don't you agree? Just to prove you are worth the sacrifice. I warn you, my fair Clarissa, I won't be cheated, and I won't let you go back on your bargain. You do realise that?'

Clarrie licked her full bottom lip nervously, but made no move to escape. The sensation of his hand on her body was sending shivers up her spine. She had never been so close to a man before, and had had no idea that it could be so very exciting.

'A kiss, to seal a bargain then,' she whispered.

Kit laughed, low and aroused.

'You are sealing a bargain with the devil.'

His lips brushed hers, smooth and cool at first, a feather-light touch at the corners of her mouth. He ran his tongue over her full bottom lip. She smelled of roses and vanilla, and tasted sweet and hot. Her breath was warm, her breathing shallow.

Clarrie sighed at his touch. She could feel the heat from his body building a slow fire somewhere deep inside her.

She wanted more.

Born and educated in Scotland, **Marguerite Kaye** originally qualified as a lawyer, but chose not to practice—a decision which was a relief, both to her and the Scottish legal establishment. While carving out a successful career in IT, she occupied herself with her twin passions of studying history and reading, picking up a first-class honours and a Masters degree along the way.

The course of her life changed dramatically when she found her soul mate. After an idyllic year out, spent travelling round the Mediterranean, Marguerite decided to take the plunge and pursue her life-long ambition to write for a living, a dream she had cherished ever since winning a national poetry competition at the age of nine.

Just like one of her fictional heroines, Marguerite's fantasy has become reality. She has published history and travel articles, as well as short stories, but romances are her passion. Marguerite describes Georgette Heyer and Doris Day as her biggest early influences, and her partner as her inspiration.

This is Marguerite Kaye's debut novel for Mills & Boon® Historical Romance

THE WICKED
LORD RASENBY

Marguerite Kaye

First published in Great Britain 2009
Large Print edition 2009
Harlequin Mills & Boon Limited,
Eton House, 18-24 Paradise Road, Richmond, Surrey TW9 1SR

© Marguerite Kaye 2009

ISBN: 978 0 263 20682 1

Set in Times Roman 16 on 17¾ pt.
42-1109-82978

Harlequin Mills & Boon policy is to use papers that are natural, renewable and recyclable products and made from wood grown in sustainable forests. The logging and manufacturing process conform to the legal environmental regulations of the country of origin.

Printed and bound in Great Britain
by CPI Antony Rowe, Chippenham, Wiltshire

Prologue

1798—Sussex coast

As the clouds cleared, revealing the moon shining high in the night sky, Kit cursed under his breath. He had counted on the cover of darkness until they safely made landfall. Under the relentless beam of the nearly full moon, the *Sea Wolf* would be in full view as she stole into the remote cove, and that was the last thing he wanted. Surely his luck would hold. After all, it always had until now.

Casting a glance over his shoulder at the two huddled figures on deck, he gestured them to go below. *'Allez, vite'*. Placing a finger over his mouth, indicating silence, he returned his anxious gaze to the shore line. No sign at present of the Revenue cutter, but there was time yet. He knew he was under surveillance.

'All quiet for the moment, John.' Kit's voice was barely a whisper, showing no signs of the tension and mounting excitement he always felt when they neared home with a cargo. He almost *wanted* to be pursued. Faith, at least it made him feel he was alive.

Even as he spoke though, he caught a glimpse of a sail just off to starboard, approaching fast. 'I think they're on to us, John.' Kit felt the rush of excitement in his blood as the *Sea Wolf* wheeled hard. 'We have the wind in our favour, we can still make it.'

John, Kit's captain, and only companion on these night runs, peered anxiously through his spyglass. 'They've spotted us, Master Kit.' Keeping his eyes firmly fixed on the course, John showed no outward sign of worry—Kit would get them out of it if the worst happened and they were boarded. The greatcoat his master wore did nothing to hide the muscular strength of the man underneath, but it wasn't just Kit's height that ... him that air of command. It was the piercing ... ck eyes under those formidable black ... the thin-lipped determination above that stro g jaw that made John fear for any of Kit's foes. He was not a man to cross, that was for sure. Almost, John could pity the cutter's crew. 'They'll know where we're headed.'

Kit laughed softly, viciously. 'Of course they

know. But we'll have time to unload before they reach us. I'll go and make sure our French friends are ready.'

The revolution in France was over, and the *Terror*, the mass slaughter of the French aristocracy, which had included King Louis and his queen, Marie Antoinette, was over too. But the *émigrés*, seeking shelter from the new regime, continued to flee to England.

The killing was not yet finished. It would go on, under one banner or another, for years. War was inevitable, and likely to be waged with England again, as anyone who even half-understood the volatile new French state could see. War would signal an end to these trips. But in the meantime, Kit was happy to do what he could to rescue those *émigrés* who made it to the French coast. He took no political sides, but believed one should live and let live.

It took but a brief moment below decks to address the two refugees. The Frenchmen listened with due respect. Kit was well known among what was left of the aristocracy as an efficient, courageous rescuer. Well known, also, for taking no payment, accepting no thanks. Addressing the men in flawless, if curt, French, Kit told them to be ready for a quick getaway. The thrill of the chase, the need for speed, the challenge of outwitting the customs men, gave a glow to his hard, handsome countenance.

He was as dismissive of the threat as he was of the men's attempts to thank him. Kit prided himself on doing this job well, down to the last detail. He had promised them safe passage and no one was going to prevent him keeping that promise. In this secret life, Kit allowed himself a sense of honour that his public persona had no part of.

A post-chaise would be waiting to take the *émigrés* to London. They would be off his hands, and it was unlikely that he'd ever see them again. The thrill was in the rescue, that was enough. They would have to sink or swim without him once he had safely landed them in England.

As he had predicted, the wind was in their favour, and the clouds too, played their part, scudding back across the moon to hide the yacht as she closed in on her berth. By the time the customs cutter came close enough to hail them, the *émigrés* were dispatched, with haste and brief adieus, to the waiting chaise. A final reminder from Kit that, should they happen to meet again, under no circumstances were they to acknowledge him, and the Frenchmen were gone. Keeping his smuggling life separate from his life in London was more important to Kit than he cared to admit.

As Kit, he could be free. In London, he was somewhat more constrained.

The other cargo, a mere half-dozen kegs of French brandy, was safely stowed in the false floor of the boat house. Kit took his time responding to the hails from the Revenue ship.

'Well, Lieutenant Smith, we meet once more.' His smile was sardonic. He knew he'd won again, and he knew too, that the Riding Officer would make no move to search the *Sea Wolf* now. Lieutenant Smith would need more than a suspicion of smuggling before taking action against the Earl of Rasenby, owner of almost all the land in the surrounding area.

'Another night-fishing expedition, Lord Rasenby?'

'As you see, Lieutenant.' Kit indicated the box that John was unloading. 'May I offer you something to keep out the cold? Or perhaps a share of my catch for your supper?'

Lieutenant Smith bit down a retort. No benefit, he knew, in riling his lordship. It was more than his job was worth. 'Thank you, my lord, but I have a job to do. No doubt we'll meet again one fine night.' Lieutenant Smith consoled himself with the knowledge that at least his informant had been reliable. Next time, mayhap, Lady Luck and the weather would be on his side.

'No doubt.' As he turned to give final instructions to John, the sparkle died from Kit's eyes, and a slight frown marred his handsome countenance. 'Twas always thus. The thrill of the chase made him glad to be alive, but after, he felt drained of energy, listless, and reluctant to return to the tedium of his other life.

It had been close tonight, perhaps too close. It wasn't fair to continue to expose John to such danger, and, if he was honest, the excitement was beginning to pall. Kit had been smuggling for years, for the fun of it—brandy usually, silks sometimes. The human cargo had been a more recent addition, but the smell of war was in the air now, and the scent of change for France in the wind. The need for his services was coming to an end.

Nodding absently to John, and slipping him the usual *douceur*, Kit saddled up his patient horse and headed back across the marshes to his estate. One more run, he promised himself, then he would have to look for distraction elsewhere. One more run, then maybe he would take up his sister Letitia on her offer to find him a suitable bride, and settle down to a life of domesticity.

Lightly touching the sides of the black horse with his heels, Kit laughed out loud. He didn't know which he found funnier. The thought of

Letitia's face at being asked to supply a willing bride. Or the thought of the poor, faceless bride, at being asked to wed and bed the most notorious rake of the *ton*.

Chapter One

Two weeks later—London

'You're surely not going out in that attire, Amelia?' The Honourable Clarissa Warrington looked aghast at her younger sister. 'You're positively indecent, I swear I can see through your petticoats.'

Amelia, the younger by six years, and at eighteen in full possession of her glowing beauty, simply laughed. 'Don't be such a frump. It's all the rage, dampening your petticoat a little. You'd know that, Clarrie, if you got out once in a while.'

'I've no wish to go out in the company you keep, Amelia. And if you're not careful, you'll find that you soon get the sort of reputation that goes with dampened underskirts. To say nothing of the fact that you'll likely catch cold, too.'

'Typical Clarrie, ever practical—I never catch cold. Now do stop and fix my hair for me.' Amelia turned the full force of her huge cornflower-blue eyes on her sister and pouted. 'No one does it like you, and it's so important that I look nice tonight.'

With a sigh, Clarissa picked up the brush. She could never stay angry with Amelia for long, even when she felt in the right of it. Amelia was attending yet another party with her friend Chloe and Chloe's mama, Mrs Barrington. Clarissa received the same invitations, but almost always declined. Aside from the cost, she had no wish to spend the night dancing with dull men who bored her to death with their insipid conversation. Or worse, having to join in with the obligatory female bickering and simpering.

Amelia was different. The latest styles and colours, who was likely to marry whom, were to her of the greatest importance. And it was just as well, thought Clarissa wryly, deftly arranging her sister's hair, that she found it all so entrancing. Marriage was the only thing Amelia was good for, really. Clarissa loved her sister, but she was not blind to her limitations. How could she be, after all? Amelia was exactly like their mama.

Marriage was in fact becoming a necessity for Amelia. Not, as their mama hoped, because she would make a fabulous match. With such a miniscule marriage portion, that was unlikely in the extreme. No, marriage was a necessity for Amelia because she had neither the skills nor the inclination to earn her own living. On top of which, Clarissa suspected that Amelia was falling into compromising company. If she was to reach the altar unsullied, a wedding must be arranged sooner rather than later.

'Who are you so desperate to impress tonight then, Amelia?'

Amelia giggled. 'I don't think I should tell you. You're so strait-laced, Clarrie, you'd be sure to run to Mama.'

'That's not fair!' Clarissa carefully threaded a ribbon through Amelia's golden locks. 'I'm not a sneak, and you know it. I wouldn't run to Mama.' No, indeed she wouldn't, she thought sadly. For Mama would be sure to say that Clarrie was a fusspot, and that Amelia knew her own business. In fact Mama, the widowed Lady Maria Warrington, would probably not even have the energy to say that much.

Lady Maria had been disappointed in life from an early age, and constant disappointment had taken its toll. Married to a younger son, then left a penniless widow not long after Amelia's birth, Lady Maria drifted through life with as little effort as possible. Only cards, and the thought of the brilliant match her beautiful younger daughter would one day make, brought any animation to her face. At the slightest sign that any sort of effort would be required from her she wilted, and even on occasions took to fainting fits. Lady Maria had relied on her practical, pragmatic elder daughter for as long as either of them could remember.

Traces of Lady Maria's beauty could still be detected beneath her raddled skin, but the years had not been kind. Amelia took after her, but Clarissa's own deep auburn hair and vivid green eyes came from her father's side of the family. Clarissa barely remembered Papa, and the little she knew came from Aunt Constance, his favourite sister. Questioning Mama simply brought on tears.

Aunt Constance, alone of Papa's family, had never disowned them, and had always taken an interest in Clarissa. It had been Aunt Constance who funded Clarissa's schooling, and encouraged her reading—histories, politics, and even romances. Aunt Constance could not like Mama, and had little success with Amelia, who refused to study anything beyond the pianoforte, but she doted on Clarissa, and was fond of telling her stories of Papa as a child.

A final twist to her sister's coiffure ensured that one golden lock fell artfully over her shoulder. Amelia's thin muslin dress was of palest pink, her little satin evening slippers dyed to match, as was the ribbon in her hair, dressed in the newly fashionable Grecian knot. Perhaps Amelia's figure was a little too full to look its best in the high-waisted style, which still seemed so strange to people of their mother's generation, but Clarissa could see that no gentleman would cavil at being faced with such a lush display of curves.

'There! You look lovely, Amelia.'

'Yes, I do, don't I?'

Amelia preened in the mirror, and Clarissa sighed. Really, her sister was displaying all too much of her ample curves, even if the low *décolleté* was all the rage. 'You don't think that perhaps a fichu…'

The scornful look was answer enough. 'Oh, very well. I hope you won't get goose bumps!' Clarissa tried to introduce a lighter note. There would be no getting anything out of Amelia if she was in the least lecturing. 'At least tell me who your beau is. For you've made such an effort, there must be one.'

'Well, I don't know if I will, Clarrie; you're bound to disapprove.'

The coy look that accompanied this challenge told Clarissa that Amelia was actually bursting to tell. Perversely, she decided not to pursue the matter. 'Of course, Amelia, I respect your confidence.' She turned to leave.

'No, no, I'll tell. Well, a little. Clarrie, you just won't believe it. I think, I'm certain—well, almost certain—that Kit Rasenby is interested. What do you think of that then?'

'Kit Rasenby? Amelia, you don't seriously mean the Earl of Rasenby? Surely you are mistaken?'

'Well, I'm not, actually.' Amelia pouted. 'He *is* interested. At the Carruthers' ball last week he danced with me three times. That's twice more than any other lady. And he sat next to me at tea. And then I met him at the theatre when we went to that boring old play you were so desperate to see. You know, the one with that old woman in it.'

'You mean Mrs Siddons?' Clarissa had been keen to attend the theatre that evening. Lady Macbeth was the part for which Mrs Siddons was most famed. But Lady Maria had had one of her turns, and Clarrie had to stay home to burn feathers under her nose and dab lavender water on her temples. Clarissa was used to self-sacrifice, even though she had long ceased to believe that these 'turns' of her mama's were anything more than habit. But missing the great Mrs Siddons had been a trial.

Amelia had no further interest in Mrs Siddons.

'Yes, well, Rasenby came to our box particularly to see me. And he spoke to no one else. Chloe said he had eyes only for me all night.'

'You mean he was eyeing you from the pit?' Clarissa's tone was dry. Gentlemen did not eye respectable ladies from the pit. The type of ladies eyed from the pit were not likely to be those offered matrimony.

'And then, today,' Amelia continued blithely, 'when he stopped to talk with us in the park, he asked most particularly if I would be at the Jessops' ball tonight. So, of course, I know he has intentions.'

'Amelia, you know what those intentions are likely to be? You do know of the Earl of Rasenby's reputation?'

A toss of golden curls and yet another pout were the response.

'Amelia, I'm serious.' Clarissa might have spurned most of the invitations she received, but no one could be unaware of the reputation of the Earl of Rasenby. He was a hardened gamester and an incurable womaniser. He was enormously rich and famously handsome, although Clarissa was sceptical about this—in her view, the rich were invariably *good looking*. Lord Rasenby's mistresses were notoriously beautiful and expensive, and,

despite endless lures and traps, he remained determinedly unattached. Quite the perfect Gothic
villain, now she thought of it.

'For Heaven's sake, Clarrie, do you think I'm
stupid? Of course I know of his reputation. Better
than you, I expect, since you're such a prude no
one would dare tell you the plain truth. But I know
he likes me. A lot! I just know!'

Nothing more could be gained from Amelia, and
Clarissa went to bed extremely worried. Her sister
was both young and naïve, and could all too easily
fall victim to the likes of Rasenby. The company
Amelia was keeping, never mind her lack of
dowry, was likely to ensure that any offer would
be strictly dishonourable.

And if Amelia was offered a *carte blanche* by
someone as rich as Rasenby, she would take it.
Clarissa turned restlessly in her bed. It was so hard
to be genteelly poor, she could understand the
temptation. To a girl like Amelia, the choice
between a brief career swathed in furs and silks
and showered in diamonds, or a safe marriage
with a no more than adequate income was an all
too easy one. But life as Kit Rasenby's mistress
would be very short-lived. Amelia's charms were
those of novelty and freshness, not likely to enter-
tain so jaded a palate as Rasenby's for long. And

who would have Amelia then? There was only one way to go, and that was down. Amelia must marry soon, preferably to someone who would take her firmly in hand. But such a person was likely to be too staid and too poor for Amelia. Even supposing she did meet this paragon, would she even look at him, when dazzled by Rasenby's wealth?

If Amelia was ruined, Clarissa would be ruined by association. Even finding a post as governess, something to which she was daily trying to resign herself, would be difficult. At twenty-four, Clarissa had set her sights on self-sufficiency as the only way to give her some element of the freedom she craved. Aunt Constance's offer of a home was tempting, but Clarissa knew in her heart that it would mean tying herself to another obligation, even assuming Mama was settled with Amelia.

Clarissa had always been the sensible one. Beside her sister's vivaciousness and dazzling looks, which had been apparent from a very early age, she felt plain. Her green eyes and dark auburn curls were no match for Amelia's milkmaid perfection. She had settled compliantly into the role of carer. When Amelia tore her dress, Clarrie stitched it. When Amelia fought with her friends, Clarrie played the peacemaker. And as she grew older, when Amelia wanted to attend parties and make her début, Clarrie scrimped and saved to provide her with the dresses and hats and all the other bits and pieces that she needed.

For years now, Lady Maria's hopes had been pinned on Amelia making a match that would save them from poverty. Having no wish to become a burden on Amelia's future household, and having no desire to find herself a suitable match, Clarissa had started, discreetly, looking around for a genteel position. Surrendering her own chance of matrimony was no sacrifice, for she had never met a man who had caused her heart to flutter. In fact, she had never met a man she had found interesting enough to want to get to know better in any way.

Clarissa's pragmatic front concealed a deep romanticism that the practical side of her despised, but which she was unable to ignore. She longed for passion, love, ardour—despite trying to convince herself that they didn't really exist! She dreamed of someone who would love her for herself, value her for what she was, not for her looks or her lineage—which was good, even if Papa's family did refuse to own them—or even her dowry. Someone to pledge himself to her for always. *Happy ever after* was hardly in vogue though. Clarrie's dreams were out of kilter with the ways of the real world. Marriage vows were taken very lightly these days—once an heir had been delivered—with affection provided by a lover rather than a husband. Clarissa couldn't help but find such attitudes abhorrent, even if it did mean being mocked for her prudishness.

Reconciling these two sides of her nature, the practical and romantic, was difficult. Even when embroiled in reading one of the Gothic romances she adored, Clarissa found herself thinking that her own good sense would be of a lot more use in assisting the hero than the tears and fainting fits of the heroines. But resourcefulness was not a quality valued in a female, real or imaginary, nor was it much sought after in a wife. Since it seemed unlikely, in any event, that she would ever be given the opportunity to play the heroine, Clarissa had resigned herself to becoming a governess, a role which would certainly require all her resourcefulness. On that determined note, she finally fell asleep.

At breakfast the next morning, Amelia was all yawns and coy giggles. 'Oh, Mama, we had such fun, and my new dress was much admired.' This, with a sly look at Clarissa.

Clarissa was in no mood for Amelia's games, having woken this morning resolved to remove her sister from the clutches of the Earl of Rasenby. By force, if necessary. 'I can well imagine that you were admired in that dress, Amelia, for it left little to the imagination.' Her jibe was, however, low enough to avoid being heard by Lady Maria, now deep in this morning's post.

Amelia, predictably, pouted, and ignored her.

'And did your beau turn up, then?'

'Can you doubt it? He can't keep away, I told you. He didn't leave my side all night, and everyone noticed.'

'Amelia, that's not necessarily a good thing. Everyone will be talking about you being so singled out. In fact, it seems to me that by making you so conspicuous, it is less likely that the Earl of Rasenby's intentions are honourable. What can Mrs Barrington have been thinking, to allow it? She cannot be a suitable escort. I must speak to Mama.'

'Clarissa, if you do any such thing, I swear, I will make you pay.' Cornflower-blue eyes bright with intent locked on to emerald-green. 'I don't care what you think of Mrs Barrington, she's all I've got, since you and your precious, snooty Aunt Constance are so determined not to escort me. And our dear mama won't move beyond her drawing room, unless there's a card table to tempt her.'

Seeing her sister's stricken look, Amelia relented. No sense in getting Clarissa all worked up and on her high horse. 'You know I wouldn't do anything silly. Mrs Barrington is perfectly respectable, I promise you. And besides, for the next couple of days, I won't be seeing Rasenby. You're right, it won't do to grant him too much attention, I have to keep him keen.' And in any case, Clarrie didn't need to know that a certain Edward was really a far more attractive companion than Kit Rasenby. Kit Rasenby was rich and powerful, but he didn't cause her heart to flutter the way Edward did. In fact, Amelia was finding herself quite distracted by Edward, whose youthful good looks appealed so much more to her than Rasenby's striking countenance, which could be rather intimidating. Rasenby's wealth was losing a little of its attraction—but she was determined to give it every chance to succeed. Edward would always be there, of that she was already sure.

'Amelia, you must know that the Earl of Rasenby won't offer marriage. His reputation, his feelings about the state of matrimony, they are all against you. And even if he did intend to marry, it wouldn't be to the penniless daughter of a cast-out younger son. It would be to someone with influence and money. Amelia, are you listening at all?'

'Lord, Clarrie, you know nothing.' Abandoning her attempt to soft-soap her sister, Amelia's voice

hardened. 'You're right—perhaps Rasenby's intentions aren't marriage.' Well, in fact Amelia knew
they weren't, for he had already intimated his offer
of a *carte blanche*. She had put him off, unwilling
to take so irrevocable a step just yet. 'But he's wild
about me, I know. And with a bit of luck, marriage
it will be, whether he wants to or nay.'

'What do you mean? What have you done?'

'Why nothing, sister dear, as yet. I don't have to.
I merely have to click my fingers and he comes
running. And if I click and he runs into a—well,
shall we say, compromising situation?—then
that's his misfortune. And best for me, too.'

'*Amelia!* The Earl of Rasenby is highly unlikely
to fall for that. Why there must have been countless such traps set for him over the years, and
never a whiff of him anywhere near wed. Please,
I beg of you, stay away from him.'

'Well, I won't. At least, yes, I will, for a couple
of days. Just to keep him on tenterhooks.' Amelia
slanted another glance at Clarrie's face. Her sister
really was such a prude.

'Do you love him? Is that it?' Clarissa was
struggling to come to terms with this new, hard
Amelia. She had always been determined to have
her own way, but she had never before been so
openly scheming. If Clarissa had known that her

sister was trying desperately to suppress her feelings for Edward Brompton, she would have been less concerned.

'Life isn't one of your romances, you know. Love is such an outmoded emotion when it comes to marriage. I can stomach him well enough to bed him, if that's what you mean. And, of course, his money makes him more attractive than he would be under other circumstances. After all, he's quite old.'

'Old? You talk about him as if he's in his dotage. Why, he can't be more than five and thirty. And if you loved him, his age would mean nothing. Now tell me straight, *do* you love him?'

'Clarrie, I tell you straight, I do not.' Amelia was enjoying shocking her sister. 'Love, I will save for my beaux after we are wed. It's what everyone does. Rasenby will no doubt carry on with his lightskirts, so why should I not do the same? I shall take great pleasure, though, in ousting that supercilious Charlotte du Pres from her position as his mistress. And I suppose I'll need to provide an heir first.' Realising she'd gone a bit too far, Amelia patted Clarrie's hand in a conciliatory way. 'I'm not a little girl any more. I can look after myself. And I know what I'm doing, I promise.' No need to let Clarrie know that the *carte blanche* would still be considered if her other plan failed. One way or another, she'd get her hands on a large part of Rasenby's wealth. But for now, she wanted to think only of the thrill of meeting Edward again. 'Let us find out what Mama has found so distracting that she has paid no heed at all to our conversation.'

Lady Maria was certainly absorbed in her post, one letter in particular holding her attention. There were plenty of others, but they were all bills. Bills that she had no means of paying. Those relating to the house and to Amelia's dresses she would hand over to Clarissa to deal with. But they were insignificant compared to her mounting gambling debts—and of these, Clarissa must be allowed no inkling. She returned again to the note from the owner of the discreet gaming house she had been frequenting of late. The sum that she owed frightened her. The letter was subtly threatening.

'Mama, what is it that you find so interesting in that letter? Clarrie and I have been plotting away, and you haven't even looked up.'

At this, Lady Maria gave a nervous start. 'What? Oh, nothing, nothing. No indeed, nothing for you girls to worry about.' Her slightly protuberant blue eyes blinked out at her daughters. Nervously, she licked her lips, and produced a somewhat ragged smile. 'Now, dears, what is it you were plotting?'

'Silly Mama, only what I would wear to the theatre tonight. For I'm going out with Chloe you know, and her mama, to the new farce. Chloe's brother and that nice Mr Brompton are escorting us.'

'Will they be calling for you here, dearest?' Lady Maria had just remembered a hint from Mrs Barrington, that there were means of paying a lady's debts that she could help—discreetly— with. 'Then I'd like a word with her myself. Just to thank her for her attentions to you, Amelia dear. She's been so good taking you out to parties when my health won't hold up.'

Lady Maria gathered together her post. 'Now, if you'll excuse me, I'm afraid I have one of my heads. Clarrie, do give my regards to your Aunt Constance, I know you'll do all that is right.' And with that, she left for the sanctity of her bedchamber with its carefully drawn blinds, and the ministering of her dear, faithful maid.

'Are you going to see Aunt Constance, then? Rather you than me, I can't abide her sermonising. I'm off for a walk in the park with Chloe.' Looking back at her sister, still seated at the table, Amelia laughed once more. 'Clarrie do stop looking so serious. I know what I'm doing, and that should be enough for you. You should get out more yourself, you know. Even at your age, your looks are more than passable, as long as you don't stand too close to me. I could find you someone suitable.'

'Thank you, Amelia,' Clarissa responded drily, 'but I'm quite content as I am.'

The visit to her aunt only confirmed Clarissa's worst fears. Lady Constance Denby lived semi-retired from society, but this didn't stop her keeping close tabs on the latest *on dits*, and today one of them concerned Amelia.

'Well, my dear, I am sorry to have to tell you that your sister is raising a few eyebrows.'

They were settled in Lady Constance's breakfast room, taking morning coffee. Clarissa loved this room, with its beautifully polished rosewood tables, the cabinets crammed with her aunt's collection of delicate porcelain. The loud ticking of the clock on the mantel, and the scent from the apple wood burning in the hearth were deeply comforting.

Her aunt had been widowed very young—before Clarissa ever remembered an uncle—and, despite numerous offers, had never married again. Her beloved husband had been a rising star in the House of Lords, and Constance had remained faithful to his memory in retaining her widowed status, as well as her avid interest in current affairs. Lady

Constance was a beautiful woman, with a little of Clarissa's colouring, although the vivid auburn of her hair had faded now, and was confined beneath her habitual widow's cap. She had been formidable, too, in her brief time as a political hostess, although that, also, had been given up upon the occasion of her husband's death. Having shared something so special, she had told Clarissa once, even for so brief a time, had been enough.

Tact, and a natural reticence, prevented Lady Constance, over the years, from being too critical of Clarissa's mother and sister. She was all too aware of how badly her own family had treated them when James, her dear brother, had died. She found Maria tedious, and Amelia wilful, but she was very fond of Clarissa, and hated not being able to do more for her than provide this sanctuary whenever her niece paid her a call.

And today the talk would be upsetting—but that couldn't be helped. 'I'm not sure if you're aware, but Letitia Marlborough, Kit Rasenby's sister, is one of my friends. A flighty thing before she was married and produced that brood of hers, but still, I've known her for ever, and keep on good terms with her.' Lady Constance waited, but Clarissa had no comment to make.

'Well, Letitia has it on the best of authority that

your sister is Kit Rasenby's latest flirt. In fact, she believes he intends to set her up as his mistress.'

Lady Constance sipped her coffee, and considered Clarissa's reaction. No surprise there, only worry. So, there was truth in it. Well, she needed to warn Clarissa in plain language. Amelia was heading for a fall, and Lady Constance could only do her best to ensure that Clarissa was not to be tainted by association. Amelia would go to the bad, she was sure of it. But Clarissa deserved better.

'I take it that this comes as no surprise to you, Clarissa dear? Has Amelia mentioned Lord Rasenby then?'

'She has, Aunt. As a—an admirer.'

Lady Constance gave a bark of laughter at this. 'Is that what she called him? Your sister, my dear, seems determined to take the road to ruin. And if you don't take me up on my offer to come and live here, she'll take you with her.'

'Aunt, please, let us not discuss this again at present. I am overwhelmed at the generosity of your offer, indeed I am. But until Amelia is settled, and my mama with her, I can't desert them.' Green eyes pleaded for sympathy. 'Aunt Constance, you do understand, don't you?'

Clarissa was so very much like her papa when she looked up, that Lady Constance caught her breath for a second. Those huge eyes set in her heart-shaped face were all feminine, but the appeal, and the colouring, they were so like James. If only he had been of a stronger constitution— and a stronger character—then perhaps they wouldn't be in this mess. But to have eloped with Maria, a mere nobody, when he should have made a good match! Well, it was done now, and James long dead. All she could do was protect his child from some of the harshness of the world.

But to do that, she had to save her from her sister and her mama. Lady Constance patted Clarissa's hand reassuringly. She was four and twenty, but had seen so little of the world. 'Of course I understand, my dear, you must know that you will always find a home here, no matter what.'

'Thank you, Aunt Constance, that means a lot to me.'

'But to return to the subject of Amelia, as unfortunately we must, I have to tell you, Clarissa, that I am very concerned.' Lady Constance was brisk now. Straight talking was required, although she was loathe to do it. 'The Earl of Rasenby's reputation is extremely bad, you know.'

'I am aware of Lord Rasenby's reputation, ma'am, but surely he cannot be as bad as they say?'

'Child, I know not what you have heard, but

believe me, whatever it is, Kit's behaviour is worse. He has been one of the *ton* for nigh on fifteen years, and master of a huge fortune for longer, his papa having unfortunately died when he was still at school. His papa, such a very dreadful man, broke his neck when he was thrown from his horse riding to the hounds. He was a bruising rider by all accounts, but they say he was in his cups at the time. Mind you, there was rarely a day when he was ever anything else. Hardly a role model for his only son. Although, to be fair, Kit seems to be rather more sober and certainly more discriminating than his father. But there is no getting away from it Clarissa, his tastes are still very, very low!'

With pursed lips, Lady Constance poured herself another cup of coffee. 'I will not sully your ears with the details, there is no need for that. But this I will say. It is not just the usual, opera dancers and mistresses. He is wild. Too quick to quarrel and too slow to make up. If you ask me, he has too little to occupy him. I have often thought he could make a most excellent politician.'

Lady Constance paused to sip her coffee, gazing into the fireplace. It was her one regret, not having a son. Not for an instant would she have wished a Kit Rasenby on herself, but a child in the image of her dear husband would have been a precious gift. Still, it had not happened. And here was Clarissa, someone who did need her help and protection. Lady Constance brought her attention firmly back to the matter in hand. 'I beg your pardon, Clarissa, we were talking of Kit Rasenby. Despite all I have said, he is still seen as a good catch by some. Yet he has avoided matrimony until now, and is like to continue to do so. Letitia tells me he is happy for Jeremy, her son, to inherit, and cares naught for the line continuing from him. It is perhaps as well.'

Lady Constance paused, once again assessing the effect on her niece. Clarissa was looking thoughtful rather than shocked.

'Aunt, I am aware of much of what you have told me, although I do truly find it hard to believe that anyone could be all bad.' She held up her hand and gave her aunt a small smile to forestall any intervention. 'I know, you think I'm naïve, but I do like to think there is some good in everyone. However, that is not the point, since I have never met Lord Rasenby.'

Clarissa thought over her next words carefully. 'There is some truth in the rumours, I'm afraid. Amelia has been much in Lord Rasenby's company, and I fear his intentions cannot be honourable, no matter what Amelia may believe. She has no love for him, but I think she is deeply flattered, and is fooling herself into thinking he may offer matrimony. I think that she must come to accept that it cannot be so.'

'My dear Clarissa, you underrate your sister. She is, I have no doubt at all, fully aware that Kit Rasenby can intend only a *carte blanche*. Which she will accept, should no other more honourable offer come her way. Your sister, whether you want to believe it or not, is avaricious before anything else. There, plain speaking indeed, but you must be made to realise it.'

'Aunt, I know you think no good of Amelia.' Clarissa blinked, trying to quieten the little voice in her head that told her Lady Constance was articulating Clarissa's own fears. Lady Constance had said only what she already knew. 'Perhaps what you say is true. But I am certain that I can prevent her ruining herself with Lord Rasenby. She is a child, she is simply beguiled by his charm and his wealth.'

'You're not thinking of doing something foolish, Clarissa?'

'No, no. No, of course I won't be foolish.' The slight laugh with which she attempted to carry off the denial fell rather flat, and Clarissa bit her lip.

She could never lie. She had the makings of a plan which Aunt Constance would certainly call foolish, but she needed to think it through.

'Enough of my imprudent sister, I have to tell you that I am not at all impressed with *Udolpho*.' Clarissa rushed into a dissection of Mrs Radcliffe's novel in an effort to distract her aunt from further enquiries. Lady Constance was, rather to her shame, an avid fan of Mrs Radcliffe, and allowed herself to be diverted into a spirited defence. The two parted on excellent terms.

Mulling over her aunt's words later, however, confirmed Clarissa in her resolution. She must separate Amelia from Lord Rasenby, and that would require desperate action, for Amelia must not know that she was being thwarted. Amelia would accept a *carte blanche* from Lord Rasenby, Clarissa no longer doubted it. And she knew, in her heart, that whatever plan Amelia had to trap him into marriage would fail. Aunt Constance would not have been so blunt with Clarissa had she been less sure. So she had to prevent both Amelia's plot and Lord Rasenby's offer.

A flicker of excitement rippled through her at the thought of taking action. It was as if she was waking from sleep, preparing for the challenge to come. Telling herself that it was the thrill of rescuing her sister, and nothing to do with meeting so notorious a man, Clarissa started to formulate her plan. The first requirement was to meet with Lord Rasenby in order to determine for herself just how much danger Amelia was in. And Clarrie knew just how to effect that meeting.

With a fast-beating heart, she flicked through the pile of invitations on the desk in the morning room. Yes, there it was, discarded at the bottom of the pile. Lady Teasborough was a friend of Aunt Constance, and had no doubt sent the invite at her request. A masked ball. Clarrie would go—incognito, and on her own.

Chapter Two

Kit, Earl of Rasenby, stared down into the limpid blue eyes of yet another eligible young lady, and tried to suppress a yawn as a wave of boredom washed over him. He should never have given in to his sister Letitia's entreaties to escort her to the ball. He had planned a quiet dinner followed by a hand or two of whist at his club, instead of which, here he was at one of the society crushes he so abhorred. With the added, and completely pointless, inconvenience of having to sport a domino and a mask.

Lady Teasborough had thought to introduce a slightly *risqué* element with this masked ball, but Kit was finding it every bit as tedious as any other social event. The heat in the room was overpowering. The candles from the huge chandeliers, the fires lit—unnecessarily, in his view—in the enormous grates at either end of the ballroom, and the crush of too many people in too little space made Kit want to fight his way out into the relatively fresh air of the terrace. He was bored. He had no interest in the latest *crim. con.* story, nor in taking part in the speculation as to who had fathered his hostess's latest brat. If his host—closeted, no doubt, in one of the card rooms—didn't care, why should he? *God, he was bored.* Despite the concealing cloaks and masks, he recognised almost everyone here. Including Miss Pink Domino, being presented to him now by Letitia.

Kit sighed, bowed over Miss Pink Domino's hand, and led her out reluctantly. His enthusiasm for fencing, which he practised regularly with the renowned Harry Angelo at his academy in the Haymarket, lent him an animal grace that singled him out on the dance floor. But his partner was, alas, unable to match him, and it would take a great effort on his part to ensure that they remained in step for the duration of the country dance.

As they worked their way down the set, Kit's mind began to wander. He knew Letitia's game only too well. His elder by some years, his sister had just successfully married off the first of his five nieces, and was once again turning her attentions to his own marital state. It was his own fault for bringing it up earlier—even though it had been in jest. Kit's reputation was too bad for him to be a great catch, of course, as Letitia took pleasure in reminding him. So Louisa Haysham, with whom he was now dancing, fell into the second-best category. *A pretty little thing with an adequate portion who will cause you no trouble.* He could hear Letitia saying it, and he knew exactly what she meant. Louisa Haysham was a nice, inoffensive, malleable female for him to trample on. She'd raise a brood of nice insignificant children for him, and he'd be bored within a week. He was bored now, and he'd been in her company for barely ten minutes.

Over and over again, Kit had assured Letitia that he'd be happy for her son, Jeremy, to inherit his estates. At thirty-five, he was surely entitled to be treated as the confirmed bachelor he knew himself to be. Lord knew, he'd made his views clear to both Letitia and his mother often enough. Matrimony simply had no appeal for him. Rather, matrimony, in the accepted form these days, had no appeal. Fidelity, even if he could find a woman he wanted to be faithful to, seemed not to be valued. And he had seen no evidence, not in his family, nor amongst his friends or acquaintances, that marriage had any rewards other than a string of brats that no one really wanted, and endless re-criminations about money. Even his sister, who claimed to be happy, was, he knew, no more than content. Content, Kit was sure, wasn't a big enough reward for the sacrifice of his freedom.

Returning Miss Haysham with a curt bow to her mother, and neatly avoiding catching his sister's eye—he couldn't bear her inevitable interrogation as to whether Miss Insipid Haysham was to his liking—Kit headed instead for the group of gen-tlemen congregated at the back of the room. His tall figure in a plain black domino and mask was easily recognisable in a crowd that favoured colour and decoration. He was in fact, infamous for refusing to decorate his well-favoured person with any of the fobs, frills and furbelows of the day.

A slight man in a deep scarlet cloak standing on the fringes of the crowd noted Kit's attendance at the ball with some surprise—it was very unlike Rasenby to turn out at these formal affairs. Kit was not aware of the depths of contempt in which Robert, Marquis of Alchester, held him. Brought up as children together, since the estates of their fathers ran parallel, Robert had been forced to play second fiddle to Kit from the start. Kit was the ringleader in all their childish pranks. Kit was the best shot in the area, the handiest with his fists, the most skilled with a sword. And it was Kit who had first call on all the females. To add insult to injury, Kit's estates continued to flourish under his generous stewardship, whereas Robert's dissolute lifestyle drained every penny from his land, now in sad want of repair. All this bitterness Robert had suppressed over the years, but it was slowly mouldering. And now, he had a card worth playing. It was Robert who had been informing the customs men as to Kit's activities. One day soon, revenge would be his.

Blissfully unaware of this enmity, Kit took a reviving draught of claret, a drink he much preferred to the ice-cold champagne cup being offered to the rest of the guests. Mindful of his resolution to give up smuggling, he mulled over, once more, the notion of matrimony. Letitia had made her point of view perfectly clear when he had raised the subject before dinner. A slight frown marred the perfection of his countenance as he thought over his sister's words from earlier tonight. His handsome features were, in fact, a major bone of contention with Letitia, and had been the trigger for her latest tirade, turning his attempt at light banter into a more serious discussion.

'What would you say, Letitia, if I asked you to finally find me a suitable bride? One who met all my needs, I might add.' He had said this with a wicked grin, deliberately intending to annoy her.

Letitia sighed. Why should Kit have it all, when she didn't? Of course, she was perfectly happy with her husband, but life wasn't exactly stimulating. So it shouldn't be for Kit, either. That wasn't what matrimony was about.

'For goodness' sake, must you always harp on about your needs. With your looks, I'm sure that sort of thing won't be a problem—ever.' It was positively painful to Letitia that Kit was so very perfectly good looking. 'It's your duty to the family to bestow yourself on one of my sex for reasons of lineage, not for—not for the reasons you're implying.'

'On the contrary, Letitia, I feel it my bounden duty to bestow myself on as many of your sex as I can. And I do my best, you know.' This was said with a rueful smile, for Kit knew that Letitia, despite her perfect breeding, liked to consider herself *risqué*.

'Kit!' She feigned shock, anyway. 'I mean bestow yourself properly. I'm not referring to your mistresses, for Heaven's sake.'

'Tut, tut, Letitia, what can you know of my mistresses?'

'Why, no more nor less than the whole of

London society, since you flaunt them so brazenly at every opportunity. Only yesterday I saw you in a carriage in Oxford Street with that shameless hussy Charlotte—harlot, more like—sitting at your side. Draped in the most gorgeous furs, too. No doubt paid for by you.' Letitia couldn't prevent the bitter note of envy entering her voice, thinking back to how stunning Charlotte du Pres had looked. Providing her husband with six children in quick succession had taken a heavy toll on what little looks she herself had once possessed.

'Yes, she really is rather lovely, isn't she? But alas, I fear, becoming rather tedious. Her demands are endless, you know, Letitia, and the rewards less attractive each time. I think that Charlotte is coming to the end of her usefulness.'

'Well, I can't say I'm surprised. She's been with you two months now. Don't you ever find a woman diverting for longer?'

'Alas, no. At least, not yet. And since I've been trying for more years than either of us, sister dear, would care to count, I'm afraid you really must resign yourself to my bachelor state. And incidentally, please don't go breaking your heart over Charlotte, she'll be more than adequately compensated for her loss.'

'Yes, you're very generous in that way, I know.

But really, Kit, you're so hugely rich that it means nothing to you. Not, I assure you, that I'm complaining myself, for you've been exceeding good to me and my children over the years, particularly Jeremy, who scarce deserves it. He may be my only son and I love him dearly but it's plain the lad is a wastrel. I just wish you took your duty to marry and produce your own son and heir as seriously.'

'Enough of this. I have no desire to be leg-shackled, it was a jest. I have no wish to be presented to yet another eligible girl who will drive me back into the arms of someone who at least can attend properly to my physical needs. And spare me your blushes, Letty, for you know perfectly well what I mean.'

'No, Kit, I do not. There is no reason why you shouldn't continue to tend to your physical needs, as you put it, outside of the marriage bed. But you must marry for the sake of the family. Jeremy is no fit heir for you. You need the stability of a wife. You need someone to care for you in your old age.'

Kit threw back his head and laughed again, running his fingers through his cropped, glossy black hair. 'For God's sake Letitia, I'm thirty-five, I don't need a nursemaid yet. I'll tell you what, the minute I show the first signs of contracting gout, I'll start looking out for a wife to tend to me.'

'By then, you'll be too old to father children, and it will be too late. Kit, do listen, since you brought the topic up. I know your reputation is bad—and indeed, well deserved—but you're still eligible. I could still find you someone suitable.'

Kit was now deeply regretting raising the subject. 'Letty, enough. You know my views on matrimony, they are not likely to change. There are but two types of women on this earth, and they live in worlds that don't mix. There are those who provide pleasure for a man, and who require payment, and there are those who provide a family—and they require payment in a different way. And I'm happy to pay for the former, if I get something out of it. But why should I pay for a family when I don't want one? Have done.'

Letitia, silenced temporarily by the stern tone of her brother's voice, had done. Reflecting on what he had said, she had to accept the truth of it, for Kit had no experience of any respectable female wanting to give more than she took from him. Starting with their mother—and, she had to admit, herself too. But Letitia wasn't one to give up so easily, either. Her brother must have an heir. He must make some sacrifices. 'Kit, let me see what I can do. I'll see if I can provide you with someone who is at least good to look at.'

'Enough. Let us forgo any further discussion. I must change for this cursed party of yours.'

Shaking his head to banish the memory of that uncomfortable conversation, Kit took another draught of claret, and cast an idle eye over the ballroom. So far, he had danced only with Miss Haysham, but he knew that he'd have to choose at least one other partner soon, or the world would think he had singled the fair Miss Haysham out. And Kit did not want that to happen. Really, the idea of matrimony was ridiculous. Apart from anything else, he had no desire to make his poor wife—whoever she might be—totally miserable. And since he could in no way promise liking, never mind fidelity, miserable she would be, and quickly. Best to focus on this last run with the *Sea Wolf* first, then think to the future after. For now, he needed to find another dance partner.

A brief flash of black domino lined with emerald green caught his eye in the far corner, and roused his attention. It was highly unusual for a female to wear black—in fact, he was the only man to do so tonight. And while he could have sworn he knew everyone here—despite the masks—she was unfamiliar. She was standing by the open window, and for some reason she seemed to be watching him. Her stance was alert, giving the impression of one on the verge of flight. Kit was intrigued. Retrieving two glasses of champagne from a passing waiter, he made his way over to the stranger.

'I fear you are somewhat warm, Miss Black Domino—can I offer you a cooling drink?'

Clarrie gave a start, then tried, rather unsuccessfully, to regain her poise. The black domino, the only other one here, had been pointed out to her as the Earl of Rasenby. He had made the first move. She couldn't believe her luck. Nor could she flee now, as she had been contemplating only a moment before. Fate had decreed that she must go through with her plan.

'Why, thank you sir. It is rather hot.' He was tall, much taller than Clarrie, and despite the domino she could see he was exceedingly well built. Somehow, she had expected him to be more dandified. But the Earl of Rasenby was obviously of athletic inclination, and favoured a simple elegance that relied on his physique and the quality of his tailoring, rather than decoration. For the first time in her life, Clarrie experienced a strong gust of sheer physical attraction that was both unexpected and unwelcome.

Looking up, she could see little of his features behind the mask, only a pair of piercing dark eyes, looking into hers assessingly. So this was the man who wanted to steal Amelia's virtue. This was the man who intended to sweep her sister—and with her, Clarissa and her mama—into a world of vice and degradation. Well, she could certainly see his appeal. What she needed to find out was just how serious he was in his intentions, before she decided to act. Clarissa still nourished a hope that Amelia had exaggerated—though in the light of Lady Constance's revelations, it was but a faint one.

'Do you not find these masked affairs somewhat tedious, sir? Why, I swear I know everyone here. 'Tis but an excuse to allow those who are so inclined to flirt a little more openly, is it not?'

Clarissa's voice, usually so low and musical, had assumed a slightly breathless quality. The combination of the role she had to play, and the physical awareness of this surprisingly attractive man, were already taking their toll. But she wouldn't fail at the first hurdle, there was too much at stake. Under no illusions about her own attractions, she had studied Amelia closely, and she knew how to flirt—even if she was about to try it out for the first time.

Kit looked down into those vibrant green eyes, surprised at the tone. He could have sworn she was nervous when he first approached her. 'And do you know who I am, Miss Black Domino?' Of course she did, else why flirt so obviously unless she knew her target?

'I will hazard a guess, my lord. You are the Earl of Rasenby, are you not?' Those green eyes looked up into his, a shadow of a doubt clouding them. What if she had been wrong? A flush of embarrassment swept over Clarissa, most of it mercifully hidden by the mask.

'And if I am not, would you be disappointed?'

'Of course I would be disappointed.' Clarrie shook out her chicken-skin fan with a flourish, partly to hide her eyes, but more practically in an effort to hide her overheated countenance, and to give her time to pull herself together. 'I'd be very disappointed, since I've heard so much about your lordship, and was counting on meeting you here.'

'Were you, now? And may I ask, are you here at the invitation of Lady Teasborough, or have you taken a chance to come uninvited?' Surely the only explanation was that she was some member of the *demi-monde* with an enterprising turn of mind?

Clarissa, forgetting her part, was indignant at the accusation. 'Of course I was invited, why would I be here otherwise?'

The genuine flash of anger from those green eyes took Kit aback. Despite himself, he felt a faint trace of interest. He didn't believe her for an instant, but any new ploy, after all, was at least a refreshing change. 'I do beg your pardon. It's just that you have the advantage of me. To whom do I have the pleasure of speaking?'

'That is not important for now. And besides…' Clarrie allowed herself a peep above the fan into those dark blue-black eyes '…it's so much more intriguing, is it not, to save a little something for later?' Nothing Amelia had told her about Kit Rasenby had led her to believe that he was anything more than a rich provider. She hadn't expected him to be quite so like the villains of her favourite romances—Clarrie always empathised more with the villain than the hero, although she never liked to ask herself why!

'So, I'm not to know your name, then? Am I to know your purpose in seeking me out?'

'Eventually, of course, my lord. But first, perhaps we should get to know each other a little. Tell me, the lady you were dancing with, what thought you of her charms? Did you not think she danced rather ill?'

'You can do better than that, surely?' He was sardonic. Praising or disparaging one female to another was not a sport that he enjoyed.

Closing her fan with a determined snap, Clarissa decided to go for the direct approach. The Earl was obviously not one for simpering females, and in truth, she didn't do simpering very well. Perhaps if she played things her own way he would take her more seriously. 'I know you not, Lord Rasenby, but you seem to me a man who prefers plain speaking. Mayhap we should dispense with the niceties and progress to my requirements from you?'

'Much better.' His tone remained sceptical, however. 'Now you at least have my attention. Perhaps I should warn you, though, that if it's money you're after, I won't be blackmailed. If you've come on behalf of one of your sisters in debauchery, you'll find scant pickings here.' Ignoring the gasp of indignation from Clarissa, he held his hand up to forestall interruption, and continued in the harsh voice of one used to seeing the worst in everyone. 'I pay my debts direct. And there's no use either, in trying to pretend that it's you I owe— I may have sampled the wares of your like many times, but not enough to confuse me. I'd know you if I'd had you.'

'Well, my lord! Well! Plain speaking indeed.' Clarissa was completely unprepared for this turn in the conversation. He thought her a lightskirt. Well, that's what she'd intended, but she hadn't expected the flush of anger that such an assumption had caused. In fact, the more she thought about it, the angrier she became. The Earl of Rasenby was an arrogant pig, and he deserved to be put down.

Forgetting all about Amelia, Clarrie gave free reign to her feelings, her temper made worse by the need to continue the conversation, in the middle of the ball as they were, *sotto voce.* 'I am amazed, sir, at your arrogance. And I am sorry, truly sorry, for any of my poor—sisters, as you call them—who would be reduced to pleading with you, for you are obviously a hard case. You tell me you pay your debts direct—well, I can only hope that you do, sir, and that you pay them fully!'

'What on earth do you mean? I pay what is owed and am generous. I have a reputation of being generous. But I won't be blackmailed, so whatever your pathetic plan, abandon it.' Kit was now more angry than intrigued. He had little reputation, and all of it bad, but one thing he had always been proud of was that he compensated—generously— any woman who had provided her services to him. He ensured, too, that there were never any consequences. To his knowledge, he had no natural children. The irony of this—that he, who had the blackest of characters, had the cleanest of stables—contributed to his weariness of the world in which he lived. He was more fastidious in his habits, and more generous in his payments, than most of his peers. It struck him, suddenly, as a poor enough boast.

'Has it never occurred to you that money may not be enough, Lord Rasenby? Has it never occurred to you that some of these poor creatures that you pay off may have feelings? That they may have hoped for more from you than a few jewels and furs?'

At this, Kit laughed. 'It never occurs to me because there are no feelings in this world that cannot be compensated for financially. I should know.' Looking down into those indignant green eyes, Kit felt a twinge of compassion. Perhaps, after all, there was some innocence there? But no, it was sure to be just another act—although a better one than he'd seen for some time. 'I assure you, madam, the type of women I get involved with don't have feelings. Simpering sentimentality appeals to me not. I trade in the more physical side of things, and that, if you don't know already, is always short-lived. So, no, I don't think I owe anything on account there to anyone.'

For some reason, this statement shocked Clarissa more than any other. More than the knowledge that her Aunt Constance had been right in her character assessment. More than Lord Rasenby's outrageously blunt speaking. The man had no feelings at all. She wondered what had forged his deep cynicism. Through the mask, Clarissa's green eyes hinted at tears. 'I'm truly sorry for you, my lord, if you do feel like that.' She touched her hand to his arm in a gesture of sympathy.

Kit shook her off, angry—unreasonably angry—at the gesture. Who was she to question his behaviour, and then to patronise him with her tears and sympathy? 'Don't waste your energy, madam. I fear that whatever it was you had planned to say to me is wasted, too, for we can have nothing in common. Now, I must go and dance with another partner, lest Miss Haysham— the lady in the pink domino, since you were so interested—has her hopes raised.'

'Forgive me, Lord Rasenby, I spoke out of turn, it was not my intention to judge you. But please, do stay and hear me out.' There was desperation in Clarissa's voice as, emerging from her own anger, she realised he was walking away and she had found out next to nothing of his intentions towards Amelia. And she needed to know, in order to decide whether the risk was worth taking.

He turned at the appeal, unwillingly softened by it. There was something genuine about her, despite appearances, that still had him interested. 'I don't make a habit of ruining innocents, you know. I take only willing partners, who understand the game, and who don't have any of these more tender feelings you refer to, I assure you. Come, what is it that you're so determined I should hear, now that you've finished upbraiding me?'

'Well, actually…' Clarissa sniffed determinedly and took the plunge. 'Well, I wanted to discuss a similar proposal with you myself.' She glared at him through her mask, her expression anything but seductive. In fact, she was so far away from the flirtatious woman of the world that she had started out to be, she was questioning her own sanity. This was most definitely not going the way she had imagined it from the security of her bedchamber.

Kit stared at her speechlessly. This slim female, a complete stranger, had sneaked into a society ball and sought him out. First she had flirted with him, then she had launched into a tirade at him, had questioned his generosity and his feelings, to say nothing of upbraiding his morals—such as they were! And now she was telling him that she wanted to make him an indecent proposal. Of a certainty she was unhinged. No matter how attractive the form under the domino and mask—and what he could see he found extremely attractive, for though she was slender, she curved most appealingly in all the right places—it couldn't be worth it.

And now she was glaring at him, as if it was he who had made the proposal to her. 'I don't think, madam, that you can have meant what you just said? Surely, you are not suggesting that you want to become another notch on my notorious bedpost yourself?'

'I—well, yes, I suppose I am suggesting just that. But subject to my own conditions, of course.' Clarissa flushed once more with embarrassment. This was not going at all to plan. For a start, her proposition was to have been later, once she'd found out a bit more about what he intended for Amelia, not something she should have blurted out at this first meeting. She hadn't even thought it through properly.

'Ah, your conditions. And what would they be, madam?' He couldn't help but be interested. This was all so very, very unexpected. Kit was glad, for once, that he'd come along to the ball. Mentally, he thanked Letitia—although he didn't expect she'd be too thrilled if she ever found out.

'Well, I'm not going to tell you right now, this is hardly the appropriate place. I thought we could discuss that on another occasion. I was supposed to get to know you a bit first.'

Kit gave a sharp laugh. She was unhinged, but she was amusing. 'Were you now? And who said you were to get to know me first? Who set you up for this, my little intriguer?'

'No one, no one set me up, I'm acting on my own.' The stamp of a little foot and the quick flush betrayed Clarrie again. Her temper, did she but know it, went with the auburn hair, and had been her father's undoing. Normally it was easy to control, but there was something about this man that got under her skin. 'I merely meant, Lord Rasenby, that I wanted to know a little more about you before we have such an intimate discussion. For a start, I wouldn't want to make you any proposal if I'm mistaken as to your current state of attachment.'

'Come now, I feel sure that someone as bold as you are would have done your research. Surely you are perfectly aware of my current state, as you call it?'

'Yes, my lord, I am aware that you have an attachment to Miss du Pres, but I was more concerned with your intentions as to your immediate future. I have heard that you have been paying court to a Miss Warrington?'

'You have been digging, haven't you? And what have you heard about Miss Warrington and my intentions towards her?'

'I have heard that you have been marking her

out, my lord. I have heard that she has been the object of your affections for the last few weeks. I have heard that you have even raised expectations of a more honourable kind.'

Kit gave another bark of laughter at this. 'Whatever you have heard, I have nothing honourable in mind when it comes to Amelia Warrington. And I cannot believe that Miss Warrington imagines any such thing either. That girl is a chit who knows only the value of my purse, and aims to dig as deep into it as she can. Can it be that it is she who has set you on to me?' Behind the mask, Kit's eyes narrowed. 'No, she does have a close companion, an insipid, simpering miss, but she bears no resemblance to you. Her name escapes me.'

'Chloe.' Clarissa realised her mistake immediately; the black brows opposite her snapped together with suspicion. 'I believe that's her name. Although I don't really know Miss Warrington personally—at least, not very well.' After today, that at least was true. Amelia was becoming a stranger to her. 'I am merely repeating the latest gossip. And the rumours are that you intend marriage.'

'I assure you, madam, I have no plans to marry. My intentions in that direction are not yet fixed. Miss Warrington is attractive, I'll grant, and more than willing, that I know. I may have a proposal for her, but it would not be honourable.' Kit smiled rakishly. Seeing Clarissa flinch at his words, he narrowed his eyes. 'Did you think her one of those innocent victims you were throwing in my face earlier? Amelia Warrington knows exactly what is on offer, I have made that perfectly clear to her. And if she thinks to hold out on me in the hope of more, then she'll quickly learn the better of it. If I ever deign to marry, it would certainly not be to someone as easy to touch as Miss Warrington.'

Clarissa absorbed this assassination of her sister's character with sadness, but a weary resignation. It was, after all, no more than what her aunt had said earlier. Even, although she hated to admit it, what she was coming to believe herself. But if Amelia could be prevented from making a fatal mistake with the Earl of Rasenby, if she could be prevented from ruining herself now, there would still be time for Clarissa to try, one more time, to establish her more genteelly. She had to secure this chance for her sister, even if it meant risking her own virtue.

'I see. Very well, my lord, then I feel that the way is clear for you and me to discuss terms.'

'You are either very naïve or very stupid. It is for the gentleman, you know, to make terms. And for the lady to accept. You cannot expect me to take you seriously.' Lord Rasenby was by now, against his will, thoroughly interested. It was a trap, he had no doubt about it, but it was a good one, and merited his attention—at least until he discovered what it was.

Clarrie, braced for rejection, was yet determined to prevent it. She had to give her sister a chance of escape. She had to get Lord Rasenby away from her for just a few days, a few weeks, enough to let him cool off, and for Amelia to have her sights pitched at a more achievable and more honourable target.

'I realise that I am being a little unorthodox. But I thought you would appreciate both directness and a change. You are, as you admitted yourself, a little jaded in your taste. Perhaps a freshness of approach would restore your appetites?' Clarrie smiled in what she hoped was a coy manner, although the effect was ruined somewhat by the pleading in her eyes.

It was the pleading that succeeded. 'I'll give you a chance then, for your boldness, if for nothing else. But you must rise to the challenge, and prove your good faith to me first.'

'How?'

'I'll listen to your proposal in private. Tomorrow, not now. That will give you time to cool your temper, and to make sure that you really want to go through with this.'

'I will be just as determined tomorrow, I know I will. Name the place, Lord Rasenby, and I will be there.' With a toss of her head, and a determined point of her little chin, Clarrie glared into those deep blue eyes. She was anything but propitiating, but she was learning, and quickly, that Kit Rasenby responded badly to anything other than direct dealing.

'Will you? I wonder?' The soft tone sounded just a little threatening. 'I don't take kindly to being deceived, I'll warn you now. I'll have no truck with games and trickery. Come and dine with me tomorrow evening. At my house. On your own.'

'Oh, no, I couldn't. Why, that would be shocking. Oh, no. Can we not meet in the park, or perhaps take a drive? I couldn't dine alone with you.'

'Ah, 'tis as I thought. You are not nearly so bold as you promise. It was pleasant, exchanging views—' his tone was heavily ironic '—but I'm afraid our acquaintance is now at an end. I bid you good evening.'

'*No! Wait!*' Once again, Clarrie was forced to take a dramatic—nay, huge—step forward. 'I'll be there. I'll dine with you.'

He was surprised at her agreeing, for it was a

mad suggestion, even for him. No one could be under any illusion about a single lady dining alone in a gentleman's house—he had never invited any before now. But he gave no sign of his surprise. 'Very well, until tomorrow evening. I take it you know the address?'

She nodded, mute at her own daring.

'And am I to have a glimpse of the face under the mask before tomorrow? Perhaps even something on account?'

But Clarissa shrank back at this, unable to comply, even for her sister. And she had achieved her objective for tonight, after all. 'Wexford, my name is Wexford. As to my face—tomorrow will be soon enough. Unless, that is, you have more than one masked lady coming to dinner?'

He laughed. Her humour had the desperate touch of the gallows about it, but she was game. 'No, only you. Until then.'

And before he could bid her good night, Clarrie fled, removing her mask with relief, oblivious to Lord Robert Alchester, following discreetly at her back. A small exchange of coins bought him the address the footman had given to the hackney driver.

Back in the ballroom, Kit realised, with a curse, that he would need to find another dance partner.

Chapter Three

On her return from the ball Clarissa went straight upstairs to bed, but the long night brought her little comfort. She dreamt of surrendering to a passionate figure in a black domino, a dream that left her hot, flushed, and far from rested. Sitting up in bed to drink her morning chocolate—her one indulgence before facing the day—she tried to shake off the mists of sleep. Kit Rasenby, she reminded herself, was not a man to whom she should surrender anything, not even in her dreams! But the image of his strong, muscular body, his voice husky and flushed with passion, pressed naked against her own flesh, remained obstinately in her mind.

In person, Kit Rasenby had been completely un-expected. She had not counted on the strong pull of attraction she could feel between them, nor had she counted on him being so plain spoken. Amelia's description had led her to expect a man of the world, that was true, but one like the rest of the *ton*. Instead, Lord Rasenby stood out from the crowd, and his attractions were not those of a primped and perfect macaroni, but of a clean-cut, athletic, very *masculine* man.

Clarissa reminded herself once again not to confuse the outer man with the inner. He only *looked* clean cut and honest. His bitter remark, that all women wanted to be recompensed for their favours one way or another, came from deep within. In many ways, Clarissa could empathise with this. In fact, thinking about her sister, she could understand completely why Lord Rasenby was so very cynical. She fought the urge, growing deep in the recesses of her mind, to prove him wrong. She was not such a woman. She could be his equal. Only by recalling her mission, to save her sister—and her virtue—from his clutches, did she remind herself that her interests in him as a man, a lost cause, or any sort of acquaintance would be of necessity of very short duration. When Kit Rasenby found her out as a deceiver, she had no doubt he would never forgive her.

But she couldn't subdue the wistful thought that during their short time together, she might prove to him that women—or at least one woman—could be different.

Sitting in the small parlour after breakfast, Clarissa attempted to put together the week's menus. Amelia's seemingly endless requests for new dresses, new shoes, and new hats, made economy an absolute necessity, which meant that their meals were very plain fare indeed. Menu-planning was one of Clarissa's most hated tasks. It was not surprising, therefore, that it took a while for Lady Maria's strange behaviour to penetrate her consciousness. Eventually, though, Clarissa became aware that her mama was a little more animated than normal. Instead of occupying her usual position on the *chaise lounge*, she was sitting upright at the little writing desk, frantically scribbling in a notebook.

'Mama, what is it that you are working on? May I help?'

Lady Maria jumped and tried, not very successfully, to assume an air of nonchalance. 'Help? No, no, dear, not at all. I'm just doing some sums, trying to look at our expenses, you know. Amelia needs a new dress, she was saying just yesterday, and her dancing slippers are quite worn away again.'

'Mama, you know that you have no head for figures. Here, let me help you.' Wresting the notebook from Lady Maria's grasp, Clarissa failed to notice her mama's aghast expression. But looking at the vast sums that had been scribbled, in writing that became less legible with each number, she turned to her in dismay.

'What on earth are all these numbers? These are far too large to be household expenses. Mama, what can they be?'

'It's nothing for you to worry about, Clarissa, dear. They're just jottings. Give them back to me.'

Ignoring her mother's desperate attempt to reclaim the notebook, Clarissa continued to look in confusion at the numbers. 'Mama, please tell me what these are. Come, let us sit down and talk comfortably. Where is your tisane, for you look in need of it to me?' As she spoke, Clarissa ushered her mother over on to her habitual seat, and, pulling up a stool, sat down beside her. 'Now, what can be so awful that you can't tell me?'

'They're my gambling debts.' The bald statement was blurted out with relief. Surely, now that she had confessed, thought Lady Maria, Clarrie would fix it. She always did.

But for once her daughter, transfixed with horror, had nothing to say.

'You see, I thought, if I could win, then I could help with Amelia's gowns,' Lady Maria explained.

'For if she is to save our fortunes through a good marriage then she needs to be tricked out properly—even you would agree, Clarrie. And she says that she's so close to finalising things with Lord Rasenby, I thought I could help. But I kept losing. And then a nice man at the party said he would assist me with my stake money, and I thought, surely I couldn't lose for ever. But I did, Clarrie, I did. And now that nice man is dunning me, and I just don't know what to do.'

'Mama, don't, please don't tell me that you've actually borrowed money to gamble with?'

The abject horror in her voice made Lady Maria defensive. 'What of it? Everyone does it, Mrs Barrington says, and why should I not do so, when I'm bound to win soon.'

'Mrs Barrington? And what, pray, has she to say to this?'

'Well, she first introduced me to the party where I've been playing. And last night, when I had a quiet word with her, she said not to worry, she'd speak to the young man who is dunning me. Except, Clarrie, I can't help but feel I'd rather have you sort things out, you're so very good at it. I'd rather not rely on strangers, even if Mrs Barrington is such a good friend to Amelia, when I know can rely on you. My own *trusty* Clarissa.'

Lady Maria beamed gratefully at her daughter. She felt hugely better, having relieved her conscience and passed the burden, as always, to Clarissa.

But Clarissa was flabbergasted. The sums she owed, if the notebook was accurate, were beyond belief. 'Mama, you have not made any more arrangements for funds with Mrs Barrington, have you?'

'No, no, I promise. I just mentioned it in passing last night, I haven't exactly committed to anything.'

'And this man who is dunning you, when does he expect payment?'

'Well, as to that, I couldn't say. He merely says that he wants something on account soon, if I am to rely on him for further stake money.'

'Mama! You must not, under any circumstances whatsoever, take more money from him. You must stop this gambling at once. You won't win, you know, you will only put us further in debt. Please, I beg you, promise me, Mama, that you will stop.'

'Well, I—well, but do you think you can fix things, Clarrie? For Amelia must have her dress, you know. We can't expect Lord Rasenby to put us in funds until after they are married, once a settlement is agreed. And that is probably at least a month or so hence.'

'There is no question of Amelia marrying Lord Rasenby, absolutely none. We must sort out this mess ourselves, and you must refrain—Mama, you *must*—from further gambling in the meantime.'

'But, Clarrie, Amelia assures me that Lord Rasenby is about to propose. And if he does not, where will we be? No, no, Amelia cannot be wrong. She was born to make a sensational match, and she will.'

'Mama!' Clarissa's temper was rising rapidly beyond her control for the second time in two days. Taking a deep breath, knowing that harsh words would only give Lady Maria one of her turns, she tried once more for calm. 'Believe me, Lord Rasenby's intentions towards Amelia are purely dishonourable, no matter what Amelia may say. I know. Nay, I am certain of it. Amelia must be made to give him up, or she will bring us all to ruin.'

'Well, dear, if you say so,' said Lady Maria dubiously, torn between doubt and an unwillingness to give up her vision of Lord Rasenby as their saviour. 'Perhaps, then, a *carte blanche*—strictly as a temporary measure, you understand—would be a good thing, Clarrie? Then we could see ourselves clear of debt, and after that, Amelia can still make a good marriage. What do you say?'

'What do I say? Am I the only sane person in

this family? Aunt Constance was right, we will be ruined.'

'Oh, don't talk to me about your precious Aunt Constance. She is so ridiculously strait-laced as to be positively old-fashioned. And anyway, she's never been short of a penny, so what does she know? You take after that side of the family, Clarissa, I have always said so. Amelia is so much more like me, the darling girl.'

'Thank you, Mama, but I am pleased to take after Aunt Constance, if it means I have some moral fibre! I beg you, please, leave this in my hands. Do nothing further to get us deeper in debt. And get it out of your head that Amelia will receive any proposal from Lord Rasenby, honourable or otherwise.'

Lady Maria was far too used to Clarissa sorting their problems to question her abilities to cope with such huge debts, so she sighed, tucked her scarf around herself more comfortably, and dozed peacefully for the rest of the morning. Clarissa retired to her room with her head spinning to try to make sense of the situation.

Amelia flounced in some time later, disrupting her meditations. 'Why so glum, Clarrie? I hope you're not still fretting over my virtue. It's safe enough—for now at any rate.'

'Did you have a nice night?'

'Yes, I did, thank you very much, and as I promised, saw no trace of Rasenby. Mr Brompton was most attentive, though. I do like him.'

'Do you, Amelia? Enough to marry him?'

'Lord, Clarrie, not that again. I've told you, Edward is a clerk in a lawyer's office, he can hardly keep himself in cravats, never mind marry me. Although, perhaps as a last little fling before I tie myself to Rasenby, he'll do well enough.' Amelia laughed contemptuously at Clarissa's face. 'You're so easy to shock, sister dear. Provided that Rasenby gets no whiff of it, why should I not have Edward first? It's not as if Rasenby would be coming to the marriage bed pure.'

Amelia paused for a moment to reflect. Really, it was too, too vile of Edward to be so poor. And virtuous into the bargain. She was not at all convinced that he would take her to bed unless it was as his wife—even if she paraded naked in front of him! He had found out from Chloe some of Amelia's doings with Rasenby, and had had the temerity to lecture her. He could lecture her all he wanted if he had the funds. But he didn't. Frustrated at the unwonted feelings of tenderness Edward aroused in her, and at the necessity of deceiving him, Amelia turned once more on her sister. 'Yes, I warrant I like Edward enough to marry him. But he has not the means. It's Rasenby or the poor house, and I will not be going to the poor house.'

Clarissa was shocked. She had not realised just how perfidious her sister had become. She was horrified, too, at how she planned to treat Rasenby. Even had she not already resolved to remove Amelia from his grasp, she would have been forced into warning Rasenby about Amelia! 'Perhaps you may find that if this Edward is so much to your taste you may settle for him after all?'

'No, I've told you, Clarissa, my plans for Rasenby are unchanged. A few more days and all will be resolved between us, one way or another.'

'He won't be trapped into marriage, no matter what your plan.' Clarissa's tone was dry. 'He is far too clever for that. Are you so sure that he is as mad for you as you say?'

'Of course he's mad for me, I'm never wrong about these things.' This with a determined toss of golden curls. 'I have him wrapped around my finger. And there he'll stay, be assured, Clarrie, until he puts a ring on it.'

'That he will never do, I am sure of it. But what of you? How can you contemplate a life of matrimony based on deceit and trickery?'

A scornful laugh was Amelia's reply to this. 'Why do you care? It's not you who's being tricked. He deserves to be played at his own game, it will serve him well.'

'No, he never relies on trickery, he is honest in that sense. Really, he does not deserve such treatment.'

'What are you talking about, Clarissa Warrington? You've never met him—what do you know?'

The suspicion in Amelia's voice reminded Clarissa of the need for secrecy. But it would seem that rather than save Amelia from Lord Rasenby, Clarissa was now intent on saving Lord Rasenby from Amelia. When had come about this switch in loyalty?

'No, I don't know him, except by reputation. But it seems to me that, rake as he is, he deals honestly with his conquests. And he does not deserve to be tricked into matrimony. It is a recipe for disaster. For all, including you, Amelia, don't you see? Dearest, you'd be miserable.'

'Lord, Clarrie, there's no reasoning with you. You like to think you're so practical, but you're the most pathetic romantic, deep down. I won't discuss it further. I merely came in to ask you to come for a walk with me. Edward gets an hour for luncheon, and he said he may take the air in the park, so I thought we might bump into him. Do come,

Clarrie, you'd like him.' Amelia's tone was conciliating, but for once Clarissa was not to be won over.

'No, I won't be party to your assignations. It sounds like poor Edward is going to be another man let down by your plotting and scheming. Take Chloe, I'm sure you can persuade her easily enough.'

Amelia flounced out before Clarissa finished her sentence. It wasn't like Clarrie to be obstinate. Well, she'd show her!

Alone, Clarissa resolved on action. She was sure that there was more to Amelia's feelings for Edward, if only money were not the issue. If money, in the form of Rasenby, were removed as a temptation, Amelia would have a chance to see more of Edward. And he sounded like a determined young man; he would surely take the chance himself to secure Amelia. It wasn't much to go on, but it was a start. And if Edward didn't come up to scratch, she could always come clean with Rasenby, tell him her sister's plan. She was not going to stand by and let Amelia trick anyone into marriage. And she was going to do all she could to give her sister a chance at happiness— virtuous happiness.

Only Rasenby stood in the way. And by now, Clarissa had a good enough idea of his character to guess at what would interest him. A challenge, that's what he would like. And a bit of intrigue. She could do it. Clarissa turned her mind towards tonight, ignoring the thrill of anticipation she felt at the contest she was about to invoke. She was excited at seeing a means to save Amelia from herself, that was all. It was nothing at all to do with pitting her wits against such an opponent. Nothing to do with the charms of the opponent either. Certainly not!

Depositing her at the front door of Lord Rasenby's mansion in Grosvenor Square, the jarvey slid Clarissa a calculating look. Single ladies visiting these mansions did not normally travel in hacks. Nor did they arrive after dark, alone and wearing evening dress. Giving up the attempt to square all of these things with his passenger's cultured voice and genteel manner, he shrugged philosophically, and headed off into the night. She might be a toff, but she was up to no good, that was for sure.

As Clarissa tugged the bell and waited nervously at the front door, her thoughts mirrored those of the hackney driver. She felt like a woman of the streets. The look of contempt she received from the butler as he removed her cloak in the spacious hallway confirmed that he too shared this belief.

The hallway smelt of lavender polish, and was warmed by a huge fire burning to the left of the door. The rugs were Turkish, the large clock ticking softly against the panelled wall antique. There was a palpable air of wealth stretching back generations. Clarissa had no money, but there was nothing wrong with her breeding, and she had pride too. A martial flush gathered on her high cheek-bones and sparkled in her eyes as she thanked the butler in frigid tones. Clarrie was getting ready to do battle, and she was not about to be put out by a mere servant.

As with the hackney driver, her cultured tones gave the butler a shock, confusing him. Handing her cloak over to the footman, his voice became more propitiating. 'Lord Rasenby is expecting you, madam. I will show you to the parlour, if you'd be kind enough to follow me.'

A quick check in the mirror reassured her—she would do. Amelia's gown of palest blue silk with an overdress of twilled sarsenet was a little too large for Clarissa's more slender frame, and the *décolletage* way too low, showing far more of her creamy white skin than she had ever done before, but none of her own gowns were grand enough— or fashionable enough—to wear. Following Amelia's example, she had dampened the skirt so that it clung to her long slim legs, making the gauzy material almost transparent in the candlelight. Her glossy auburn hair had been cajoled into a Grecian knot, the curls falling over her white shoulder, and her slim arms were covered by long kid gloves. She had forsworn any cosmetics, fearing that she had not a light enough touch, but there was an attractive natural flush across her cheeks.

It was now or never. Head high, Clarrie entered the room and glided gracefully over to Lord Rasenby, hand extended. He was standing with his back to the fireplace, dressed simply but elegantly in an impeccably cut dark-blue coat, his pantaloons of a biscuit hue and glossy Hessians adding a touch of informality. Taking her gloved fingertips, he pressed a whisper of a kiss on the back of her hand, then quite blatantly looked her over.

'Well, Miss—Wexford, I think you said?' A quizzical raised brow told Clarissa he knew perfectly well that she had given an assumed name. 'You've surprised me on two counts.'

'I have, sir?' Clarissa retrieved her hand and, placing it behind her back, retreated a few paces, finding Lord Rasenby's presence somewhat overpowering. The tilt of her chin, did she but know it, was challenging.

'Yes, you have.' So, she was a little on edge, the

fake Miss Wexford. Well, he wasn't surprised—it was a brazen enough act to dine with him, and he admired her courage, if not her honesty. 'I wasn't convinced that you'd come, for a start. And, seeing you without the mask for the first time, I'm also surprised at just what perfection you kept hidden from me.'

Clarissa flushed. Tricked out in Amelia's finery, even she had to admit that she looked well enough. But having no great opinion of herself, she was inclined to dismiss his lordship's compliment as flummery. 'Thank you, sir, you are very kind.' A small curtsy of acknowledgement. 'At least I can be sure now that you will listen to my proposal without disgust.'

Kit laughed, finding himself once again confused by this woman. She was beautiful, although not in the common way. Her hair was not a fashionable gold, but burnished copper in the firelight, and the reddish flecks in it hinted at a temper. Those huge emerald eyes were too wide open, a little too perceptive, and had a disconcertingly honest look. Her mouth, with its full bottom lip, was not the cupid's bow that society decreed beauty, but it was, to Kit's eyes, far more sensual. And that chin—it was determined and defiant at the same time. Definitely not a simpering miss, but one with a real spark of fire.

He had been right to make this assignation. He was going to be anything but bored, dealing with the challenging Miss Wexford and her proposition, whatever that turned out to be. Having just this day made the arrangements for his final trip to France on the *Sea Wolf*, Kit was aware that he was in dire need of distraction. It pained him already, knowing this was to be the last of such adventures, and he knew he would miss it sorely. He worried that boredom would turn him to old quarrels and to new depths of depravity. And that thought, too, bored him.

Almost as an afterthought, he had paid off Charlotte du Pres. She didn't know it, but Miss Wexford's timing was excellent—she was just what he needed right now to take his mind off things. 'So, madam, you have no taste for compliments. We shall deal well then, for I favour plain speaking myself.'

Handing her a small glass of Canary wine, Kit ushered Clarrie into a seat by the fire. 'I thought we'd dine here, without the aid of servants. So much more comfortable, if you don't object to helping yourself?' Seating himself opposite her, he watched her take a nervous sip of the wine, and nod her assent. 'I thought, too, that we'd postpone our discussion until after we've eaten. It would be nice to become better acquainted first, don't you agree?'

Clarissa was staring into the flames, wallowing in the all-enveloping warmth, and only nodded, absently, at his words. The room was beautiful, in a restrained way. The furniture was light wood and highly polished, with a marked absence of the rococo gilt and ormolu currently so à la mode. With a sensuality she didn't even know she possessed, Clarrie snuggled deeper into the chair, and stretched, her white skin picking up a glow from the flickering flames, the red tints in her hair alive with colour. A small smile curled up at the edges of her mouth, and she sighed, deeply.

'Perhaps, you would prefer I left you to the comfort of the fire, and your own company?' Kit had been at first beguiled, then disconcerted, at her behaviour. He was not used to being ignored. He was a little piqued, and more than a little aroused. She was like a sensuous cat, stretching luxuriatingly in front of him.

The sharpness of his tone recalled Clarissa to her situation. She sat up abruptly, spilling a little of her wine on to Amelia's dress. 'I am so sorry. It's the heat, it's a little overpowering.' She rubbed at the dress with her handkerchief, but was succeeding only in making it worse.

'Here, let me.' Lord Rasenby bent over her, his own large handkerchief of white linen in his hand.

'There, that's better. Now, if you can force yourself to stay awake for a while, we'd better dine, I think.'

His touch, light as it was, made her shiver, and she drew back abruptly. 'Thank you.'

Kit eyed her quizzically. She was as nervous as a kitten under that veneer of calm. More and more, he was intrigued. But he would let her set the pace. For now, he was content to watch—and be entertained.

Over dinner, of which Clarissa partook little, confining herself to the duck and peas, she set out to charm. She had a fair idea by now of Kit Rasenby's preconceptions of her sex, and rather than make the expected idle small talk, conversed instead on the politics of the day. Her conversation was informed, thanks to her Aunt Constance's tutelage, and she was not frightened of expressing an opinion.

'I can't help but feel that things in France are not as settled as they claim. It seems to me that there will be another war, do you not agree? And then, perhaps all the *émigrés* presently here in England will become our enemies?'

'Yes, war seems to be inevitable. As to the *émigrés* I have no views at all. Some will turn, some—those who have found a home here—will not. 'Tis human nature to follow the easiest path.'

'That is a sadly cynical point of view, my lord.

Do you grant no room, in human nature, for loyalty to a cause? Must everyone be so selfish?'

'Do not tell me you are a do-gooder, for you are far too pretty. You are obviously an intelligent woman, and unaccountably well informed, but believe me when I tell you that the French are no different than anyone else. People do what is easiest and most lucrative for them, naught more.'

'Well…' Clarissa pursed her lips and frowned '…I think that we will simply have to differ on the subject. For I choose to believe there is some good in everyone that is not simply self-interest!'

The challenge was accompanied again by that tilt of the chin, and a flash from those green eyes. She looked so sure of herself that Kit almost laughed. He contented himself with an inward smile, however, and merely offered her a dish of cream. She helped herself with relish, blissfully unaware of her naïvety.

'You sound like the heroine in one of those dreadful novels my sister raves about,' Kit said. 'Virtuous despite the overwhelming odds. How would you cope, I wonder, locked up in a castle like *Udolpho*, faced with the vile Signor Montoni?'

'So you've read it, then, *Udolpho*, although you despise it? I'd like to think I'd have a bit more presence of mind, and would escape. And I don't believe in blind virtue, just that there's more to people than self-interest.' Temporarily distracted, Clarrie wondered whether to continue this line of conversation, but quickly abandoned the idea. Ruefully, she realised that a discussion of virtue didn't really fit with her proposition for his lordship. 'We were talking of the French. Do you know anything of them, personally, Lord Rasenby—the *émigrés*, I mean? I have often thought that they must have such romantic tales to tell of escape. Far more exciting than Mrs Radcliffe's novel.'

'On the contrary, it's not at all romantic. They escape with no wealth, often only the possessions they can carry. And they have to rely on the goodwill of friends and relatives in order to survive when they land abroad. To see it as romantic is to persist in holding an uninformed point of view.'

'And yet, I cannot help but do so. I would so much like to see for myself what such rescues involve.'

'I think you wouldn't find it such fun if you were present. Have you eaten sufficient? I think it's time we *talked terms*, as you called it last evening.' Kit's tone brooked no argument.

'Yes. Yes, you are right.' Now it came to the bit, Clarissa was more than a little apprehensive. She knew what she had to say, but she wasn't convinced it would work. And if it did, she was worried it might work too well—for this man would want more than talk. How to go through with her plan and keep her own virtue intact? Especially when, it seemed, she was becoming less inclined to do so. Kit Rasenby was not just attractive, he was *interesting*. Becoming better acquainted was proving no hardship at all.

Taking a deep breath, Clarrie launched into her proposition with no thought for preliminaries, determined on seeing it through before her courage failed her—or her common sense intervened. 'I think, my lord, that it would be no exaggeration to say that you are rather bored with your life? Well, I wish to offer you a temporary diversion.'

'Bored? Well, that's one way of putting it, yes. I think you should realise there's not much you can offer that I haven't tried, one way or another, though. You are no doubt aware, madam, of my very dreadful reputation when it comes to your sex? After all, we touched on it last night.'

'Yes, and if you don't mind me saying so, I think that you're rather maligned by society, my lord.'

A cynical smile twisted Kit's lips, as he looked down into her honest-seeming emerald eyes. Was she truly naïve, this woman, or was she just an excellent actress? 'You know, if you hope to redeem me in some way, there's no point. I am, according to my mother and sister, long past redemption.'

'Oh, no, no one is *ever* past redemption. I can't help but think, Lord Rasenby, that you cling rather too much to your reputation. You seem to actually enjoy being an outcast. By your own admission, you do have principles, although you keep them well hidden. You deal far more honestly than some, but you don't like people to see that, do you? You like to be the bad Lord Rasenby. And I can quite see why that would be convenient.'

'Pray do give me the benefit of your insight, then—why would my being bad be convenient?'

'Why, it means people expect less of you, of course. They can't rely on you, and therefore they won't be likely to turn to you when they need help, will they?' Clarissa held up her hand, as Kit tried to interrupt, too taken up with her line of argument to let him. 'I know what you're going to say, you told me yourself, that people do rely on you—for money. I'm sure that your mama and your sister and your mistresses all get plenty of that from you. But that's easy. What you don't give is anything of yourself.'

'I'm not sure I follow. Is bleeding me dry not enough of myself to give?' There was bitterness in the words. Kit was so wealthy that it would take more than his mama and Charlotte du Pres to ruin him, but they certainly tried. Paying Charlotte off had cost him a fortune and a diamond bracelet to boot, and his mother was hinting at new hangings for the Dower House. To say nothing of his nephew Jeremy and his regularly accumulated bad debts.

'You understand me perfectly well, my lord.' Clarissa's voice was terse. She hated deliberate avoidance, and Lord Rasenby was no fool. 'You substitute money for everything, and then you don't like it when you get nothing back.' Seeing his brow crease, she realised that she'd gone too far again. Lord Rasenby might like plain speaking, but he didn't like home truths. Clarrie cursed her blunt tongue, it was always getting her into trouble. And it wouldn't get her anywhere with this man.

Biting her lip, but failing to look totally contrite, she apologised. 'I beg your pardon. I get carried away sometimes, and speak without thinking. Let us talk of more congenial matters.' She smiled cajolingly up at him.

'Yes, but you're not truly sorry at all, are you— it's just that you've realised you've angered me.' With an effort, Kit dismissed the idea that she'd managed to see through him with ease—and that she'd echoed, almost to the word, his own thoughts. It was just luck. He wasn't so transparent. He was more than ever sure she was playing some sort of game, but it was a deep, and therefore challenging, one.

'Come clean, Miss Wexford. For a start, I know that's not your real name. What can I call you? If we are to talk openly, I would like *some* element of truth in our conversation.'

'Very well, you can call me Clarissa. Since we are to be informal.'

'So we are to be informal, Clarissa? The name suits you. And will you call me Kit?'

'Kit. It too suits you.' The humour was reflected in her eyes as she echoed his words. 'I think, since our relationship is to be both informal and of short duration, that we can manage on such intimate terms. It's not as if there will be any witnesses.'

'You intrigue me. I take it, then, that you do not aspire to Charlotte du Pres's position?'

A flash of anger was quickly disguised. 'No, I want no such relationship with you. Nor do I want any financial recompense, nor any presents nor anything at all of that sort. Let us be clear on that now, Lord—Kit, please.' She reached out, touched his arm lightly with the tips of her fingers, then quickly withdrew. Even such a tiny touch sent tingles up and down her skin.

'I can see you are serious. You are not someone who lies easily, are you? Whatever your game, you have honest eyes,' Kit said wryly. 'So, no presents. Well, it will be a refreshing change, certainly. But you are happy for Charlotte's position to remain unchallenged?' Kit had already decided she didn't need to know that Charlotte was already history.

His question gave Clarissa pause. If he got rid of Charlotte du Pres, then it created a vacancy, and it was likely he'd offer it to Amelia. It had been no part of her plan to comment on his current mistress, but perhaps, now that the opportunity had arisen, it was worth while?

'Are you contemplating a replacement? I thought you said last night that the rumours concerning Miss Warrington had no substance?'

'I said she would not be my wife. I have no need of a wife, when I can take my pleasures outside the marriage bed. From what I have seen of matrimony, there are few pleasures to be had there. Daily, the scandal sheets give us another tale of adultery and bastard children. And behind it, heartbreak for someone—the children, at the very least. Matrimony does not require affection. I have no wish to sample the insipid and dutiful caresses of a virgin wife. There is naught to substitute for experience. But you already know my feelings on this subject. I'm more interested in why you bring Amelia Warrington into the conversation again. Has she put you up to this?'

'No, no, I assure you she has not.' At least that was the truth. In fact, if Amelia found out, she would never forgive her. 'But I am a little acquainted with her, and I cannot feel she would make you a very good mistress. She wants to be your wife—she is hardly likely to be happy settling for less. No, on consideration, I think Charlotte du Pres is much more suited to your needs.'

Kit smiled, humour lurking deep in his midnight-blue eyes. Looking into them, laughing complicitly, Clarrie was suddenly breathless. His mouth, which he normally held in a firm, hard line, had softened, and there was a slight growth of stubble on his jaw. She had a sudden urge to run her hand along it, to feel the contrast between the roughness there and the smooth contours of his lips. Clarrie felt her mouth go dry at the thought, and licked her own lips nervously. She had never felt such blatant attraction emanating from a man.

Reminding herself that it was exactly this attraction he traded on, she looked away. 'I didn't come here to give you advice about your mistresses, but you did ask. I am aware that this is not really a conversation we should be having.'

Kit laughed out loud at this. 'My dear Clarissa, you shouldn't even be here, let alone discussing such intimate matters with me. But that hasn't stopped you. However, I think you're right about Amelia Warrington, I think she is likely to be rather too demanding. And virgins, you know, can be so unsatisfying. I prefer my women to know what pleasures a man.'

'Oh! Well—well, I think then you can quite safely dismiss Amelia Warrington.'

'You seem sure of her. She won't be a virgin for long, you know. It may not be me, but she will be plucked soon. And likely not by a husband. She aims high.'

'Is she really so bad? She is young, you know, but not—not calculating.'

'You don't know her at all well if you think so. She is a pretty and very ambitious young woman. Though in my experience, she has the kind of looks that fade quickly. Any man can see that he has no need to offer marriage to have her. It's just a question of how high she'll sell herself. I'm not personally convinced it's a price worth paying.' Looking at Clarissa, he was surprised to see the hurt on her face. He possessed himself of her hand. 'It's the way of the world. She will take me not because she likes me better, but because I have more money. You are wasting your energies, concerning yourself with such a one. She will go her own way, and no friend will stop her.'

Looking into Kit's eyes, such a piercing, deep, dark blue colour, and for once showing such genuine concern, Clarissa acknowledged that he spoke the truth. But Amelia was her sister. She couldn't give up on her, it wasn't yet too late. And if nothing else, she could make sure that Amelia didn't throw herself away on this man.

With a sigh, and a renewed determination to get her proposition finally out of the way this evening, Clarrie smiled up at Kit. 'We've wasted enough time discussing other women. I've no aspirations to replace them in your affections. What I want from you is temporary.'

'You're frank, at least. Tell me then, precisely what is it you want me for—temporarily.'

'I will, then. But you must hear me out without interruptions, for it is vital that I make the terms as clear as possible—do you understand?'

His lips twitched as he repressed a smile, but Kit simply nodded his assent and sat back to watch her. This was proving to be worth every minute. Not once this evening had he been bored.

'I said I did not want to replace Miss du Pres, or anyone else—any of your opera singers or bits of fancy or whatever term you prefer.' Clarissa looked up, flushing. 'You're laughing at me?'

'No, no, I promise. I am merely impressed at your opinion of my prowess. Just how many of these bits of fancy am I supposed to be maintaining at one time? I am but a man, you know.'

A small gurgle of laughter escaped Clarrie. Shocking as this conversation was, it was more shockingly fun. 'Well, you told me yourself that your reputation is very bad, so I naturally assumed that you would place quantity over quality.'

At this, Kit gave an amused chuckle. 'No, I assure you, Clarissa, you are mistaken. I very much prefer quality, it's just that it is so difficult to come by. However, I am interrupting you once again. Please do continue, this is most—most—intriguing.'

'Well, I'm glad to hear you say that you would prefer quality, because that's what I'm offering. I'm four-and-twenty, and it is way past time I was married. But marriage, as you've said yourself, is a lifetime commitment to boredom, and for a lady, especially, promises no real pleasure.' A deep blush was stealing over Clarissa's cheeks, but she was determined to get this over with, no matter how embarrassing it all was. 'However, married I must be, and soon, or I will be too old.'

Looking up, Clarissa saw unease writ large on

Kit's handsome face. She hastened to reassure him. 'Fear not, I have no matrimonial expectations of you. I am under no illusions there, and must aim rather lower, for I have neither dowry nor traditional beauty. I have someone in mind, you know, but the problem is that he is just a little staid and more than a little old.' Ruthlessly thrusting her neighbour Bingley Smythington into the role to give her lies some authenticity, Clarrie shuddered effectively. Bingley had clammy hands, and such a bumptious manner, as well as being nearer fifty than forty, that she had no qualms about using him so ill. 'So I thought, while I resigned myself to a life of propriety, that I might indulge myself first, and have one little adventure.'

Clarrie stopped talking, and looked at Kit, trying to assess his reaction to her words, but he merely raised an eyebrow, indicating that she should continue. She had thought through this approach so carefully, knowing she had to come up with something that would surprise him, that she forgot her modesty in her determination to make him agree.

'So, you see, that is why our relationship would have to be kept very private. And of short duration. I must on no account be publicly compromised. And I picked you because you said you had no qualms, you see, about seducing virgins, provided that they were willing. And I *am* willing, provided that it's fun. And of course, I know it will be—fun, that is—since your reputation as a ladies' man must mean—well, you know what I mean.' Clarrie paused, flushed at the path her thoughts had taken. Of course it would be pleasurable, sharing herself with this man, she had no doubt at all on that score. But she wasn't actually going to go that far, she had to remind herself. So really, she had to stop thinking about it.

With a shake of her curls to dispel the images she had conjured up, Clarrie returned to her proposition, finding that Kit was watching her with an amused, and slightly bewildered, look upon his face. 'I must insist that you promise to abandon— for just a little while—your pursuit of any other females. Indeed, I must make it a condition of your acceptance that you do so. What I want first and foremost is for you to surprise me. I want an adventure, not just a liaison.'

Once again, she held her hand up to stop him speaking. This was the tricky bit. 'I know you said that lack of experience was not something you relished. And I can't pretend that I have the skills of the likes of Charlotte du Pres. But I'm willing to learn, and I'm sure you won't find me bashful or— or unsatisfying, if you're willing to take a chance.'

She sat back, amazed at her own temerity. She had said it. She had been as blunt as she could be, and as clear about her terms. Surely he wouldn't resist the challenge? This evening had shown to her, if nothing else, that he was ripe for a change, and surely she had offered just that?

'Let me get this straight—for I have to tell you that I've never heard anything like it in my life.' Kit ran a distracted hand through his hair. He didn't believe her, but he was tempted, just to see how far she'd go. The claim of virginal innocence, he dismissed immediately. No virgin discussed such things so openly. It was a mere ploy to whet his appetite. And it was working. Virgin or no virgin, he wanted her.

'I have to forgo all other women for the duration of our acquaintance. I must see you only in secret. And you want nothing from me other than this— no recompense, only my silence?'

'Yes.'

'Further, you wish what you call an adventure in my company. I take it you mean something other than the adventure of sharing our bodies?'

She was blushing furiously now, and managed only a slight nod. Really, she was an excellent actress.

'And you cannot be more specific as to the nature of this?'

'No. That is your payment, you see. You arrange something out of the ordinary, something illicit, something thrilling, something I can remember when I'm old. And something too that you will enjoy, of course. As a prelude. I thought that you'd relish the challenge, that it would help, for a while, to ease your boredom. I thought—well, I thought we could have some fun together.'

'Fun? Good God, I don't think I've ever had fun with a woman. I'm not even sure I would know what you mean by it.'

He was looking at her assessingly now, and Clarissa desperately wanted him not to turn her down flat. The whole idea of an adventure was just a delaying tactic. The longer he took to organise something, the more time she had to separate Amelia from him. And until he could arrange whatever he was going to arrange, Clarrie was free from any threat to her virtue. She also needed time to think over what she had done—for she really had no idea yet how she was to manage to pull this off.

'Perhaps it would be best if I were to leave now, and we can discuss this further once you have reflected?'

'You're right, I need time to think. I'll meet you in Hyde Park tomorrow at four.'

'No, no,' Clarrie said agitatedly, 'that is the fashionable hour. We will be seen. I will meet you at the gates of Green Park—no one goes there at that time.'

'Very well.' Kit stood and raised a hand to help her out of her seat. Taking her by surprise, he pulled her close, one arm around her slim waist, cool on her skin through the thin fabric of her dress, the other tilting her chin upwards. 'No women other than you? You ask a lot of me. I think a sample of the merchandise would be appropriate, don't you agree? Just to prove you are worth the sacrifice. I warn you, my fair Clarissa, I won't be cheated, and I won't let you go back on your bargain. You do realise that?'

Clarrie licked her full bottom lip nervously, but made no move to escape. The sensation of his hand on her body was sending shivers up her spine. She had never been so close to a man before, and had no idea that it could be so very exciting. 'A kiss to seal a bargain, then,' she whispered.

Kit laughed, low and aroused. 'You are sealing a bargain with the devil.' His lips brushed hers, smooth and cool at first, a featherlight touch at the corners of her mouth. He ran his tongue over her full bottom lip. She smelled of roses and vanilla, she tasted sweet and hot. Her breath was warm, her breathing shallow.

Clarrie sighed at his touch, leaning closer in to the hard wall of Kit's chest, inviting him to deepen the contact. She could feel the heat from his body building a slow fire somewhere deep inside her. Experimentally, she let the tip of her tongue run over Kit's lower lip, mimicking his actions, feeling him groan in response. His lips took possession of her mouth fully, one hand on the sensitive nape of her neck, holding her carefully close, the other at her waist.

Clarrie surrendered to temptation and let an instinct she didn't know she possessed take over. Tongues met in a kiss that took them both by surprise. In an instant, Clarrie moved from warm tingles to searing heat. Kit's lips were soft and hard at the same time. He was kissing and licking her mouth in a way that left her weak with wanting. His tongue flicked to the sensitive corners of her lips, then back to tangle with hers. He licked along the length of her lower lip, then his mouth fastened fully on hers again.

She wanted more. She ran her hand over the nape of his neck and up into the short cropped hair on his head, relishing the rough feel of it, contrasting it with the soft, hard, smooth feel of his mouth on hers. Her nipples hardened as she pressed into his chest, rubbing against him, relishing the small shivers and the pleasure-pain feeling that the contact gave her, even through their clothes.

Kit groaned softly, and pulled back. His breathing slowed. He eyed her through heavy lids, careful not let her see how much she had aroused him. All her pretence of virginity must be at an end. This woman knew exactly what she was doing. 'Enough. That is definitely enough for now, I think. You have proved yourself entirely, madam.'

Clarrie, still trying in vain to control her overwhelming and totally unexpected response to his kiss, could do no more than blink up at him, confused. 'I—I—I'll get better in time, sir.'

'A word of warning. I will play these games only so far. You can abandon, once and for all, this pretence of innocent virginity, for the passion in your kisses prove you to be far from innocent.' Looking down at her, he was taken aback to see a sheen of tears glazing her speaking emerald eyes.

'Rest assured, your lack of innocence does your case no harm. Had you really been the virgin you claim to be, I would have hesitated. I need now have no scruples, and can consider your proposition with a clear conscience. The footman will call a hack for you. Good night.'

With a slight bow, he turned away from her, ringing the bell for the servant. Clarissa stumbled out to the waiting hack, her mind a swirl of abject confusion and unexpected hurt.

So distressed was she that she failed to notice the figure turning the corner into the street. Lord Robert Alchester, returning home early of necessity since his pockets were to let, from the tables of the hell in St James's currently favoured with his patronage, was most intrigued. Well, well, the woman from last night, if he was not mistaken, and emerging alone from Kit Rasenby's town house. This development was worth keeping an eye on.

Chapter Four

Clarissa rose heavy eyed the next morning, having slept only fitfully, haunted by the memory of Kit Rasenby's kisses and her own shocking response. What was it about the man that made her act so out of character? Needing to clear her head, she eschewed her usual morning chocolate and settled instead for a brisk, invigorating walk around the park. This fever her body had succumbed to was but a passing fancy, surely. Triggered, like as not, by the novel experience of being kissed for the first time, and nothing more. It was not that Kit was irresistible at all. It was just that she had never had such contact with a man before. He was a novelty, that was all.

Entering the little breakfast parlour an hour later, she was grateful to find that both her mama and her sister were as yet abed. Resolutely putting all thoughts of Kit to one side, Clarissa partook of coffee and warm rolls, finally able to mull over the events of the previous night with something approaching her usual rational calm.

Kit's ruthless assassination of her sister's character she acknowledged to be sadly all too accurate. There could be no doubt that Amelia would accept whatever Kit Rasenby offered, proper or improper. What would count with Amelia would be the recompense in purely financial terms. And the higher the terms, the less Amelia would concern herself with the loss of her virtue. Kit Rasenby was right. Amelia would be *plucked*—she shuddered at the awfulness of the term and all it implied. If not by him, then certainly by some other opportunist with a large and generous purse and a taste for virgin flesh.

Ruefully, Clarissa realised she would not wish Amelia as a wife on Kit Rasenby even had he any such intentions. It would be the road to misery for them both. Not, she cautioned herself, because she had any feelings for Kit herself, mind you. No, it was merely that she was sure they would bring only unhappiness to each other. And even a rake, after all, deserved more from matrimony. No, Amelia and Kit must not—*would not*—marry.

Amelia herself put an end to these musings, storming into the breakfast parlour in a state of high dudgeon, bright flags of anger flying in her cheeks. She was not yet dressed, and though she had discarded her nightcap, her hair was hanging loose, and the muslin wrapper she wore over her chemise was only loosely tied.

'Clarrie, there you are. I've been looking for you everywhere—where have you been? I've had the most dreadful night, I've hardly had a wink of sleep.' Throwing herself into a chair, failing to notice that her sister looked singularly tired from her own restless night, Amelia's mouth puckered in temper that boded a storm of tears in the near future. Reaching for a roll from the basket, she discarded it again petulantly. 'These are cold. And I expect the coffee is too! I want fresh. Where is that dratted maid, she's never here when I need her? Honestly, Clarrie, is it too much to ask that we employ servants who can actually fulfil their duties? I swear that woman hates me. How I detest being poor!'

Pulling the bell to summon fresh coffee, Clarissa eyed her sister with an impending sense of gloom. The last thing she needed was one of Amelia's tantrums, which were not only exhausting, but all-consuming. And unstoppable. There was no point in trying to do anything other than let them run their course, so she simply sat back and waited.

'Don't look at me like I'm some tiresome child to be indulged. I won't be ignored! Oh, Clarrie, you don't know—how can you know?—how truly dreadful it is to be me. Sometimes I almost wish I wasn't so beautiful. If I was merely pretty, like you, then it wouldn't be so bad.'

Clarissa, inured to such casual insults, continued quietly with her breakfast. Amelia slumped into her seat, causing her to hope that a full-blown tantrum was to be avoided, but this was dashed when, with a long drawn-out 'Ohhhhhh' of frustration, her sister rose abruptly, pushing her chair over, and started pacing in front of the fire place. With a sigh, Clarissa gave Amelia her full attention.

'Come Amelia, what ails you? Won't you sit down and tell me?' She patted the chair invitingly, but Amelia continued to pace.

'I tell you, Clarrie, I am positively sick to my teeth of my life. Look at me!' Pausing to inspect herself in the mirror above the meagre fire burning in the grate, Amelia looked temporarily gratified at what she saw. Really, she was simply beautiful, even with her hair uncurled and her nightwear in disarray. But that was just the problem. 'I mean, I'm lovely. I'm not being vain, Clarrie, I can see it myself. And everyone says so—Mama, you, Chloe, *everyone*. I can't be this beautiful if it's not for a purpose, can I? I *must* be meant to marry well, I don't want to be an ape-leader like you.' Her breathing quick and shallow, Amelia paced, determinedly nursing her anger. 'It's my destiny, a good marriage. The end to all of my problems.'

Wryly Clarissa noted that Amelia concerned herself only with her own fate. No thought, as usual, for Mama. But then, when did Amelia ever think of anyone but herself? Last night Clarissa had accused Kit of escaping all responsibility by using his money to pay people off, everyone from his mother to his mistress. Sometimes she wished she had the means to do the same thing. Kit's wealth would do a lot to ease the many responsibilities she carried on her slim shoulders. Her mother's debts. A dowry for Amelia. Even enough to put adequate coals on the fire, or something other than rabbit and onions on the table for dinner.

Amelia unwittingly echoed her thoughts. 'I need money. I was born for luxury. I can't go on like this, I just can't. I'm fed up with wearing the same old clothes all the time, and never having nice jewellery. I'm eighteen, for goodness' sake, I'm practically on the shelf. I mean, look at you, Clarrie—what have you got in front of you except life as an old maid, or a governess, or married to some ancient old fossil and having to spend your days changing his gout bandages? I've got to get out of here. I've got to get married. *I've just got to!'*

Giving her temper full reign, Amelia's voice rose shrilly. Her face became unattractively red and tears flowed rather unbecomingly down her cheeks. A bout of crying was one of the few things that drew attention away from her charms. For a few moments, there was silence in the parlour, interrupted only by hearty sobbing. Amelia cried with a passion, her shoulders heaving, her face hidden in her arms, as she sprawled once more on a seat at the table.

Eventually the tears turned to hiccups and she looked up, a sorry sight, hair tangled and lying damp on her cheeks, eyes puffed and red, to continue her lamentations. 'And if I'm to marry without a dowry, then it stands to reason that I'll have to resort to some *underhand behaviour*, as some people have called it. It stands to reason that I'll have to be *less than honest* in my dealings, as some may accuse me. It's just that fate needs a helping hand sometimes. And if *some people* can't see that, well, that's their problem, not mine. And what's more, if that's the way *some people* think, well…then they'll find that I'll refuse to see them again. Not ever! *Then* they'll be sorry.' The sobbing resumed, but more quietly now. The storm had almost worn itself out.

Smiling inwardly, Clarissa realised they had finally come to the crux of the matter, the real reason for Amelia's tears. Amelia's plans for tricking Kit into marriage had obviously been in part revealed to Edward last night. And Mr Brompton, bless him for the honest man he must be, had obviously severely upbraided Amelia. The fact that Amelia had listened sufficiently to be able to quote his reservations back word for word this morning was evidence enough of her affections being engaged, would she just admit it. With satisfaction, Clarissa realised that Amelia was, rather astonishingly, falling in love with this sober and righteous young man.

Trying to persuade Amelia that Edward and his reservations should be paid heed was, however, beyond Clarissa's capabilities for the present. With resolution borne of experience, Clarissa decided to sit back and let Amelia cry herself out, inwardly calmer herself now in the knowledge that she was right to pursue a course of separating her sister from Kit Rasenby. And hopeful too that Edward had played a part in putting at least some obstacles in the way of Amelia's plot to trick Kit.

* * *

But it took the rest of the morning and well into the early afternoon for Amelia's tears to run dry. Only then did she allow Clarissa to dose her with hartshorn and water, tuck her up in a darkened room, and leave her to sleep off the damage done to her complexion.

Which left Clarissa with little time to continue her own reflections before having to ready herself for her assignation with Kit in the park. He would say yes, he *had* to say yes. And if he turned her down—well, that simply wasn't an option. She told herself, with more bravado than conviction, that she would persuade him—somehow—to come round to her way of thinking.

Had she been aware of just how Kit had spent his extremely busy morning, Clarissa would have been more than a little perturbed. As it was, she set out for the Green Park by hack, looking smart in a pale green merino walking dress and matching spencer, a gift from her aunt. Her feet were clad in boots of Morocco leather, and a reticule of her own design dangled from her wrist. A treasured pair of kid gloves and a simple poke hat completed the outfit. Clarissa was content with her appearance, and happy that she looked her best. She carried no muff, it was a luxury she could not afford, but the day was none too cold, and she was not anticipating being in the carriage for long.

With a heart fluttering with anticipation, despite having given herself a stern talking to on the subject of attractive rakes, their kissing abilities, and the need to avoid all such intimate contact in the future—somehow or other—Clarissa paid off the hack, and stepped lightly through the park gates.

Lord Rasenby was waiting in a high-perch phaeton to which two glossy, perfectly matched chestnuts were poled. They were restless, contained with some effort by the small tiger at their heads, and Clarissa looked up at their master, carelessly lounging in the seat of the vehicle, impossibly high off the ground, with some trepidation.

'Don't be alarmed, I assure you I have them well under control. Any rake worth his salt, you know, is an expert at mastering even the freshest of fillies.' The sardonic look that always accompanied any mocking reference to his reputation was tempered by a slight smile. 'It's not so high as it looks, just place your foot on the step and I'll help you up.' Leaning over to take her hand, Kit pulled Clarrie easily into the carriage and briskly tucked a rug over her knees. His touch was cool and impersonal, but she flushed slightly all the same. With a curt nod of dismissal to the tiger, he jerked sharply on the reins, and the chestnuts set off at a brisk trot.

The few moments it took to get the horses under control allowed Clarissa to rein in her own feelings at the proximity of this man. His thigh brushed hers through the rug, for the seat was narrow. She could not but be aware of that hard, muscled body which his caped great-coat did nothing to hide. He was every bit as overpowering as she remembered. Every bit as attractive. *And every bit as dangerous,* she chided herself. Think only of what you have to achieve, and make sure you do it with regard to your own safety, Clarissa Warrington.

'I congratulate you for your punctuality Clarissa, it's not a trait common to your sex.'

His words startled her from her thoughts, and she replied with unthinking asperity. 'As I believe I have been at pains to point out to you, sir, I am not inclined to be taken for the common herd. I pride myself on being punctual.'

'And frank, too. You could not be accused of reticence.'

She laughed. 'Yes, that too. I'm sorry, I didn't mean to be rude. It's just that—well, I hate being judged. I know you'll think me foolish, but you've no idea how irritating it is when people assume you are just the same as every other young lady. I try not to be so predictable.'

'You do me a disservice, madam. I sympathise with your frustration and assure you I understand only too well both your feelings and your reaction. But are you not being a little hypocritical, for did you not so judge me—as a rake—when first we met, in exactly the same way?'

'Yes, I did, and it was wrong of me. Although I have to say that you've been at great pains to confirm me in my assumptions, have you not?' A glance at him showed, from the lips firmly suppressed, that she had hit home. 'And when I did point out that you were hiding behind your reputation, you were not best pleased.' Another glance showed that he was not best pleased again. Oh dear, her unfortunate tongue—when would she learn to guard it? 'I'm sorry. I fear I have offended you once more. And I so meant not to—offend you, I mean. I meant to be more *propitiating*.'

A crack of laughter made her look up, an answering sparkle in her own eyes.

'You think that's funny. I know what you're thinking.'

'I doubt it. Pray tell me.'

'That my behaviour is hardly conducive to achieving my goal. Getting you to agree to my proposition, that is. And I do most abjectly apologise, for contrary to what I may have said, and even with the benefit of a night's reflection, I *do* want you to agree.'

'Actually, I was thinking that you're the most unpredictable woman I've ever had dealings with. And I was thinking that I would very much like to kiss you again. So you see, my fair Clarissa, you're not as able to read my mind as you think you are.' A smile, warmer than before, softened the words.

'Oh.' A blush stole across Clarrie's pale cheeks, for his words roused such pictures in her head as she had been trying to suppress since last night.

As she looked up at him, her eyes wide, her soft mouth trembling slightly, Kit was surprised at the sharp gust of desire that ripped through him. The combination of honesty—or the appearance of it, in any case—and the undercurrent of passion, the fiery nature that must surely accompany those auburn locks, was captivating. Once again he reminded himself that he was no doubt being embroiled in a plot of her making. Once again he decided that whatever it was, it was a small price to pay for the use of the exceedingly comely body being offered to him.

Raising a dark winged eyebrow in query, he

smiled. 'Oh? Is that all you have to say? You are not normally so succinct.'

'No. That is…well, Lord Rasenby—Kit, I mean, there must be no kissing yet, for we have not sealed our bargain. We were to discuss it further, were we not? Then, in case you need reminding, there was to be payment in advance on your part, in terms of our adventure, before any more such—intimate contact.' Ignoring the blush that heated her face despite the cold wind, Clarissa tried to pull the conversation back on track. 'So, there will be no more talk of kissing at the moment, if you don't mind. We have other things to discuss.'

'You would concede then that our kissing last night was exceptionally pleasurable?' He was enjoying the act in front of him, she was squirming in seeming embarrassment. Really, the woman should be on the stage.

'As I told you last night also, sir, having no other kisses with which to compare yours, I cannot say whether it was *exceptional*, or merely mundane.' The sparkle in her eyes and the challenging tilt of her chin belied the put-down. Clarrie could not help it, she enjoyed sparring with this man. She ignored the added *frisson* of awareness that such very *risqué* subject matter aroused, deciding that since no one else could possibly overhear them, she had naught to be ashamed of.

And she was rewarded for her barbed witticism with another burst of laughter. '*Touché*, Clarissa. But your kisses gave you away last night. Your claims to virginity are both false and unnecessary. So once again I will remind you to cast off that part of your repertoire. Your passion and your experience are what I desire. And what I shall have. For, having considered your terms, I have decided to accept your offer.'

His capitulation was so unexpected and so sudden that his determined disbelief in her innocence was cast momentarily from her mind. Clarissa was betrayed into a small crow of delight. She would do it. She would keep him away from Amelia. Edward would have his chance. *And she would spend some more time in his company. His exclusive company.* Ignoring this inward voice—for it was of no relevance, she told herself—Clarissa tried, rather belatedly, for composure. 'Thank you, Kit. I look forward to our adventure, when you've had sufficient time to arrange it.'

Kit merely smiled and gave his attention to the horses, relaxing his grip slightly on the reins to give them their heads. 'Since our business is concluded for the moment, then, let us relax and enjoy the ride.'

The phaeton was built for speed, and responded so smoothly that it was quite some time before Clarissa, deep in her own thoughts, became aware of their change from sedate trot to swift gallop. Even longer before she became aware that they had left the confines of the park, and even the traffic of the city, and were now traversing open countryside. How long had they been travelling thus? 'I'm afraid we must turn back, sir, I'm expected at home. I hadn't realised you intended more than a drive around the park. I'm not dressed for a longer journey.'

'Not far now, my horses need some exercise. Be patient, and enjoy the scenery.'

Suddenly Clarissa became aware of how foolish her behaviour must seem, alone in an open carriage with a notorious rake. Fleeting thoughts of abduction passed through her mind, to be dismissed summarily. She was being foolish. Kit had no need to take her by force when she had already offered herself so freely. After all, he did not know that she had no intention of fulfilling her promise. And while he was a rake, he was surely no villain. No, her imagination was simply overwrought, what with lack of sleep and too many lurid novels. Clarissa tried to relax and follow Kit's advice to enjoy their surroundings, but it was a relief none the less when, a short time later, the carriage slowed to a halt as they approached a whitewashed and thatched inn set prettily by a bridge over a lazily flowing river.

The small seed of doubt as to his intentions died. They would partake of some refreshment here and he would return her safely home. He had merely wished to try the paces of his horses, that was all. Well, they had certainly had a good run. How long had they been on the road? She was chilled. The horses being released from the traces by two uniformed ostlers were steaming with sweat. She had no timepiece, but Clarissa was starting to worry, from the darkening sky, about returning home in time for dinner.

'My lord, I—'

'Inside, Clarissa, where there is a fire. Come along, you're cold. I must see to my team first, then we may talk more freely.' An imperious hand in the small of her back propelled her forward, and she went with him, more reluctant with each step.

'I had no idea we had been driving for so long. We must turn around quickly, my lord, for my mama will be expecting me.'

A curt nod was his only response. He would brook no discussion in front of the servants. But *what*, exactly, was in need of discussion? Surely they were just waiting on fresh horses? That was it, of course. Fresh horses. And some warming coffee while they were poled up. With a lighter step, Clarissa preceded Lord Rasenby through the door of the inn, and towards the reassuring warmth of the fire in a small private parlour.

'I won't be long.' A stiff bow, and she was suddenly alone.

But as she stripped off her gloves to heat her chilled hands at the blaze of the fire, Clarissa was beset by doubts. He hadn't needed to command the parlour. What was it the innkeeper had said when he had welcomed them at the door? *Everything is ready, just as you requested, my lord.* Well, perhaps he had decided in advance that they would take a drive. No harm in that, was there? And he was obviously well known to the proprietors, so it wasn't as if he was concerned about his identity becoming known. So the growing fear Clarissa was trying to subdue, that she was being abducted, was ridiculous, wasn't it?

Of course it was. And here to prove it was the landlady herself, bustling in with a pot of hot steaming coffee and a large jug of foaming ale. She busied herself, putting another log on the fire and fussily adjusting one of the porcelain ornaments on the large mantel. No sign at all of anything untoward.

'Will that be all, madam? Lord Rasenby said to tell you to take your coffee while it's hot, he is just making sure his horses are stabled properly. If you require anything else, just ring the bell to summon me.' At Clarissa's nod, she bobbed a curtsy and left.

There, seeing to the horses, the woman had said. Making sure the fresh pair were ready for a quick departure. She would be home, if not before dusk, at least before full dark. With a sigh of relief, Clarissa snuggled down on to the settle before the fire, and poured her coffee. The warmth of the flames after the cold outside lulled her body into comfort and her mind into a calmer acceptance of her situation.

It was not until she was pouring her second cup from the pot that she realised Kit had been gone an overlong time. And the doubts awakened again, with renewed force. Nervously, she stood and peered out of the window into the growing gloom. Judging from the light, it must be near six of the clock. They had driven nigh on an hour and a half. It would be well after dinner before she was back. What on earth was he thinking? And where on earth was he? As her worries grew, so Clarissa's temper also rose.

The object of her ire finally walked back into the

room, bringing with him a blast of cold air and the faint smell of the stables. 'Ah. I see you are a little warmer. An open carriage for such an extended period at this time of year is not ideal. I apologise.'

'Had I known you intended such a long drive, sir, I would have cautioned you against it. As I have told you twice now, I am expected at home.'

'Yes, and I heard you the first time. I am not dim-witted, Clarissa, I do understand simple English.'

His bland tone provoked rather than calmed her. 'Then you will understand the simple fact that we must leave at once and return to London, sir.' This, through gritted teeth. 'I would not wish to be at odds with you, but we seem to have rather different inter-pretations of the phrase *a short drive in the park.*'

He smiled at this sally, but she received no other response. Kit seemed more intent on the refresh-ing draught of ale he had poured himself, and the warmth of the fire. His very indifference made her throw caution to the winds. Clarissa stamped her foot in a fair imitation of her sister that very morning, had she been inclined to notice. It did not occur to her, however, so intent was she on gaining Kit's attention. She really needed to get back home.

'If you will not rouse yourself from your beer, then I will just have to commandeer a carriage myself.' She had nowhere near sufficient funds in her purse to do so, but she tried not to think about that obstacle for the moment. Clarissa moved purposefully to the looking glass above the fire in order to adjust the strings of her bonnet.

He moved like a cat. One second he was lolling in a hard wooden chair, drinking from a brimming tankard, the next he was on his feet, standing all too close, his presence dominating her slim form, his face not angry exactly but stern. Forbidding. The full extent of her predicament struck Clarissa forcibly. No one knew where she was or who she was with. She had little money. And this man, this impossibly attractive, intimidating, overpoweringly strong man, was in full command of the situation. Nervously, Clarissa licked her dry lips, and decided to try a different tack.

'You are teasing me Kit, I know you are. But really, the joke has gone too far. I must go home now. We have agreed terms. You are happy with my proposal, you said so yourself. You'll be wanting your dinner soon. And surely your horses will be rested by now. You will no doubt wish to have a think about our adventure too, to spend some time planning it. So we should go now, and make arrangements to meet in a few days. Should we not?' Her voice faltered, seeing no change on his face, no response at her attempt to lighten the mood. 'Kit?'

He was looking down at her, scrutinising her closely. There was confusion and fear lurking in her wide-open green eyes. He knew perfectly well what she was thinking, for he had fully intended to frighten her just a little, to let her know that whatever her game was, she wasn't going to have it all her own way. But he had been unprepared for this feeling of pity, tenderness even, that her fear invoked. With difficulty, Kit resisted the sudden urge to reassure her, to soothe her anxiety. He reminded himself that she was an excellent actress. All the talk of Mama, the show of bravado, even the slight tremble of that full, sensuous bottom lip. Really, Mrs Siddons could not have acted better than this wench. She had no need of tenderness.

Grasping her small determined chin, he moved closer, feeling her light breath on his hand, inhaling that alluring combination of roses and vanilla. His thumb stroked the corner of her mouth, and ran over her full bottom lip. She was staring up at him, those huge green eyes pleading, the lashes so dark and long that she must employ some artifice, no matter how natural they looked. He could drown in those eyes. For a timeless moment they stood thus, Clarissa silently pleading, Kit coolly assessing, implacable.

'Kit, please take me home.' Her words were spoken softly, a gentle request, for somehow she was no longer frightened.

'I'm not planning to abduct you Clarissa, although I know you fear that is my intention. I have no need to take you by force. Anything we do together, you'll do willingly or not at all. I would not have it any other way, and you know it.' As he spoke, Kit pulled Clarissa to him, holding her with one hand lightly by the waist. 'You can leave directly, only say the word. Ask me again, I'll take you home and we can forget everything. Our adventure. Our kisses. The union of our bodies will be consigned for ever to our imaginations. It will be as if we had never met. We can forgo it all, Clarissa, if you tell me that is what you truly desire.'

The closeness of their bodies invoked memories of last night. His words were a whisper on her face. His mouth, his tempting, cool, hot, mouth, was inches away. His thumb continued its slow, languorous caress as he spoke, the line of her jaw, back to her mouth, over the planes of her cheek. Brushing gently. Soothing her. Distracting her. Hypnotising her. But the clasp on her waist remained light. She could leave now, she believed him. Instead of turning away, Clarrie moved forwards, drawn closer as if mesmerised, casting aside all doubts and reservations, any sense of the danger of her situation, in the need to taste him once more.

Her tongue flicked over the tip of Kit's thumb. And flicked over it again, her teeth just grazing the skin, before she closed her lips around it and sucked with a slow, sensuous and purely instinctive movement. She sucked harder, drawing the length of his finger into her mouth, closing her eyes to delight all the more in the sensations it was arousing all over her body. She moaned slightly as his finger was withdrawn, only to purr with satisfaction when it was replaced by the lips she craved.

Opening her mouth to receive his kiss, Clarrie gave a mewl of frustration as Kit's lips moved slowly, deliberately, delicately, when she wanted hard, hot, fast. Reaching up to pull his head down more firmly, relishing the rough graze of his chin on her tender skin, Clarrie drew tight against his hard, aroused body, and stopped thinking. Their kiss deepened, rocketing her body temperature, causing the flames that had flickered somewhere in her belly to strengthen and focus lower down. She could feel the male hardness of him between her thighs through the delicate wool of her walking dress, and tilted slightly to press herself against him.

The action was too much for Kit's self-control. Suddenly she was free, a cold distance between them, the room silent save for their ragged breathing. The flame of passion was replaced by a deep blush of shame.

Clarrie looked up to find Kit's eyes on her, that sardonic, devilish look of his accentuated by his slightly raised brow, the half-smile on his mouth. 'Well? Are you going to persist in your demands to be taken back to your mama? Have you decided, after all, that to deal with so notorious a rake as me is just a mite too dangerous? Speak now, Clarissa, or for ever hold your peace. Is it to be safe home? Or is it to be onwards into the unknown with me? Think carefully, for if you choose onwards, my bold Clarissa, *your adventure begins this very day.*'

Chapter Five

What on earth had she done? Clarrie wondered. Broken all her resolutions, and some she hadn't even thought she'd need to make, for a start. Betrayed by her own body, tricked by her own desires, she had placed herself in a position of real peril. She had thrown herself—quite literally—at this man, when only moments before she had been terrified of abduction, and protesting her innocence. Clarissa turned to look bleakly out of the window. How stupid her plans had been. How poorly she understood her own true nature. A few hours in his company, and here she was launching herself at Kit like one possessed. If she persisted in such brazen behaviour, he would tire of her far too quickly and return to his pursuit of Amelia, and then she'd have sacrificed herself for nothing.

Leaning her hot cheeks against the cool of the

glass, Clarissa realised that her scathing denunciations of romantic heroines had been naïve in the extreme. Here she was with a notorious rake, and succumbing to his charms—nay, hurling herself wholeheartedly at them—with nary a thought for the consequences. Stupid, stupid Clarissa!

As if that wasn't enough, she had walked with eyes wide open into this impossible situation. A situation, she was forced to acknowledge, of her own making. She had asked for an adventure. It was natural to assume that adventures involved surprise, and foolish of her to suppose that one so impetuous as Kit would do anything other than rise immediately to her challenge.

What on earth was she going to do? Return home and forget her plan? Clarissa had no doubt that Kit would take her back if she wished. He might be a rake, but he was an honest one, she was sure of it. He said he would not abduct her against her will and she believed him. But to return home was to put an end to everything. She would have failed in her attempts to save Amelia. And she would never see Kit again. Never. At the thought, a huge chasm seemed to open at her feet. Never share a joke with him. Never test her wit against his. Never see that smile, so rarely given, of genuine amusement, which lit up his face, changing him from devilish to absurdly, over-whelmingly handsome. Never taste his lips on hers. Never feel his hard body pressed against hers.

Reminding herself that she had no intention of succumbing to more intimate advances did not prevent Clarrie from craving more of the forbidden fruit she had already tasted. Surely a few more kisses would be no compromise? Surely a few more hours, a few more days in his company, would satisfy her, and suffice to save her sister? Suffice to subdue this fire. Surely a better acquaintance with Kit would cure her of this irrational infatuation? A surfeit of his presence would ensure she saw him in a more rational light, and would have the happy consequence of doing Amelia good too.

Lost in her thoughts, Clarissa stared unseeingly out of the window. Kit watched, judging it best to give her this time to adjust her thinking, refusing to attempt further persuasion. She would come, of that he was certain. She would accede to his terms. He had neither the desire nor the need for an ab-duction. She would come. He was sure of it.

Checking his watch, he tugged the bell by the fireplace, summoning the landlady. 'We will dine in twenty minutes. You'll oblige me by bringing some writing materials immediately, and some brandy too.' The woman curtsied and left.

'Dine?' The words startled Clarissa from her musings.

'Yes. I know it's early, but we have a long journey ahead of us. If you're not hungry now, you should be. And I'm ravenous.'

'But we can't be much more than an hour from town. I'd rather wait if you don't mind, Kit.'

'We're not going back to London. I had credited you with more wit than that, Clarissa. You demanded an adventure, but you also demanded secrecy you may recall. You may not be particularly well known in town, but I am. How can we conduct any sort of private liaison with the eyes of the world upon us?'

'Yes, I suppose—that is, I had not thought…'

'You had not thought? I find that difficult to believe. Well, you can think now. We are not going back to London unless it is to abandon all. And if we are to continue, we must dine. So Clarissa, for the last time, do you wish to continue?' He was growing weary of her prevaricating. Had she not been so very tempting, he would have readied them both for the journey home with no regrets. But he was finding her inordinately tempting. And he wanted, more than he realised, for their liaison to continue. 'Well?'

It was *yes*. It had to be *yes*, she knew that. But

some instinct for self-preservation made her stall. 'What about Mama? I can't just disappear. She'll be beside herself with worry.' Actually, Mama would probably indulge in a fit of the vapours, then simply assume Clarissa had forgotten to inform her of a visit to Aunt Constance, but that was neither here nor there.

'You can write her a note. You forget, I am already familiar with your ability to deceive. How else did you manage to escape your mama's tender care for two evenings in a row, and on your own? I am sure you can think of something to allay her fears.'

'Yes, but why the need for haste? I don't understand, Kit, why could you not have informed me in advance of your arrangements, then I could have been prepared, packed a bag, told Mama some tale. Surely there was no need for such a rush?'

'Where would be the adventure then? You wanted a surprise, something memorable—you were most specific. Isn't the unexpected part of the thrill?' Kit had been sitting by the fire, watching her from a distance, but now he moved to stand beside her at the window. His voice became huskier as he looked at the small, defiant, and strangely alluring woman at his side. 'The kisses you bestowed so willingly a few moments ago, my lovely Clarissa, simply confirmed what I already knew. I wish to have the preliminaries of our liaison over as soon as possible in order to enjoy the fruits of my labour more quickly. Your charms, as I am sure you are perfectly well aware, are considerable, and I wish to wait no longer than necessary to sample them more fully. I was persuaded by our kiss last night you know, although your reminder was very pleasant—I thank you.' A brief, ironic bow accompanied this last remark.

'I'm sorry, I hadn't meant to—I don't know what came over me.'

'No? Well, whatever it was, I'm grateful. But it might be best to save it until a more convenient time. You won't have to wait long, Clarissa, never fear. Nor will there be any gainsaying me when it happens. Once I have fulfilled my part of the bargain, I won't let you renege on yours.'

The glint in his eye was uncompromising. She had known it from the start, he was not a man to cross. Yet she had tried to ensnare him. He had pulled the ground from beneath her feet, but still she fought to recover it, as a general rallies his troops even at the eleventh hour. 'You are premature, my lord. I won't go back on my promise, but I must remind you that you have an obligation to fulfil first. My adventure, lest you need reminding.'

'Strangely, Clarissa, I need no reminding at

all. Your adventure has already started. Had you not realised?'

'I had not mere abduction in mind, and well you know it. I particularly remember, for 'twas but last night, that we said it should be fun. Lest it has escaped your notice, this is not fun for me, and I am not enjoying myself. So you must try harder, sir, or you will have failed.'

'This is no mere abduction madam, I assure you. No matter what you may think of my morals, or lack of them, I pride myself on my finesse, as you will find out when the time comes for me to bed you. No, this is but the preliminary to the fun you are so intent on receiving.'

He was angry, frustrated at her refusal to give an inch, unused to being cross-questioned. It made him all the more determined that she would comply. With an effort, Kit bit down on his temper, deciding wisely that an explanation would be more likely to result in co-operation. 'We drive tonight to the coast, and thence we board my yacht, the *Sea Wolf.* You seemed so interested in the plight of the French refugees that it seemed only fair to allow you to experience first hand the kind of daring rescue mission required to deliver them from the fate that surely awaits them. It is an illicit undertaking which I confess I am intimately familiar with.'

'Why, Kit, I had no idea you were involved in such work when we discussed it last night. How exciting. And how very noble of you.'

'Don't be deluded, Clarissa, there is naught noble in my motives. 'Tis a sport to me, is all, but I hope it will be an exciting adventure for you. Especially since we'll be clapped in gaol if we're caught. I trust you will find the experience *fun* enough. Now, you may write your note to your concerned mama to ensure you are not looked for. Then we must dine and be on our way.'

Silencing the words of protest forming on her lips with a swift, brutal kiss, Kit grasped Clarissa's chin and looked straight into her troubled eyes. 'I will brook no further discussion. Write your note and we shall dine. The innkeeper's wife is famed for her table, we would not wish to disappoint her.' A smile curled his sensuous mouth, but did not reach his eyes. 'And you will need sustenance, my dear, if you are to make the most of your adventure.'

Clarissa vouchsafed no answer, but she sat obediently to write her note, consigning her worries about the future to the back of her mind. Her adventure was indeed about to begin. She might as well make the most of it, now that she was committed.

* * *

As Kit had promised, the landlady's cooking was a delight, but the neat's-tongue, the platter of delicate sole and the side-dish of artichokes sautéed in butter might as well have been cooked in ashes, for all Clarissa could taste. Conversation was desultory, both Kit and Clarissa being distracted by their own reflections.

Despite his earlier threats, Kit had no wish for an unwilling companion, and no taste for a resistant lover. Watchfully, he poured himself another glass of the excellent claret and waited for Clarissa to come to terms with the situation. She had been bested and she was not happy to have been forced to relinquish the reins, but she was yet determined on her course. She would go along with his scheme, he knew that, yet her real intentions were still unclear.

She was a puzzle, this beautiful woman before him, and one he wished to unravel. Her claims to virtue and the preposterous tale she spun him last night about wishing to enjoy herself before settling to the boredom of matrimony, Kit dismissed out of hand. She was no innocent, that was for sure. And if perchance there was some unsuspecting dotard waiting in the wings to wed her, he was sure she would continue in her scheming, wanton ways, whether she was married or no. Her plotting would come to light in the end, and he would deal with it then. For the present, he resolved simply to enjoy himself as much as possible.

Rather to his own surprise, Kit found himself reconciled to postponing their physical union for the present, content enough as he was with Clarissa's company. She was challenging. Her habit of speaking without thinking, of never saying quite what he expected, even her frankness, all were a refreshing change. And she seemed to understand him too—her attack on his rakish reputation had so nearly reflected his own cynical view of himself as to make him wonder if she could somehow eavesdrop on his very thoughts.

To be plain, he wanted to know more of her. Once they were bedded, he doubted not, he would become bored. Putting Clarissa from him when their kiss got so out of hand, when she had rubbed so sinuously against the throbbing evidence of his desire as to almost overset him, had not been easy. But passion was enhanced by anticipation, so postponement there would be—for a day or so, at least. Pouring the last of the claret into his glass, Kit looked up to find Clarissa's green eyes fixed on him with resolution. 'Speak, fair Clarissa, I can see you are pregnant with words. I am, as they say, all ears.'

This was said with a lurking smile that she found reassuring, as he had intended. She was in no danger for the present. Returning the smile tremulously, Clarissa pushed aside her plate. 'I take it, sir, that there is no point in my wasting time trying to persuade you to delay this undertaking?'

A shake of the head was her reply. Well, she had resigned herself to this. She knew she had taken a risk when setting out on this whole preposterous journey, and she had been foolish enough to ignore the warnings her Aunt Constance had delivered as to the perfidious nature of the man before her. Beguiled by his physical attractions, drawn on by her desire to know him better, Clarissa had fashioned her own fate. And now she would pay for it. But at least if Kit was aboard a boat sailing for France, he would not be in London waving his plentiful purse under her sister's nose.

And, oh, she so much wanted to go! There, she had admitted it to her deepest soul. The Earl of Rasenby understood her desire for adventure very well. He could not, in fact, have selected a more enticing trip. To sail out to sea on his yacht, to be part of a rescue mission, perhaps to be chased by the customs men—it was so much like a romance she could not resist. And she would not, simply would not, behave like a simpering miss when faced with the challenge. If she must go—*and she must, she must*—then she would go with flags flying and battle colours held proudly aloft. Kit would not intimidate her. On the contrary, she would make sure to enjoy every minute of it.

Kit watched in amusement, reading Clarissa's face fairly accurately, surprised and more than a little impressed at her courage in the face of adversity. He had thwarted her, but she would not submit easily to his will. 'Well? Your eyes give your thoughts expression, but really I would rather have them spoke plain, lest there be any misunderstandings between us. Are you ready to commit to our adventure, Clarissa?'

An answering smile, tinged with something— fear? Again, he repressed the urge to reassure. She did not need it. He would play along with her only so far.

'Yes. You give me no choice, Kit, but I will not pretend to go unwillingly when you are offering something that interests me so much. In fact, I'm already looking forward to it. How long shall we be gone?'

The question, almost casual, did not fool him. The lady was already planning her escape. 'One night only, if the winds are with us—and they usually are. Two at most, I believe. Had you something of longer duration in mind?'

'No, no, not at all.' Short enough a time, but surely sufficient for things between Amelia and Edward to flower? Resolving to put Amelia and Edward and everything else aside for now, and to extract the most from the situation which would surely be the adventure of a lifetime, Clarissa gave Kit a direct and steady look. 'You could not have picked anything more exciting for me, you know. I was not in jest last night when I told you that I find the idea of rescuing these poor *émigrés* completely enthralling. Since reading Mrs Wollstonecraft's account of the revolution, their plight has moved me. I've never been to sea before, though—I hope I'm not taken poorly.'

He made no comment on her reference to the infamous and now dead Mrs Wollstonecraft, being unsurprised at her sympathies with that lady, but stored the information up with which to annoy her later. He enjoyed pitting his wits against Clarissa, so rare it was to find a woman with a brain worth testing. Sea sickness, however, had not occurred to him as a possible issue. Immediately it was brushed aside. 'I am very sure, Clarissa, that if you decide not to be sick, then you will not be. I imagine there are few things—or people—you cannot subdue to your wishes.'

'What a strange thing to say. If you knew more of

me, you'd realise just how constrained and burdened with other people's wishes my own life has been. I am not used to indulging myself, you know.'

'Well, if I am your chosen indulgence then I am flattered. But be aware, Clarissa, that I am not an indulgence to be abused. Once and for all, I remind you of your promise. When we go forward from this inn, you are not just committed to a trip to France. You will pay for it with that delectable body of yours. And you will not pretend that the payment will be anything other than desired by us both. Are we understood?'

The urge to tell the truth passed fleetingly across her mind, followed quickly by the urge to admit that she would be delighted to pay with her body. Both urges were suppressed. There could be no question of it, and she would deal with denying him later. But the lie that her tremulous agreement required sat heavy on her conscience.

Kit noticed, but ignored it. Time was against them. Checking his pocket watch, he rang the bell and demanded the bill. Clarissa, clad once more in her less than adequate spencer and gloves, was ushered out through the passageway and into a closed carriage. A hot brick was placed at her feet, and a fur rug tucked around her legs.

'I will ride alongside. There are not usually highwaymen on this stretch of road, but I prefer not to take the chance. Try to sleep for a while, we have a journey of some hours ahead of us.'

'Kit?'

'Yes?' The terse voice was intimidating. He was impatient to be off.

'I trust you.'

'What am I to take from that?'

'To keep me safe. To share the experience with me—properly, I mean, don't just bury me below decks. To leave me unmolested for the while. I trust you.'

'Then you are a fool. Rakes, my purported innocent, are never to be trusted. But I will allow you to be right, just this once. You may trust me thus far. But no more.'

'Yes, but you will keep me safe. For now.'

Leaning back into the warmth of the carriage, Clarissa was unaware of the anger she had aroused in Kit. And confusion. The urge to tell her he would keep her safe always had been unaccountably strong. Once more, Kit's instincts warred with his mind, as he told himself she was merely a very clever actress playing him like a professional. 'For now', however, was the only reply he vouchsafed.

The door of the chaise was banged shut. The

ostlers let go of the horses, and the carriage leapt forward into the dark of the falling night, the tall man astride his powerful black stallion riding alongside. Clarissa was left to her own reflections, but the long day and her lack of sleep the previous night took their toll. Exhausted, the gentle rocking motion of the carriage soothed her and, to her surprise, Clarissa drifted into a sound sleep.

The carriage was stationary when she woke, and she could smell the salty tang of the sea air. Rubbing her eyes and casting off the rug, she descended to a scene of ordered but frenetic activity. They were at a small quayside. The boathouse, doors open and an oil lamp blazing inside, was waiting to shelter their carriage. There was a stable at the back for the horses, but no other sign of buildings, and the track they had come ran through deserted marshland.

On the quay she could see Kit, wrapped in an enormous black greatcoat, barking out orders to two men, one on the deck of the sleek yacht, and one beside him on the jetty. It was a cloudless night, and the stars were bright, much brighter than they ever were in London, where lights dimmed them to a soft glow. Here in the middle of nowhere they glared like so many burning braziers lighting up the heavens.

Shivering in the cold wind, Clarissa picked her way carefully down the jetty, avoiding the coils of rope and boxes of supplies stacked ready to be taken on board. Calling out a final instruction to the man on deck, Kit came towards her smiling, his eyes shining with anticipation as he trod with cat-like grace on the boards. He was obviously in his element here.

'Take care not to trip on those nets. When we're not out on these night runs, John and I—that's my captain, on the deck there—take the *Sea Wolf* out on fishing expeditions. You'd be surprised at what we catch. And, of course, fishing provides an excellent cover, should we meet a customs cutter. Are you rested?'

Shivering now, for the cold was biting, Clarrie looked up into Kit's face, her own eyes reflecting his gleaming anticipation. 'Yes, thank you, I slept almost the whole journey. Please, will you show me around? And tell me everything? I want to make the most of this trip, for it's unlikely I'll ever get the chance of another. Tell me about your yacht.'

Laying a small gloved hand on his arm and making to urge him forward, she was treated to one of Kit's rare, genuine smiles. 'Very well. But wait here for a moment. You are ill equipped for the cold; I have a cloak in the boat house.'

Returning quickly, he fastened the enveloping wool around her throat. 'There, that should keep out the chill, although you must take great care not to trip on it, especially when we're on board. I would hate to lose you to the sea!'

Laughing as the wind whipped her hair from under her bonnet, she snuggled the soft folds around her and turned back towards the gangway. 'Since I can't swim I would be lost indeed, and you would lose out on your payment. Even I am not such a prize as to risk a wetting in a rescue attempt.'

'I'm beginning to think that you're more of a prize than I realised. But rest assured I wouldn't get wet myself. I would send John in. Or more likely I'd pull you back with the boat hook I use to haul less alluring catch on board.'

'Well, I'm flattered indeed to be held more attractive than a fish, my lord,' Clarrie said with a grin, but her words were lost in the sudden gust of wind that swept in from the sea.

'Tide's on the turn, Master Kit,' John said, 'we'd best be going.'

The *Sea Wolf*, riding high against the jetty, was straining at the ropes that held her. The constraining hawsers creaked. John was looking anxiously at Kit, keen to be away. He had a bad feeling about this trip, and it wasn't just because of the close call with customs a few weeks ago. Someone was informing on them, he knew that. Bringing a woman on board, obviously one of Master Kit's flighty pieces, was a new departure, and one he could well have done without. He didn't hold with women on board unless absolutely necessary. They got in the way, to say nothing of bringing bad luck.

Standing at the foot of the gangway, Clarissa was shaken by a sudden attack of nerves, unable to move, one hand on the rail, but both feet still firmly on shore. Boarding this ship was madness. What was she thinking? The wind ripped across the bay, making the yacht pull, anxious to get away now that the anchor was up. The riggings creaked and moaned, and the gangway shifted, to Clarissa's eyes, treacherously.

'Last-minute qualms, brave Clarissa?' Kit's words were mocking.

The taunt was sufficient to urge her to action. With a defiant toss of her head and a silent prayer, Clarissa put first one foot, then the other on to the slippery walk way, and boarded the *Sea Wolf.* Feeling none too steady, for the deck rocked and swayed even though they were still berthed, she stood still for a moment, trying to find her balance. Aside from a curt nod, Captain John ignored her, making his resentment at her presence clear.

Carefully clutching the cloak around her, and taking care to avoid the plethora of ropes, boxes, and goodness knows what else that made the deck an obstacle course, Clarrie found her way to stand by Kit at the wheel. A distracted smile was all she received, for they were in the process of putting to sea. John was casting off, making the ropes safe, loosing the sails, and in an instant the yacht responded to her freedom and leapt towards the open sea, riding the waves effortlessly.

As they left the cove behind, tacking to catch the wind, the waves rose higher, the spray soaking their faces, the *Sea Wolf* tilting up, then down, in a rhythmic, lulling motion that filled Clarrie with a wild joy. Lifting her face to the wind, she looked up at the stars with a strange, exhilarated expression on her face. This was what freedom must feel like. Freedom from all the trammels of her mundane life. Freedom from her mama, from Amelia, even from her staid Aunt Constance. Freedom from her past and her depressing future. There was only here and now. This man. This open sea. These stars.

A gust of wind blowing directly over the starboard side jolted the yacht, and would have knocked her over but for an iron grip on her arm. Looking up to thank Kit, Clarissa caught an unguarded expression of pure, unadulterated lust on his face and blinked at the sheer force of it. She blinked again and it was gone, replaced by his usual sardonic expression.

'You should go below. The crossing is likely to be fast but vicious, and I have to give my full attention to the *Sea Wolf*—I have not the time to be constantly making sure that you are safe.' Nor the time to be constantly distracted by the wild joy on the beautiful face beside him, if truth were to be told.

Deflated by his cold words, Clarissa turned to hide the hurt on her face. She had expected to stay above decks in order to see and experience everything to the limit. Being confined below was not her idea of an adventure. But she was too sensible to argue, for she could quite see that the stormy conditions were likely to be taxing. Quelling an instinctive protest at the command, therefore, she bit her lip and turned obediently towards the stairs.

Her obvious disappointment was too much for Kit to bear. He felt like an ogre stealing sweets from a babe. He had been watching her face more closely than she had realised, gratified to see the look of unadulterated pleasure that suffused it when the yacht set sail. Gratified and aroused to perceive his own feeling of joy at the freedom of the open sea reflected there. And disturbed, too, for it was not an emotion he had expected to share with a woman. And now she was thwarted yet uncomplaining.

'Clarissa.'

She turned at his call, a hopeful smile curling her full mouth, her skin bright with the sting of salt, her curls entrancingly dishevelled around her heart-shaped face. 'Kit?'

'Once we are settled in to the journey, I'll hand over to John, and you can come back up on deck, then, if that is what you wish.'

She clapped her hands with excitement, leaving him in no doubt.

'Contain yourself. If the weather worsens, you must stay below. Now go, before I change my mind.' He turned from her as she made her way gingerly below decks, before he could call her back regardless of the danger. Having Clarissa by his side at the wheel felt just a bit too right for his own comfort. Some space between them was a sounder idea.

The spartan cabin was built on practical rather than luxurious lines, with few fixtures other than the bunks that doubled as seating. Not a place for seduction, that was for sure. In fact, Clarrie thought with wry humour, as the yacht rolled with the waves, they would like as not end up on the floor, even had they managed to cram two bodies on to the narrow bunk. Still, having nothing else to occupy her mind for the while, she gave some time over to imagining how such adversities could be got over. She had just concluded that with determination two people could overcome such difficulties as a narrow mattress on a heaving yacht, when the door opened and Kit entered, bringing with him a cold gust of air.

Blushingly thankful he was not privy to her thoughts, Clarissa stood rather hurriedly, her foot catching in an uneven board, and fell unceremoniously on to the opposite bunk. Lying sprawled there, presenting Kit with her deliciously rounded posterior, Clarrie managed a soft laugh at the indignity of the situation. Her attempts to scramble to her feet were hampered by the continued rocking of the boat, and her sense of humour finally got the better of her. She succumbed to laughter, and lay for a few moments helpless, face down on the bunk.

'Kit, help me up, for goodness' sake. Now I know you're no gentleman, standing there and watching me.' Another abortive attempt had her on all fours on the bunk.

'You present such a very attractive picture that I'm loathe to move, Clarissa. Your position may be uncomfortable, but I should tell you that it displays your curves very well.' Extremely well, in truth. His body was reacting rather vigorously to the display. Had it not been for the circumstances…

Restraining an urge to lift her dress above the bottom so pertly presented and thrust himself into her sweetness there and then, Kit reminded himself that John was above decks, and they were in the middle of the English Channel in a storm. That there was a cargo awaiting them in Normandy. That there was likely to be an excise cutter waiting for them on their return. That Clarissa was a perfidious, scheming actress. That… None of it worked.

Like an automaton, he moved towards the tempting bundle sprawled in front of him and grasped her by the waist, pulling her rear into his hard body, noting her laughter change to a surprised gasp, and then a soft, accepting moan. Clarrie wriggled slightly against him, causing him to throb almost uncontrollably. His hands tightened on her waist to pull her close, and his breathing quickened, coming in harsh gasps in the confines of the cabin. Steadying his knees against the base of the bunk, he allowed one hand to trace the line from her tiny waist along the curve of her spine, and to cup one soft buttock through the wool of her dress, aware, from the soft panting of her breath, that she was as aroused as he. Bracing himself more securely, Kit moved to the hem of her dress, preparing to lift it up over her in order to grant him the access he craved. He met with no resistance.

The sea saved her. A violent movement that sent them both sprawling, as John called urgently for help. Kit was gone at once, leaving Clarrie alone again. Alone with her feelings—of despair at her easy submission, of anger at herself for her lack of resistance. But most of all, the one that really scared her, a feeling of deep frustration at the unconsummated act. Clarrie could fool herself no longer. When Kit decided to take her, there would be no question but that she would submit. No matter what the consequences.

Chapter Six

The tossing of the ship had become less violent, or perhaps she had simply accustomed herself to it. In any case, to stay below and nurse her feelings of frustration would, Clarrie decided, be as fruitless as it was a waste of the precious time she had on board the *Sea Wolf*. She prepared to brave the upper decks and to pretend that nothing of note had happened below.

The yacht was holding a steady course in the face of the wind. Kit had the wheel, idly maintaining conversation with John, whose talk was of the future, his plans for life once this last mission was completed.

'I'll not be sorry, Master Kit, I tell thee true. It's old bones I've got now, too old to be chasing after them Frenchies and running away from the excise men. I've enough set aside to buy my own smack and do a bit of legal fishing for a change. Won't net me a fortune, but it'll keep us well enough, I reckon. I've my eye on a little beauty I spotted for sale down Romney Marsh way, fore-and-aft rigged like the *Sea Wolf*, but smaller, just big enough for me and a lad to handle. And Sal, she'll be glad to have me home at night regular again.'

'How is the lovely Sal, your good lady wife? The last time we met, she threatened me with a rolling pin for getting you into mischief.'

A gruff laugh greeted this remark. 'Aye, you know her ways, Master Kit, she means no harm, just frets for my safety is all. She's never liked me going off on jaunts like this, but she's not one as would ever complain neither. A good woman, Sal, she knows her place. And she deserves some peace of mind, after all these years. She's earned it.'

'You both have, John. I really envy you, the way you've got your life all mapped out. I have no idea what I'll do without these trips. My sister wants me to marry, but lord, what a dreadful husband I'd make. I'm afraid I'm destined to be the devil's own, one way or another. I'll miss these trips more than I can say.'

'Aye, well, Master Kit, like as not summat'll turn up, you'll see. I'm a great believer in fate, myself.' With this laconic reply, John turned his attention seawards, scanning the horizon for signs of sail, leaving Kit free to pursue his thoughts.

As if summoned by them, Clarissa appeared head first, ascending the cabin steps gingerly, struggling to contain the cloak that whistled around her in the wind. She had abandoned her hat, and her bright auburn tresses whipped around her face, temporarily obstructing her view. Tottering, she grabbed the rail and righted herself before smiling and offering a tentative greeting. 'I thought I'd take you up on the offer of a tour. That is, if you are not otherwise occupied.'

A terse nod from John, who took over the wheel, gave Kit no option but to accede to her request. 'We're about an hour away from landfall, we've made excellent time. I'll be happy to show you round—she's small but beautiful, my *Sea Wolf*— and then you can stay on deck as we berth."

The technicalities were lost on her, but she listened with intelligent interest as Kit explained everything from the rigging to the sleek lines of the yacht, comparing it favourably, and with obvious pride, to the slower, clinker-built cutters still used by the Revenue. Pointing out the key navigational stars high above them, he talked a little of his early sailing days, his fishing trips with John when he was no more than a child, sailing his first skiff and learning the hard way about the tides and vagaries of the coast line. That Kit loved the *Sea Wolf* and was an expert sailor, Clarrie had no doubt. That she too could learn to love sailing, she had no doubt either. At his side, with his tuition, she was sure she would quickly become adept.

Standing at the guard rail, watching the yacht cut cleanly through the waves and the coast of Normandy looming into view in the distance, Clarissa felt a rush of freedom like champagne fizzing through her blood. At home, so far away as it now seemed, freedom had meant her sister married, her mother comfortably settled and herself earning a living as a governess. Such a vision seemed merely a new set of fetters compared to this. How had she ever imagined that life at the beck and call of an employer would be any different to life at the beck and call of her family?

No point in thinking about such things now though, no point in spoiling this moment. Turning to Kit, standing so close she could feel the heat of his body even through the thickness of their clothing, Clarissa asked about the people waiting for them on the French shore.

'We can never be certain that they'll be there when we arrive,' he explained. 'There are so many things that can go wrong. On occasion we've had to wait—usually a few hours, but once it was a whole day and night. We went ashore, but John did not take to the French cooking!' Kit laughed at the memory of John's face when presented with a huge piece of beef, the blood pooling beside it on the plate. 'Tonight, we're to pick up a man and his daughter. Their name is Renaud. Madame Renaud is dead by the guillotine, and Monsieur Renaud and his daughter have been in hiding on a country estate in Burgundy. He is a classical scholar; of her I know naught more than that she is young and unwed. Needless to say, they are rich no more. They are alive, that is the main thing. Or they were when last I heard a few days ago,' he added bitterly. 'To come out of hiding and journey north to the ports is hazardous even after all these years. There are informants everywhere.'

'They cannot have been in hiding all this time, surely? It is almost ten years since the revolution.'

'Aye, ten bloody years. But remember, the *Terror* grew slowly at first. The wholesale slaughter only really started when Louis was beheaded, four years after they revolted. For many, especially those of the lesser nobility such as this family, it seemed possible to keep their heads down—if you'll forgive the gallows humour—

and survive the killing. Monsieur Renaud, whom you will meet tonight, God willing, is not himself of high rank, but his wife was the younger daughter of a duke. The blue blood was hers. And so, in the end, it was she who sealed the fate of the whole family. 'Tis certain they would not have been spared had they been found.'

'But is it not safe enough now in France under the Directorate? Are they not more tolerant? Surely it's becoming possible to start again in their own country, rather than to take such a drastic step as these people make tonight?'

'For some, yes, perhaps you're right. But for others, those who have lived the life of privilege, to accustom themselves to the new regime seems unnecessary, when in England they can bear their titles proudly once more.'

'With no money, how can that mean so much? Money is by far more important than a title, as I should know, Lord Rasenby.'

'And what, Clarissa, do you know of such things?'

She shrugged. 'My own father was titled, my widowed mother still bears his name. It means naught, for he was cast off and poverty-stricken just the same. At times, I would happily swap my birth right for the wealth of a merchant family— at least that way I wouldn't have to worry about avoiding the coal seller at quarter time.' An embarrassed laugh concluded this admission. She had not meant to say anything so revealing, being merely caught up in the need to understand more of the situation in France. But looking into those piercing eyes above her, Clarissa realised Kit had missed none of what she had said.

'So you claim to be of noble birth? And may I be allowed to ask what this family name is, for I know—have known all along, of course—that the name you gave me is false.'

'No, there's nothing to be gained for either of us in that. Rest assured, my real name is Clarissa. That should suffice, for the duration of our brief acquaintance.' Smiling nervously, for she had no wish to continue this turn in the conversation, Clarissa resolutely faced away from that all too penetrating look, back towards the approaching land. 'You were telling me about Monsieur Renaud. If he has no title and his poor wife is dead, I still don't understand the need for him to leave France.'

Thrusting aside the urge to probe into Clarissa's background—for like as not it would only lead to more lies—Kit focused instead on the Normandy coastline, anxious to catch the first glimpse of their destination, a tiny fishing village, where a beacon to guide them would be lit if all was safe. 'The likes of Renaud leave because the future is still so uncertain. True, he has no title, but he has a daughter to protect. And he has the sense, as anyone who has studied the situation can see, to realise that this regime is every bit as volatile as the last. There will be war soon, do not doubt it. In England he'll be sleeping with the enemy, but at least there is less chance there of invasion, more chance of a respite from bloodshed. France has not come to the end of its sufferings, mark my words. For all these reasons, and others, too, these trips on the *Sea Wolf* are, however, coming to an end. I must find some other occupation to sate my appetite for danger.'

The bleakness in his voice betrayed his true feelings. Giving up this life was hard for him. Having tasted the thrill of it for herself, Clarissa was not surprised. Laying a hand on his arm in an attempt to convey her empathy, her words were yet hesitant. 'I can see that you'll miss this life. But you must take comfort in the good you have done, the lives you have saved. All these *émigrés*, they must be so grateful. I expect, when you meet them in London, as you must often do afterwards, you are something of a hero to them.'

'You are much mistaken, Clarissa, to set me up

for a hero.' The habitual cynical drawl had returned. 'I don't rescue these people for any more noble motives than a desire for adventure spiced with danger. I care naught for their fate. I take no sides in their politics. Their country can gnaw at its own entrails until it has consumed itself in the process for all I care. Do not attribute to me any heroic virtues, for you will find yourself far from the truth. These people are just cargo, like the silks and brandies we will carry tonight alongside Monsieur and Mademoiselle Renaud. And as to recognition from those I rescue? Never. They are under strict instructions not to acknowledge me once they leave the *Sea Wolf*. I am not, nor never will be, a hero.'

'You may choose to deny it. Indeed, to do so is in your character for you are overly fond of your raking, care-naught reputation, Lord Rasenby, as I have pointed out to you several times now.' His determined cynicism was having a rousing effect on Clarrie. She would not allow him to be so harsh on himself. He was not a complete villain, no matter how much he played the part.

'I notice that I become Lord Rasenby and not Kit when you are lecturing me, madam. I do not take to it kindly either, for you have not the right to lecture. No one has that right but myself. And believe me, no one could be harder on me than myself either. But to no avail. I am destined for the devil. You would learn, if you chose to spend more time in my company, that I can neither be reformed, nor am in wont of it.'

'No, you're not in need of reform, because you're not anything like as black as you paint yourself. You are not stupid, you told me so yourself. Well, neither am I! You would not have continued with these trips, which put John as much as yourself in danger, had you not felt they were worth while—and I don't mean for the brandy. These rescues mean something to you, would you but admit it, if only to your own heart. To these people at least, you are a hero, I doubt it not. The only need you have of reform is to think as well of yourself as you are entitled.'

'You persist in this belief at your peril, foolish Clarissa, but be warned. Such determinedly positive appraisals of my character will not change it one jot. Nor will you, by applying such soft soap, beguile me into releasing you from your promise. Now let us have an end to this conversation, for we have important work to attend to. Look straight ahead and slightly to starboard—there is our beacon. We are expected. You may watch, but you must keep silent and take care not to get in the way.'

With that he was gone, joining John at the wheel and leaving Clarissa to her reflections. Anger at his abrupt dismissal and pity for the contempt in which he held himself were foremost in her mind. But there was, too, a growing desire to be the one to bring him to a sense of his own worth. Not to reform him, that phrase he so despised, but to raise his sadly low esteem. *She* believed in him, and she could prove it to him, too, if only the situation was different.

But to wish things were different was to wish their whole adventure away. Increasingly all Clarissa wanted was for their time together to go on—and on. The thought of an ending to it was a thought she thrust firmly from her mind. A future without Kit Rasenby was not a future she wished to contemplate just yet.

John dropped the sails, and the ship glided smoothly into calmer, shallower waters, navigating by a beacon lit at the end of the harbour wall. Watching Kit's face as he guided the yacht through the treacherous rocks that guarded the bay, Clarissa realised how truly handsome he was when his countenance was not marred by his habitual cynical frown. Kit's eyes sparkled with anticipation as he steered the difficult course confidently. The gleam of excitement was contagious, stirring her own heart with a longing to be at his side, to face the danger with him. Here was a Kit released from the constraints of his London life. Here was the real Kit, the bold rescuer, not the dissolute rake. Like a shooting star brightening the cold, crisp night sky, Clarissa saw the truth. Here was her Kit. The Kit she had begun to love.

Breathless with the realisation, she clutched the rails, trying not to allow the elation that the admission brought reflect in her face. For just a moment, the thrill of finding herself truly in love was all-encompassing. She was soaring upwards towards the stars, the brilliance of the flame inside her outshining even the brightest of lights in the night sky.

But her spirits plummeted back down to earth all too quickly. That man standing so proudly at the helm of his yacht felt more for the ship shifting beneath them than he could ever feel for any woman, especially not the deceiver he believed Clarissa to be. He wanted her body, nothing more, a wish that would no doubt prove both fleeting and quickly sated.

Even Clarissa's dauntless spirit was downtrodden by such a thought. For a moment she stared blankly ahead at the approaching shore. But long experience of coping in the face of adversity stood her now in good stead, and, ever the optimist, she resolved to enjoy the present, and to let the future take care of itself. It was enough for now to be here with Kit, sharing this experience. Enough to know that he desired her body, at least. With resolution renewed, Clarissa turned to the scene before her, determined to extract the last ounce of enjoyment from it. Enough to last her a lifetime.

They had reached the bay and were dropping anchor, the tide being too low for the yacht to pull alongside the jetty. The night was still, the wind almost gone, the only sound the gentle splashing of the oars from the small boat that was making its way towards them, two passengers huddled together in the bow. John was lowering a rope ladder over the side, and as the small dinghy neared, called a greeting in rough French to the oarsman, obviously a familiar face.

Responding to Kit's nod, Clarissa moved to stand alongside him at the wheel, which he held steady with one hand, his other outstretched towards her. 'Well? Are you enjoying yourself, fair Clarissa?'

'Oh, yes, how can you think otherwise? It's perfect.'

All enmity was gone from him, caught up as he was in the thrill of the rescue, the constant aware-ness of danger, the unaccustomed warmth of sharing the experience with this feisty, self-assured female at his side. One minute passionate wanton, next as curious as a child, and next again launching into a defence of his character like a lioness guarding her cubs. Nary a trace of fear at their situation, never a hint of a tear, not a single recrimination had he heard from her, only staunch fortitude and sparkling enjoyment. It was a potent mixture.

Clarissa was watching the small boat and its precious cargo tie up alongside. She was right, of course, these people *were* precious. Transporting *émigrés* to the safety of England's shores was of deeper import to him than he cared to admit even to himself. Her hand remained tucked in his own as she watched, and she nestled close, the length of her body safe against him.

'They look so frightened huddled down there,' she said softly. 'How much they must have been through to get here. It's a humbling thought, but they must know they are safe, now you are here.'

She looked up at him with such trust that he could not restrain himself. Bending down, Kit kissed her softly on her lips. A gentle kiss without the heat of passion, a kiss one would give to a child, designed to—what? He wanted to keep her safe, not to betray the trust he saw writ in her eyes. She persisted in seeing him as a saviour. Fleetingly, he wished it could be so.

He was bewitched. She needed to be saved from nothing except her own wiles, and whatever this scheme was she had embroiled him in. Hardening his heart, Kit stepped briskly away. 'Wait here. They'll need help coming aboard, and John will need help with the rest of the cargo too.'

Left alone to watch, Clarissa could only admire the sleek process of loading from the tiny dinghy tied loosely to the *Sea Wolf*'s side. The men worked in silence, broken only by hushed instructions from Kit to John and the French oarsman, as Monsieur Renaud and his daughter were guided with care up the ladder and on to the deck. Several casks of brandy, boxes of tea, and bales of fabric— silk, she assumed—followed, handled by Kit and John effortlessly and with a practice born of familiarity. The cargo was stowed in a small compartment reached via a trap door on deck, which was hidden beneath some fishing nets. The *émigrés* were ushered to the cabin below. The dinghy cast off back to shore, the oarsman having received a generous *douceur* for his troubles. John and Kit were preparing to up anchor and away.

Clarissa watched all of this with fascination, taking in every detail while at the same time trying to reconcile Kit's strange behaviour. He believed her to be a fraud, and did not trust her, that much was obvious. Nor did he believe her story—and who could blame him, for it was indeed flimsy. Yet he had gone along with her proposition, none the less, for reasons she could not fathom. He was bored, true. And he found her amusing, that was also true. And tempting. That, too, Clarissa knew to be true, although she found it harder to believe, so many real beauties had he had, and no doubt would continue to have. Yet he told her she was beautiful, and she believed him, for he did not lie.

Well, the novelty would no doubt wear off, but it was flattering all the same. Still, none of this explained why he went along with her scheme. He wanted her, but he trusted her not. He seemed, as when he kissed her just now, to be fighting against more tender feelings, but each time he pulled her close he pushed her away all the harder. He believed her to be false, and she had herself conspired to ensure that he would do so.

There was nothing to be done. The situation was of her own creation and she would have to accept the consequences. It had been no part of her plan to fall in love, but she could not regret it, even if Kit would never know how she felt.

The rocking beneath her feet told her they had turned back out to sea. Sure enough, the sails were set and the land was falling away behind them.

Monsieur and his daughter were below decks. Clarissa decided the best way to assist was to provide what comfort she could to the French family on the long journey ahead. They would be chilled, and no doubt hungry. She could do something about that. She slipped away from the rail and was below decks before Kit had even noticed she had gone.

Monsieur and Mademoiselle Renaud were huddled together on one of the narrow bunks, fatigue etched on their wan faces. Mademoiselle was young, fifteen or sixteen, and bid fair to being a beauty, but at the moment all Clarissa saw was a girl at the end of her tether and in need of comfort. Pinning a bright smile to her face, and summoning up her schoolroom French, she set about providing it.

Warm blankets were retrieved from a locker beneath the bunk, and the supply box Kit had tucked into a corner was opened, revealing a ham, cheese, bread and wine. The *émigrés* fell on the food with obvious relish, and were considerably cheered by the time they had made a good repast. The sea was smoother for the return journey, and fortunately neither of the new passengers was subject to sickness. Clarissa poured herself a glass of burgundy and settled down to conversation with the father and daughter, keen to find out their story for herself. Keen also to discover their opinion of their rescuer without Kit himself being privy to it.

It was as sad, sordid and harrowing a tale as she had ever heard. Yet *Monsieur* emerged from it with a quiet dignity, a respect for life and a trust in humankind despite all his experience. He had no wish to dwell on the details of the past, the worst of times, when his wife was held in captivity, the only certainty that of her death by the blade. He focused instead on the goodness of the people who kept his daughter safe in the country while he pleaded in vain with the authorities in Paris. Of their kindness in providing him with a roof over his head, food, even some work tutoring the village children. And the generosity of the people who offered him a new home in England.

Monsieur spoke perfect English. 'Over the years before the revolution, my studies led to friendship with some eminent professors at Oxford university. It is these very good friends who offered sanctuary to myself and Lisette, my daughter, as soon as we got word out that we were alive.'

'So, you've been planning your escape for some time then, *monsieur*?'

'Yes, for more than a year now. My wife, Lisette's *maman*, was killed by the guillotine three years ago. Until she died, we had hoped to survive in France, to simply wait until this madness, this *terreur*, was ended. But when my dear wife was executed—murdered…'

'Papa, we must think of the future now, it is what *maman* would want.' Lisette's gentle voice, full of compassion, roused her papa from his maudlin thoughts.

'You are right, *ma petite.*' Monsieur Renaud heaved a sigh, and, fortified with another draught of wine, resumed his story. 'We heard of the English *monsieur* and his rescues through another of my countrymen, but it proved difficult and time-consuming to make contact and the necessary arrangements. Easy to understand, given the need for secrecy and the danger to all concerned. But now, thank God, we are finally here.'

'The expense must have been a big problem for you?'

'Oh, no, *mais non, madame*, there was no cost. *Monsieur* never takes a fee for his rescues, nor even a gift—and he has been offered many. Not once, in many, many attempts, has he been caught. Not one passenger has he failed, even when he had to wait in France, at great danger to himself. He is a hero.'

Clarissa smiled, wishing just for a moment that

Kit was present to hear himself being described in the very terms he had denied so vehemently only hours before. She had been right about him, but it was reassuring to have it confirmed.

'Yes, I believe he is a hero, *monsieur*, would he but admit it.'

'We are not even permitted to know his name, *madame*.' Lisette joined in the conversation now, her pretty face animated, the only traces of the frightened little girl who had boarded the yacht showing in the lines of exhaustion. 'He is known as the *Loup de Mer*, the name of this yacht, and I think it suits him, *non*? He is just like a wolf, is he not, so dangerous, and so brave. But you, *madame*, you must know him well to be here on the boat with us. Tell me, is he of noble birth, as they say he is?'

Clarissa blushed, for Lisette was obviously curious as to her relationship with Kit, even if she was too polite to ask. 'I think, *mademoiselle*, that if he wished his name to be known he would tell you. It is not for me to give away his secrets.'

'Well spoken, my dear, my secrets are nobody's property but mine.'

Kit entered the tiny cabin with his usual cat-like grace, making the room suddenly seem much smaller. The cynical smile was firmly in place, the slight frown drawing his black brows together demonstrating clearly that he had overheard enough of the conversation to know Clarissa had been asking questions.

'My aunt always told me that listeners hear only ill of themselves, you know. You are fortunate you didn't arrive any earlier.'

'Ah, so you have an aunt, as well as a mother. Quite a little family gathering there will be awaiting you on your return from your trip. And what, pray, would I have overheard that would have been so unwelcome to my ears?'

'Why, sir, only what I told you myself, and to your face. You are a hero. And it came this time not from my lips, but from those of Monsieur Renaud here.'

'And, oh, *monsieur*, it is true. To us you are a hero, *je vous promis.*' The worshipful tone of Lisette's voice could not be ignored, but instead of taking umbrage with her, Kit laughed.

'*Merci du compliment, mademoiselle.* But I didn't come here to discuss my character, I came to remind you of your promises to me. We will be in England soon. A chaise awaits you, to take you to London and thence to Oxford. Once you are dis-embarked, you must not discuss this journey, nor may you tell any of your friends still in France how you came to contact me. From tonight, the

Loup de Mer is no more. You have the honour of being my last passengers. And after tonight, even if we meet in the street, you must not recognise me. Is that understood?'

'But why? *Monsieur*, I do not understand why?'

'Lisette!' Monsieur Renaud laid a constraining hand on his daughter's shoulder. '*Tais-toi*. I speak for both of us, *monsieur*, when I say that it shall be as you demand. But I beg you, if you should ever be in need of a friend yourself, to consider me your eternally grateful servant.'

'Thank you, *monsieur.*' Only Clarissa realised that the curt tone hid Kit's own pleasure at the compliment. 'Now, I will bid you adieu. I will be busy on deck until we disembark. I am sure that *madame* here will look after you well. She is adept at it, I can vouch.' A brief nod and a smile, and he was gone.

Clarissa settled Lisette down to sleep on the narrow bunk, letting her head rest on her own lap, soothing her into slumber by stroking her hair as she had done with Amelia countless times. After a while, Monsieur Renaud slept too, more fitfully, uncomfortably upright on the bunk opposite, and Clarissa sat watching over them, her own mind too tired to grapple with the travails that lay ahead when they arrived back in port.

Finally she too dozed off. She woke briefly to

see Kit hovering over her, tucking a blanket round her, but he put a finger to his mouth and left as silently as he had arrived, so she smiled faintly, and turned to a troubled sleep once more.

When Clarissa next opened her eyes, the porthole revealed a choppy iron-grey sea rising to meet the pale dawn sky. It was morn, though she had no idea what o'clock. Even with a poor wind, they must be near home. Gently, so as not to disturb Lisette, still soundly asleep on her lap, Clarissa rose and stretched, stiff and sore from lying on the rough planks that passed for a bed. Her eyes felt gritty from the briny salt of the sea-spray, and she was ravenously hungry. She had not eaten since the inn, which seemed like long ago now, though it was only yesterday. But breakfast would have to wait until they landed, and she had a suspicion that once they were safely ashore, breakfast would be the last thing on her mind.

The yacht was slowing, but she could see nothing from the porthole to tell her their position. Steadying herself to go above decks, she was stilled by the sound of strange voices, and waited, suddenly alert to danger. The cabin door opened abruptly and John appeared, his face creased in worry.

'Master says to stay down there, and make no

sound. There's a cutter coming alongside, they mustn't find you.'

'A cutter? Do you mean a customs ship?'

'Aye. They've been tipped off, must've been, as they were lying in wait for us. I warned the master after the last time that someone was informing on us. And this time they want to board. They must be certain sure of their information.'

'But can't you prevent them boarding?'

'Master Kit'll try, lady, but they do seem mighty determined this time. And Master Kit, happen he's riled that Lieutenant Smith once too often. The lad's got summat to prove.'

Looking desperately round the tiny cabin, Clarissa realised there was nowhere for them to hide. The brandy casks were in the hidden compartment on deck, but no Riding Officer worth his salt would fail to discover the hiding place if he was permitted a thorough search. Looking anxiously at the still peacefully sleeping *émigrés*, Clarissa knew that if the customs men found the brandy they would almost certainly want to search the cabin too, where, unknown to them, a much more valuable cargo was stored. They must be prevented from searching or the game was up for them all. And if Kit couldn't stop them, she thought, a plan forming in her mind, well, then she would have to.

Something of her thoughts must have shown on her face, for John was entreating her to remain in the cabin and stay quiet. 'Do as Master Kit commands and don't even think of doing anything silly or you'll get us all hanged.' With this, he closed the cabin door firmly on Clarissa's face and returned above decks.

'I must command you to allow us to escort you into port, Lord Rasenby. We have a warrant to search the *Sea Wolf.*' Lieutenant Smith stood stiffly on the deck, his dinghy tied alongside in the calm waters of the channel, his cutter swaying a few yards off and behind the yacht.

'This obsession with my night-fishing trips is becoming tedious, Lieutenant. I thought you would have better things to do with your valuable time.'

'You have been less fortunate than usual, my lord, from what I can see?'

'I don't take your meaning.' Kit's temper, usually so cool under pressure, was frayed. Never before had they been unable to outrun the customs men, and he cursed the ill luck which had seen the wind drop suddenly. The thought of the Renauds and Clarissa hidden below decks made him nervous, more nervous than the thought of the cargo concealed in the secret locker. He had no clear idea of the law regarding the *émigrés*, but he had a very clear idea indeed of what would happen to his reputation if this story got out.

'My meaning, my lord, is simple. Where is your catch?'

Cursing volubly under his breath, Kit turned helplessly to John, who shrugged in consternation. They had caught no fish.

'As you say, I was unlucky last night, Lieutenant. Come now, we both know this is foolish. I am in need of my bed, as I'm sure you are of yours. Nothing can be gained from searching us, for there is nothing to be found.'

'Perhaps your catch is below decks, my lord?'

'Devil take you, Lieutenant, what are you implying?'

'You know very well, Lord Rasenby. You are carrying contraband and this time nothing will prevent me from discovering it.'

'I'm afraid you're going to be disappointed all the same, Lieutenant.' Clarrie's husky tones, as she stepped boldly on to deck, startled the men into silence. John, standing behind Kit, looked on slack-jawed.

'Lord, Kit, I thought we'd never get back to England. I've missed you darling, it's no fun below decks on my own.' Laying a proprietorial arm on Kit's, Clarrie pouted. Her hair was loosened to curl freely down her back, and her dress unbuttoned sufficiently to add to her air of abandon. There could be no mistaking that she had this moment arisen from a night of passion.

Lieutenant Smith's jaw dropped in imitation of John's at this lush display, but Kit, quick to take advantage, merely pressed Clarissa's hand in acknowledgment of the ruse, and smiled tauntingly at the Riding Officer. 'My cargo, Lieutenant Smith, as you see.' Taking Clarissa's hand in his, he raised it to his mouth and planted a lingering kiss on her palm. 'Good morning, my love. I'm afraid this gentleman was rather intent on searching your quarters.'

'Oh, please, Lieutenant, let me preserve some modicum of dignity. The cabin is—how can I put it delicately—a little untidy.' There could be no mistaking her meaning. Lieutenant Smith blushed as scarlet as his uniform.

'You can see now, Lieutenant, why I had no time for fishing last night. I was rather more agreeably occupied with this particular little piece of bait.' A rather unnecessary pat on her bottom made Clarrie start.

'Please, Kit, not in front of the gentleman. You can see he's embarrassed.' Indeed, the Lieutenant was playing with the collar of his coat as if suddenly finding it too tight. 'I'm so sorry, Lieutenant—as you can see, I'm having a little difficulty in taming his lordship here. What he needs is his bed.' This accompanied by a wink, which made even Kit raise an eyebrow.

'I—well, I—yes. Excuse me, Lord Rasenby, it would seem that once again I was misinformed. Please accept my apologies, ma'am, for disturbing you—I mean, for disturbing your…'

'My rest, I think you mean,' Clarrie said with a saucy smile.

'Yes. Your rest, ma'am. Of course.'

'Lieutenant?'

'My lord?'

'A word, if you please, before you go. I would ask you to keep this encounter to yourself for all of our sakes. The lady, you understand, belongs to another, and it would grieve him greatly should he find out about this night's fishing trip.'

Realisation dawned in the officer's eyes, and they widened at the temerity of the man standing shameless in front of him. Lord Rasenby's reputation was well known to those hereabouts, of course, but never before had Lieutenant Smith been faced with such blatant evidence of his raking. And she so young and pretty too! Nodding wisely in an attempt to pass off the encounter as he was sure a man of the world would do, Lieutenant Smith thrust the proffered note away in confusion. 'My discretion does not need to be bought, Lord Rasenby. I am a man of honour. You can accept my word that I will not discuss this encounter.'

Kit's brows rose in surprise. 'You are a credit to your uniform, sir, and I honour you for it. And in return, I'll tell you something to your advantage.'

'Sir?'

'It will perhaps relieve you to know that my night-fishing trips are at an end. You may wish to share that knowledge with the Marquis of Alchester, your informant.' Raising his hand to forestall the confused denial, Kit continued. 'I have been aware for some time that he has been keeping you apprised of my movements. Rest assured, I will be taking the matter up with Alchester personally. But for now, I trust, you take my meaning? The *Sea Wolf* will not be going fishing again.'

'I thank you sir. I take your meaning well. Now I must bid you good morning." A blushing nod to Clarissa, and the lieutenant was gone, over the side to the waiting dinghy, and back to his cutter.

He was barely back on board before Clarrie turned, exultant and bursting with excitement, towards Kit. 'Oh, Kit, I can't tell you, my heart was thumping fit to burst. Just for a moment there I thought he—'

Kit cut short her excited torrent of words with an imperious wave of his hand. 'You were told to remain below. Can I not trust you to follow even the simplest of instructions? I would have found a way to deal with Lieutenant Smith. John, make haste for the quay. We are long overdue. Clarissa, go below and make sure the Renauds are prepared to disembark.'

Curtly dismissed, Clarissa stumbled below, blinking back the tears. Kit turned to take the wheel, confused at his own sudden temper.

'Don't you think you're being a mite hard on the girl, my lord?' John asked gravely. 'She got us out of a pretty pickle there and no mistake.'

'I know John, I know. Your point is well made.' She had saved them all from a perilous situation with her quick thinking, cool head and bravery. So why, then, was he so angry with her?

Chapter Seven

'Can you finish up here on your own, John? This way, Clarissa, we have unfinished business to attend to.' Kit, his expression impassive, ushered Clarissa towards the awaiting chaise. His tightly reigned temper had been in evidence ever since the *Sea Wolf* docked. Monsieur and Mademoiselle Renaud were disembarked and dispatched in a separate post chaise with uncommon haste, allowing Clarissa time for only the briefest of fare-wells. John was kept busy amid a flurry of barked orders from Kit, unloading the remaining cargo, securing the yacht, and then finally the boathouse.

Aside from pointing Clarissa towards the chaise, Kit had said nothing to her. Deducing correctly that she was the source of his anger, although having no clue as to how she might have provoked it, Clarrie felt her own temper starting to rise, fuelled by a sense of injustice. She wheeled to confront him.

'What have I done to incur your displeasure this time, my lord? At least have the decency to tell me to my face. I thought you would be impressed by my actions when we were boarded by the Revenue. My motives were of the purest, I did it only to protect all of us—you, me, John and the Renauds. Would you have me in the wrong for that, would you have me apologise for trying to save you? For it worked, didn't it?' She added proudly, 'The look on poor Lieutenant Smith's face was priceless!'

'Yes, it worked. But you were lucky and, more to the point, extremely reckless, for things might easily have gone awry after your impulsive behaviour. This is not merely a game, some sport for your entertainment, Clarissa. Innocent people's lives are at stake. Lives that you put at risk.'

'I thought you cared naught for these people yourself. Did you not make me a pretty speech that it was all sport to you and you were indifferent to their fate?'

'Well, I care for John, at any rate,' was his lame response. Confound the woman, Kit thought, looking distinctly uncomfortable now. First she knows my thoughts, and now she seems able to look into my very soul and read what lies hidden within.

Clarissa pressed on, warming to the task, recognising that for once she held the upper hand. 'As usual, my lord, you would be better served aiming your words at a more deserving target—yourself! Putting innocent lives at risk for sport and pleasure! For shame sir, is that not exactly the fate you intended for Amelia Warrington?'

'Her again,' Kit exploded. 'What is your obsession with that girl? As I've said before, I pride myself on amply rewarding those with whom I play such games.'

'Indeed you do, Lord Rasenby. But have you ever considered that what you proudly call generosity is, in fact, conscience and guilt?'

Kit stepped towards Clarissa, grasping her by both elbows, looming over her threateningly. 'That may be so Clarissa, but we are embroiled in a game of our own, remember. One we both chose to play willingly and in which neither of us could be called innocent. A game that is about to resume.'

Giving her no time to reply, Kit nodded farewell to John, ushered Clarissa into the chaise, and mounted his own horse. Almost before the door was fastened shut, the chaise started forward. They were journeying back to London, that much seemed certain. But how was she to forestall Kit to give her plan more time to succeed with regards to Amelia and Edward, while keeping her virtue intact? Kit would be expecting payment soon, that was plain. So much had happened in the last twenty-four hours, Clarissa could not find it in her to care at this moment. Mentally and physically exhausted, she fell into a deep dreamless sleep.

She awoke to the heat of a fire and the rattle of a tea tray. Sleepily she sat up rubbing her eyes, to discover that she was no longer in the coach, but on a sofa in a small parlour. The curtains were drawn, giving no indication of the time of day. For a minute in her confusion Clarissa imagined she was back home. But as she gradually took stock of her surroundings, noticing the tasteful, opulent furnishings, the paintings and ornate tapestries that adorned the walls and the huge roaring fire with its impressive over-mantel, she realised this was not her own humble home but somewhere much grander, redolent of money and privilege. Clarissa also became aware that she was not alone. Kit was studying her quietly from the comfort of the generously upholstered leather armchair opposite.

'Where am I? What is this place?'

'This is my home, Clarissa—or the one closest to the coast, in any event. Thornwood Manor to be exact, although, if you wish, you may call it *Castle*

Udolpho.' Kit closed the book he had been reading while she was asleep. 'I have been familiarising myself with Mrs Radcliffe's novel, of which you seem so fond. Naturally I wish to ensure that I live up to the villainous Signor Montoni. Bringing you back to my lair while you slept seemed rather appropriate.' His smile was twisted, every bit the unrepentant rake.

Clarissa felt a small curl of trepidation clutch the pit of her stomach. But to show it, she knew, would be to surrender. Challenge, and if she could manage it, a cool approach to quell his ardour would be the most likely weapons to succeed. She yawned and sat up properly on the sofa, pushing the cashmere shawl that had covered her to one side. 'Lord, Kit, you take me too seriously, I fear. Mrs Radcliffe's novels are much too dramatic for me—'tis my aunt, really, who has a liking of them. Perhaps you should abduct her instead.'

'Very good, Clarissa, but I know you better than you think. This latest act does not fool me, nor will it put me off. I was happy to play the wicked Montoni, but I think, do not you, that the wicked Lord Rasenby will suffice just as well?' The smile that accompanied this remark was bleak, curling his sculpted mouth only slightly, but he made no attempt to move, seeming content with talk for the present.

'I know you well enough by now, Kit, to know that you are not, nor never shall be, the wicked Lord Rasenby. I presume you brought me here that we may partake of refreshment before the journey back to London. A sound idea, I am badly in need of a wash and some sustenance.' Watching him cautiously from under her lashes, Clarissa was not encouraged. Kit was showing no signs of relaxing.

'Several times now, Clarissa, I have warned you to ignore my reputation at your peril. You persist in doing so, but that is your look out. Do I need to remind you that we struck a bargain? A bargain with the devil it may be, but one that you must see through, none the less.'

Licking her dry lips nervously, Clarissa forced herself to relax against the cushions, feigning an indifference she was far from feeling. He had no intention of letting her go, and would insist on their union here in this house, and soon. For all she knew they were alone, although common sense told her there must be servants around somewhere. But servants in Lord Rasenby's employ were not likely to come to her rescue.

Rising to make the tea, Clarissa noted with relief that at least her hand did not betray her as she carefully measured out the delicate bohea from the wooden chest and poured the hot water from the little copper kettle into the delicate Chinese porcelain pot. Handing Kit a dish and settling gratefully to sip on her own, Clarissa frantically reviewed her options. They numbered two in total, and she was not confident of the likely success of either. She could stall, persuade Kit to postpone their union until some later point, and then somehow manage never to see him again. Or she could simply tell him the truth, and beg him to release her from her promise.

Actually, there was a third choice. She could submit. The thought brought a flush to her cheeks. To experience true passion just this once. To succumb to Kit's love-making. To bring this flame lit by Kit's kisses to a fire. To know real fulfilment. Oh God, it was tempting. Clarrie shivered at the thought.

But it was a fantasy. Impossible. For she knew that one taste of Kit would leave her desperate for more. One slip and she would be wholly in his power, incapable of refusing him aught. Kit would use her and discard her, of this Clarissa was certain. She had to refuse him at any cost, no matter how much her body begged her to say yes to him.

Postponement, then, is what she would aim for. Taking another sip of the beautifully scented tea,

Clarissa tried to relax. 'Do you think the Renauds will be safe, now? *Monsieur* told me a little of their troubles. Despite all he has been through, he seemed to me a kind man. He looks for good in everyone, even his enemies. I am not sure I could be so forgiving.'

'No? You surprise me, I thought that seeing good in people, despite ample evidence to the contrary, was something you took pride in doing yourself. Your determination to cast me in a positive light, for instance?'

She was nervous, Kit realised, looking for a way out, that much was obvious. Like a cat toying with a mouse, he decided to humour her. The outcome was inevitable—why not enjoy seeing her writhe in his clutches?

'That's different,' Clarissa replied. 'I merely pointed out to you that you have good qualities as well as bad. That is not at all the same thing as believing in goodness when faced with true evil, as Monsieur Renaud must surely have been. Were it my husband locked in a prison, condemned to death for no reason other than his birth, I would not be so forgiving.'

'Would you not? And what, fair Clarissa, would you do?'

'I have no idea. It would depend on the circumstances, I suppose. But if I found harm had been done to the man I loved, I would seek revenge.'

'I'd like to see it. I had no idea you could use a sword. Or would you choose pistols at dawn?'

'Of course not, I did not mean a duel. I meant— oh, you are infuriating! You take nothing seriously, there is no point in this discussion.' Petulantly, Clarissa placed her tea dish on the side table. So much for trying to involve him in conversation. All he seemed to do was aggravate her.

She took a calming breath and tried again. 'This is a lovely room. Is it a large house—Thornwood Manor, I think you called it?'

Only the slight twitch of his sculpted mouth betrayed Kit's amusement at this latest sally. 'Not large by the standards of my other properties—a mere cottage, some would say—with only ten bedrooms, and really quite small grounds.'

'And do you stay here often?'

'Not as often as I'd like. I spent my youth here. Nowadays I come when I want to sail, or to escape the tedium of London for a spell.'

'Oh.' The silence grew as Clarissa searched her mind desperately for another topic.

'You could always ask me about the weather.'

Looking up at this taunting remark, she could not help but smile, acknowledging the hit. 'Oh, no, for I feel I have not yet exhausted the possibilities of asking about your other residences first. The weather is far down the list. I'd be surprised if we reached that topic before we returned to London.'

'We are not returning to London for a while yet; you really must resign yourself to that fact. We are staying here, Clarissa, in the solitude of this ten-bedroom house with its small but beautiful park, until I have received my payment from you. To return to London without it would, I very much fear, be to give you the chance to disappear while still in my debt. And I have no intention of allowing that. You should not play if you cannot pay. Every gambler knows that.'

Would that her mama had followed that advice, Clarissa thought bitterly. But Mama and her debts seemed so far away. And unless she could escape from Kit, and soon, Clarissa was not sure she would ever be able to face them again.

'I can't stay here, it's not practical. I have nothing with me but what I stand in. No clothes, not even a toothbrush. No, no, Lord Rasenby—Kit—I must beg of you to return to London. I *will* pay you, but not here.' She was frightened, but it was tinged with a strange excitement. She did not fear hurt. He was making her suffer to tease her, perhaps even frighten her a little bit. But he would let her go, surely? He would not really make good his threat to keep her here against her will?

'A toothbrush I can supply you with. As to clothes—what need will we have of those? You need no adorning other than the glow of love-making. Lying naked in my arms, I have no doubt you will look your most beautiful.'

'Oh!' The thought was shocking, but the picture it conjured up, crystal clear in its detail, was more shocking still. A flush stole across Clarissa's pale cheeks at the idea of Kit naked beside her, his hard masculine body starkly contrasting with her own feminine curves. She felt a slow burning heat suffuse her. A rhythmic pulse picked up an insistent beat deep within that refused to be dispelled. Shaking her head in an effort to clear the fog clouding her brain, Clarissa looked up to find Kit watching her knowingly, perfectly well aware of the direction he had given her mind.

'Well, Clarissa? Have you any other objections? If so, I would prefer that you raise them now, for pleasant as I find it to talk with you, there are other more—pressing—things we must do together. I find I am growing impatient with waiting, and wish to conclude our bargain.' Kit rose and crossed the room to stand before her. 'Come, Clarissa, enough of your excuses. You have a promise to fulfil.'

'I can't, I…'

'You would do well to co-operate, you know. I have no wish for an unwilling partner.' His words were spoken low, but the threat and the iron will behind them were unmistakable. Kit was annoyed at this show of reluctance, and could not understand it. She had never intended to pay at the start, that much was certain. But she wanted him now, he could not have mistaken her response to him. So why this pretence of reluctance? Surely she could not be planning to trap him into a commitment?

The thought gave Kit sudden pause, for it had never occurred to him that this could be her purpose. That she had some secret scheme he doubted not, as he doubted not that this maidenly modesty of hers was a ploy. But that the plot could have been a honey trap! No, he could not believe it. 'Come, Clarissa, it is time. I know not why you are feigning reluctance, you were eager enough in the cabin last night. You know full well this will be no ravishment, nor seduction even. Better to show good grace in defeat. You will enjoy yourself with me, I promise.' This time his smile was wolfish.

Taking his hand reluctantly, Clarissa stood. She was trembling, a combination of fear and antici- pation mixed with desire making her unsteady on her feet. She stumbled, clutching Kit's arm to steady herself, and found herself drawn close when she would have made to pull away. 'No, no, I can't, I—'

'Oh, I think you'll find that you can.' His arms were around her, pulling her tight to his chest. His breath was on her face, and his lips captured hers in a sweet, tempting kiss before she had time to reply.

It was a kiss that promised of delights to come. A prelude, an appetiser of a kiss, softening her lips, forcing her mouth gently open, making her sigh softly as she melted.

Anchoring Clarissa to him with a hand placed firmly in the small of her back, Kit carefully stroked the soft curls on her forehead with the other, soothing, caressing away her resistance. His mouth left her lips to nibble gently on her ear lobe, and then to whisper light kisses on her brows, her eyelids, down to the swan-like line of her neck, licking the tender hollow of her shoulder.

It was a kiss that threatened to be her undoing. Clarissa unfurled like a spring flower in the bright March sunlight, slowly turning to the heat of the sun after the long cold winter. The defences she had thought so strong melted under this slow, sensual assault. As Kit slowly licked his way back up the white column of her throat to find her mouth once more, Clarissa sighed again, more deeply this time, surrendering to the inevitable. His tongue swept slowly along her lower lip, now pulsing with response, and she opened her mouth in anticipation of his onslaught.

To her surprise, it didn't come. Kit pulled back, just enough to look into her face, but the break awoke her to the extreme danger of her situation. Once more, fear battled with desire. Once more, she tried to pull together the tattered shreds of her resolution.

'No, you don't, Clarissa.' The arm around her waist tightened, preventing her from moving away.

'Let me go!'

'No. I didn't stop in order to resume this tedious pretence of reluctance on your part. In fact, quite the opposite. I want you willing. I know you are willing, and you know it too. I have no wish to force you, but I think we both know I won't have to. Admit it, damn you!'

'No. I won't. Let me go.'

'Don't make me lose my temper. I am fast approaching the end of my tether with you, I warn you. Now, admit that you are willing, for the love of God, woman, for in case it had escaped your notice, I am more than a little in need of satisfaction.'

Indeed, she could hardly be unaware of his arousal, pressed so close as she was against him.

Clarissa shifted slightly, trying to move away from him, but succeeded only in rubbing herself more intimately against him, causing him to wince.

'If you don't stop struggling like that, we will not make it to the bedroom.' Kit's tone was urgent, his voice husky with passion, but his eyes were hard, dark pools of determination.

Clarissa knew she could not fight such a man with subterfuge any longer. If she was to escape from here with her virtue—what was left of it—she must confess all. 'Kit, please let me go. There is something I must tell you.'

'I thought I had made it singularly clear that the time for talk is over, Clarissa. I am not interested in words at present, I am more concerned with the other things our mouths can do. I need one word only from you, and that is yes. Just say it, Clarrie,' Kit said urgently, 'say yes.'

'No! I won't. Let me go.' Her voice betrayed her desperation as she twisted in his grip. 'Kit, you've got to listen to me. If you don't you'll regret it, I promise.'

'The only thing I'll regret is that I stopped when I did. I am tired of your tricks. I want to hear no more of your lies. Your kisses tell me clear enough that your answer is yes.'

Clarissa's struggles became more determined.

She felt the flounce on her petticoat rip as Kit held her effortlessly tight. One long curl escaped its pins, and she shook it impatiently from her face. Her heart was beating so fast she felt it must escape the confines of her rib cage, and she could no longer hide the apprehension in her eyes. 'No! I am not who you think I am. I am not here for the reasons you believe. Kit, please, you must listen to me. Please!'

The single tear, the first he had seen her shed, was so surprising that he released her abruptly. Thrusting her back on to the sofa in confusion, Kit watched as she wiped it away. Even in extremes, it would seem, Clarissa was not a female to fall back on the traditional ploy of waterworks. Striding to the side table, he unlocked the tantalus and poured brandy into two glasses, downing his in one swift gulp before taking the other glass to Clarissa. 'Here, take this.'

She pushed it away, still intent on regaining some measure of control over the panic that was engulfing her. 'I don't want that. There is no need to get me drunk, my lord, it will not make my consent any more forthcoming.'

'I have no intention of making you drunk, damn it! You are upset. The brandy will calm you. And before you even think about it, no, it is not laced with any drug. I am not, after all, such a villain as Signor Montoni. Now drink up.'

The fiery liquid made her gasp, but it did help calm her. Trying rather ineffectually to push her hair back into its pins, Clarissa looked up to see that Kit was watching her, a grim look on his face. 'I must look a fright.' Her voice was shaky.

His hand reached out to grasp hers, his fingers wound round the curl, and tightened, just enough for her to sense the threat. Despite the concern he had shown, he had not softened towards her. Idly twisting her curl round and around those long, shapely fingers, Kit watched Clarissa, his eyes like cold chips of flint, a slight frown between his dark brows, giving her no hint of his thoughts.

She shivered. She had badly miscalculated; he would not be swayed from his purpose. Her only hope was in making him listen to the truth before his temper took control. If she was going to speak, now was her only chance.

Clarissa took a deep breath. 'Kit? I know you're angry, but, please, won't you listen, just for a moment?' Forcing herself to look up into his face, she was taken aback at the bleakness there. His eyes were expressionless, his mouth a hard, grim line. His breathing was harsh and he trembled with a mixture of barely suppressed anger and frustrated desire. The urge to reach up, to place a small, soft hand against those grim lines on his brow, to try to smooth them away with her thumb, was irresistible.

Kit closed his eyes at the touch, but almost immediately swatted her hand away and sat back from her, as if the contact gave him pain. 'Another of your tricks, Clarissa, pity? I have no need of that. If anyone is to be pitied, it is you.'

The frown deepened, the brows drawn together to meet in the middle, giving him a satanic look that made her retreat, truly afraid for the first time. Noting her reaction, Kit gave a harsh laugh. 'Yes, now you see before you the real wicked Lord Rasenby. Just as I see before me the real, treacherous Clarissa. I have but one advantage over you, my sweet. At least I played fair.'

'What do you mean?'

'I never pretended to be other than what I am. Whereas you... Well, I still don't know what your game is, but I no longer care. I knew you lied when you sought me out. I knew you lied about your reasons for wanting this little *adventure* as you called it. But I thought—hoped—had come to expect, in any case, that you would play fair, that at least your more intimate dealings with me would be honest. It seems I was mistaken, and you are simply a better actress than I thought.'

Kit ran a hand through his thick black hair and shook his head in an effort to clear his brain. He was exhausted, had barely slept for almost two days. Against his will, he had begun to like this woman in front of him, to honour her for her courage and her quick wits. He enjoyed her company, but that made her treachery all the harder to come to terms with. Subtly but surely over these last few days, this woman had got under his skin, and he thought she felt the same. Now there could be no doubt that it had all been an act. This determined blowing of hot and cold, even the meagre tears, all were mere trickery, designed to make him take pity and to let her go. But he would not!

No longer caring about the means, Kit was determined that the end should be as she had promised. He would have her, and she would admit that she was willing, would admit that she wanted him as he wanted her. He had to have her, his blood would not be cooled without her. Then, thank God, it would be over. She would be out of his system, and he could go back to his life— whatever that turned out to be.

Kit stood to pour himself another measure of brandy. Looking over as he drained his glass, he saw she was crying, silent tears, which she was frantically trying to mop with her sleeve. Her shoulders were hunched, and her breathing uneven, and she looked so forlorn, with her crumpled dress and her hair in disarray, that he had to quell the urge to go over, to wrap her in his arms, and tell her no harm would come to her. Hardening his heart, reminding himself it was just another of her games, he returned instead to the armchair opposite, and waited for her to gain some control over herself.

A loud sniff and a final surreptitious wipe of her nose informed him that she was ready to speak.

'I'm sorry,' Clarissa muttered, 'I don't usually cry.'

'No, and you wasted your effort, you know. Your tears move me as little as your protestations of maidenly modesty. Both are false.'

'You're quite wrong, Kit, but I can see that it will do me no good to protest.' She had ruined everything with her lies, she could see that. What little trust there had been between them was spoilt. What tiny, faint fantasy she had clung on to for some kind of future happiness was an impossible dream. 'I need to tell you the truth—will you listen?'

'The truth? That will be a novelty.' The harsh, cynical laugh, almost a snarl, with no trace of humour, proved she had lost him for ever. 'I'll listen, but it will make no difference. By the end of tonight, you will be mine. By the end of tomorrow, you will be gone and we can both say good riddance. I wish to get the whole thing over with, for this game begins to bore me—sooner than I had thought. So, please, tell me your tale and then let us talk no more.'

The words sounded a death knell to her hopes, faint as they had been. The only thing now was to try, at least, to extract his promise to leave Amelia alone. With a deep breath, she began. 'My name is Clarissa Warrington. I am Amelia Warrington's sister.'

With many pauses, stumbling over the words, and all the time waiting in vain for a reaction, any reaction, from Kit, silent and brooding in the chair, Clarissa told her story. Making little of her own trials, she still gave away enough to paint Kit a sorry picture of her circumstances. 'I just feel that if Amelia had the chance to meet an honourable man who would be a calming influence on her, she would marry and could be happy. There is someone, a good man who loves her, and I am sure his feelings are reciprocated. But she has been so spoilt, and she is so beautiful, that the kinds of riches you can offer make it difficult for her to choose the honourable path.'

Lacing her hands together as she concentrated on putting Amelia in the kindest light, Clarissa frowned. 'She's not a bad person, she's just weak. So I thought if I removed temptation from her, it would give Edward a chance.' Realising just how foolish this plan sounded, now that she told it aloud for the first time, made her shoulders sag with despair. What a fool she had been!

Kit echoed her thoughts. 'Well, if that really was your plan, I can only say that you must have windmills in your head. For God's sake, Clarissa, do you really believe for a moment that my absence will make any difference at all? Merely, it means that Amelia will look for a replacement, and I can assure you that it will not be this worthy Edward, unless he has miraculously come into a fortune over the last couple of days.'

'I know, it sounds so stupid now.' Looking back, Clarissa was hard put to understand her own behaviour. To have believed that Kit's mere absence would make a difference was ludicrous, not just stupid. With hindsight, of course, it was clear to her that her proposal to Kit had not been to save her sister, but to save Kit. Worse, she realised now, she had wanted Kit for herself from the first moment she had met him at the masked ball.

'But you are not stupid, Clarissa. In fact, you are

a very intelligent, well-informed young woman. I find it difficult to believe that you came up with this madcap idea merely to save your sister from an indecent proposal. And despite what you have said, I cannot believe either that you thought Amelia to be so very innocent. She is a scheming wretch, and you know it.'

His words, so nearly reflecting her own thoughts, caught her unawares. Looking over at her, Kit saw a slightly hunted expression flit across her face. 'I'm right then, Clarissa. The story you have told is not so simple, is it?'

'I don't know what you mean. I've told you the truth, I wanted to save Amelia. There is nothing more.' Terrified that Kit had some inkling of her feelings, Clarissa sought desperately for something to say that would assuage his curiosity—anything but the real truth, the truth that was only just becoming apparent to Clarissa. She had thrown herself in Kit's path from the start, not for her sister's sake, but for her own. He must never find out.

'Look at you. The lies are writ large across your face. What twist have you left out of your sorry story?'

'I—well, if you must know, I—the truth is, my lord, that I discovered from my sister that she planned to trap you.'

'Trap me? In what way, trap me?'

'Into marriage, my lord. She knew, you see, that you intended only a—a dishonourable proposal, but she was sure that she could persuade you into matrimony but some underhand means.'

'What means, exactly?'

'I don't know, I swear I don't. I only know that she had some plan, something that was to take place over the next few days, and she was certain that you would fall for it. I—I could not condone it, I had to stop it. Marriage should not be based on deceit and lies. I tried to reason with Amelia, I tried to find out what she was planning, but she merely laughed at me.'

'And knowing your sister so well as you say you do, did you really think she had the brains to carry off such a scheme? Did you think for one single minute that I would fall for anything that trollop had up her sleeve? You vastly overrate your sister if you do. I don't believe you.'

The temper on which Kit had been keeping such a tight rein was leased suddenly and wholly unexpectedly. 'Do you think I'm so stupid? That a simpering girl with cotton wool for a brain, so obviously determined to sell herself to the highest bidder, would find a way to coerce me into marriage? *Well, do you?*'

Without waiting for an answer, the words coming in a cold, harsh voice, Kit continued, all the while towering over her, his face a mask of white anger. 'No, I don't think for one second that is what you thought my fair, deceitful Clarissa. You are more like your sister than you admit. Though your plan was not quite so crude, was it? Not quite so obvious, but with the same intention.'

'I don't understand, I—'

'Don't bother to deny it, I am sick of your lies. You knew perfectly well Amelia could not succeed with me. But you thought *you* could, didn't you? Well, *didn't you?*'

'No! No, oh no. Kit, no, I wouldn't, I—'

'Oh, spare me the injured innocent, madam, it cuts no ice. I see it all clearly now. It was you who were planning to seduce me all along. Not to save your precious sister, oh, no, this was no sacrificial seduction. No wonder you were so desperate to get back to London. You had never any intention of fulfilling your promise to me, but you had every intention of blackmailing me, did you not? No doubt your so-respectable aunt, or more likely your poor frail mama, was to be brought into play. A sad and sorry tale of abduction, perhaps? Yes, that would be it. A night away in my company, and then you return home, your mama cries rape, and you await my proposals. Not bad, as far as these sorts of things go, but it wouldn't have worked, Clarissa. I've told you many times, I'm every bit as bad as my reputation. Mama could have published your tale of woe in a scandal sheet for the *ton* to read and it would have provoked no reaction from me.'

Silenced by this onslaught, Clarissa sat, motionless and appalled at what she had done. Kit fell silent too, gazing unseeing into the fire, trying to come to terms with his own anger, which seemed out of all proportion to Clarissa's crime. After all, he had known her to be deceitful from the first. Eventually, the black humour of the situation got the better of his temper. The scheme had at least the spark of originality he had come to expect from Clarissa. Placing himself at her side, Kit took hold of her cold hand. 'Let us have done with all pretence. Admit I have discovered your plans, then we can kiss and make up.'

Snatching her hand away, Clarissa moved as far from Kit as the sofa would allow. She did not trust herself to stand. 'I admit nothing other than the truth. I wanted to protect Amelia from her own foolish self. And I wanted to save you from being tricked into marriage. I had no intentions, none whatever, I assure you most vehemently, of tricking you into any sort of proposal for myself.

I meant it, Kit, I promise you, I do most truly believe that no relationship, marriage or otherwise, can be built on deceit. As to my mama's involvement—well, all I can say is that if you knew my mama, you would know her incapable of any sort of plotting.'

'Ah, I assume that Amelia takes after her then?'

A subdued giggle gave him his answer. Clarissa's sense of humour did not fail her, even in the midst of such emotional trauma. 'I'm afraid so. Mama is rather—well, suffice to say that I am the practical one.'

'The only one with any brains, you mean. It is time you put them to use. Admit that you have failed. Come clean with me, and we will call it quits.'

'You mean I can go?'

'No, I mean I will not be angry with you any more. I will save my energy for more enjoyable emotions. I still expect you to come to my bed. You can't seriously have expected me to change my mind?'

'But I never intended, I never meant—I mean, I didn't think it would come to this. I can't—please don't ask me to, please, Kit.'

Her green eyes were for the second time in a short period drowned in tears, but she would not look away, nor shed them willingly. Beseechingly, Clarissa looked up at him, silently begging for mercy. But she could see no signs of softening in the harsh mask of his face.

'Your tears won't sway me, so dry your eyes. You've tried every trick in the book over the past few days, and this sight affects me no more than any of the others, save I am in awe at the breadth of your talents. And before you try the virtuous maiden on me once more, may I remind you that your kisses have given you away several times. You are no more a maiden than your sister.'

Gently pulling Clarissa to him, Kit produced a large square of linen from his pocket, and applied himself to wiping her eyes. She lay compliant under his ministrations, almost drained of resistance, unable to think of any way out of this mesh she had woven.

'There. Your plans have gone awry, but that is no reason to prevent us enjoying each other's company.' His hand tilted her chin towards him, and he looked close into her captive eyes. 'No more tears. No more lies. Tonight you will fulfil your part of the bargain, and tomorrow you will go home. We will enjoy our coupling, you know we will. If our kisses are an indication, then it will be more than enjoyable, for we are extremely compatible, and I have tasted enough of you to know that you have been well schooled in the arts of pleasing a man.'

'I can't, Kit, please don't make me.'

'I won't make you. I won't have to. You will come to my bed of your own accord. You know you will.'

'No! Once and for all, you are mistaken in me. I have no such experience. If you take me, it will ruin me. Please, my lord, I beg of you, let me go.'

The hand on her chin tightened as his eyes darkened with anger, and something else. Dark desire, selfish need, frustrated passion—all the pent-up emotions Clarissa had roused, then dampened, then set on fire, then quelled, then blown once more into life until they burned as an inferno. Without warning, without thought, with only base, urgent need, Kit surrendered all restraint. Pushing Clarissa back on the sofa, trapping her under the hard length of his body, his mouth descended on hers in a revengeful, possessive kiss.

She struggled, her hands beating ineffectually on his chest, his shoulders, his arms. The kiss went relentlessly on, his lips hard, his tongue seeking, controlling, his body taut, pushing against hers, demanding a response. And surely, as surely as a drug injected straight into her veins, mixing with her blood, he was having an effect. She fought, but more weakly. Her mouth softened, compliant under his, if not yet responding to his demands. Her body arched into his, relishing the feel of pulsating muscle, hard bone, rough skin, all the evidence of his overwhelming masculinity against her wholly feminine softness. With every second his mastery of her became more complete.

Sensing the change in her, Kit's kisses became more sensuous, his tongue more teasing, his hands stroking her into submission rather than holding her to ransom. Clarissa sighed, her own hands ceasing their fluttering against his back, to drop boneless by her sides. She was drowning, lost, swirling deep into the eddy of their mutual desire. The fingers of her right hand trailed on the floor beside the sofa, feeling the soft pile of the Turkish rug beneath them, the texture of the wool rough against her skin like the growth of Kit's beard on her face.

The strings of her reticule caught in her hand. It must have been under the sofa. Her reticule. She clung to the last desperate shreds of her weakening resistance and pulled the strings open, groping inside as Kit continued his assault on her mouth, as her own mouth started to co-operate, poised on the verge of making her own demands. A kerchief. Her purse. A small mirror. And something else, heavy, cold and sharp.

Summoning a last strand of resolution, Clarissa extracted the small, jewelled dagger from the reticule. Calling on all her strength, she clutched it tight to the hilt and brought her hand up, the deadly blade glinting in the firelight. At the same time she placed her other hand on Kit's chest and pushed with all her might, struggling free from under him. Taken by surprise, he rolled over onto the floor with Clarissa landing on top of him. Without thinking, she reached out to break her fall. The dagger slipped from her grip, glanced off the large brass button on Kit's coat, and plunged into his arm.

Chapter Eight

'Kit! Oh, my God, Kit! I've killed you.'

'Don't be ridiculous, Clarissa. You've barely scratched me.'

'Oh, you're not dead. Thank you, God. Are you sure?'

'Have you any idea how ludicrous a question that is? Do you think it's my ghost talking? You do not kill a man by sticking a knife into his arm. It's hardly even bleeding.'

'Let me see. No, no, don't stand. Sit there. No wait, take off your coat so I can bind it. No, wait, perhaps I should call a doctor? Or get you some brandy?'

'Stop! Sit down, take a deep breath and for the Lord's sake just be quiet for a minute and let me have a look at this grievous wound you have inflicted on me.'

'But, Kit, I think you should—'

'Clarissa, if you don't just shut up for a few seconds, I swear I will be forced to murder you with that toy of yours. Where in damnation is the thing, anyway?'

Reluctantly Clarissa sat, only to stand again instantly as the point of the dagger jabbed her thigh. 'Ouch! Here, I think.'

'Give me that. Serves you right.' Kit grabbed the dagger from her hands, inspecting it with raised brows. Not a toy after all. Had it not been for his coat, she could well have injured him, seriously, if not fatally. Reluctantly, he was impressed. He had to give her top marks for originality, if nothing else—no one had ever managed to knife him before, though he was sure there were many who would have taken pleasure in it.

'It was my father's. It's one of the few things of his that haven't been sold off. I had it in my reticule. I'm sorry, truly sorry, I didn't mean to hurt you.'

Kit raised his brows questioningly, a gleam of humour lurking in his dark eyes. 'I find that difficult to believe, and I'm not sure a jury would take your side too readily. If you did not mean to hurt me, why did you try to stab me?'

'I didn't! I mean, yes, I did have the knife in my hand, but my intent was only to threaten you. I slipped, it was an accident. I just thought you would take me more seriously—I just thought—oh, I don't know what I thought. I'm sorry.'

'Well, it's certainly a drastic measure to take to escape my advances. I had no idea that you found me so unattractive.'

'I don't.'

This time the denial was a whisper so soft he was not sure he had heard it. And even as he took it in, she had reverted to her concern over his injury.

'Does it hurt? I think I should take a look, even if it is just a scratch. It will need to be dressed, you'll probably need a sling.'

The hopefulness in her tone was unmistakable. So, despite everything he had said, all that had passed between them in the last few hours, Clarissa was still determined to escape. Well, she could for now, for he was in no fit state for love-making at present, in need of some time to cool his temper, if nothing else. Some rest was what they both needed. 'Very well, do your worst.' With difficulty, Kit shrugged obligingly out of his tight-fitting coat, ruefully surveying the damage the knife had done to the expensive fabric.

The wound was small and bleeding sluggishly, situated in the fleshy part of his left arm. At his behest Clarissa rang the bell, and to her astonishment it was answered in a remarkably quick time by a liveried servant. The man betrayed no sign of surprise at the sight of his master, wounded and half-undressed on the sofa, in the company of a somewhat dishevelled and tearful young woman. Her request for fresh linen, hot water and basilicum powder were received as if she had ordered tea and biscuits.

'Are your servants used to seeing such sights?'

'Hardly. I have never been wounded before nor am I accustomed to bringing my mistresses here. That is two firsts for you.'

'I am not your mistress.'

'No, but you will be soon.'

'No, I won't. I can't. *You* can't, that's what I mean. Your arm, it will be in a sling, so you won't be able to—well, you won't want to—I mean, you won't be up to—'

'I think you'd better stop there, don't you?' His grin was tinged with wicked humour, but his voice showed signs of fatigue. Stifling a yawn, he smiled wanly. 'I think you're safe for the moment. You may bind my arm, then we could both do with some sleep—alone. When you are rested, you may command the servants to draw you a bath. We will dine together later. No—' he raised his hand as she tried to speak '—do not, I beg of you, argue with me further. We are not returning to London tonight. Apart from anything else, your over-eager attempt to defend yourself has ensured that I am not fit to travel. And before you ask, no, you cannot go on your own. Now, once and for all, accept your fate and let us have an end to this futile discussion.'

And for once Clarissa judged it best to take his advice. She vouchsafed no reply.

The servant returned, placing a bowl of water on the table in front of her, the bandages, lint and powder to the side. His countenance, and the nod he gave to her as he did so, showed no trace of disrespect towards her. 'Will that be all, my lord?'

'Yes, thank you, Robert. Wait. Tell Mrs Hatchings that we'll dine at seven. And warn the kitchen that Miss—er—Warrington here, will be requiring a bath later. Oh, and before all that, get the housekeeper to prepare the red room for Miss Warrington as soon as possible.' Turning to Clarissa, he held his arm out in resignation. 'I hope you know what you're doing. I wouldn't put it beyond you to make it worse for your own devious purposes.'

Ignoring the gasp of indignation aroused by this remark, Kit leaned back and closed his eyes.

* * *

He awoke to find himself alone. His arm had been efficiently bandaged and mercifully left without a sling. The room was dark, the fire a heap of glowing embers. He must have been asleep for some time. Rising, Kit rang the bell, demanding hot water for his own bath, issuing a series of brisk, clear instructions for the morrow as he strode across the hallway and up the wide staircase. Refreshed by his sleep, a quiver of desire arrowed through him as he thought of Clarissa asleep in the room adjoining his own. He tried to remember the last time he had felt such a rush of anticipation, and couldn't. He must needs make the most of it, for tomorrow she would be gone and out of his life for good.

Clarissa had slept soundly in the huge four-poster bed, oblivious of her surroundings, save for the comfort of the feather mattress, the warmth at her feet from the warming pan, the crisp Holland sheets and the reassuring weight of the soft, luxurious quilt of eiderdown which had been fashioned to match the bed hangings. She awoke, feeling refreshed. The room was large, lit by a brightly burning fire in the gleaming grate. The curtained bed faced an enormous picture window, which must look direct to the sea over the marshes, for she had been aware of the soothing murmuring as she slept. Aside from the usual chests, there was a pretty lacquered writing desk in one corner, and an array of delicate Oriental porcelain on the mantel. The rich Turkish rugs were warm under her feet, and by her bedside there was a beautiful array of flowers.

The overall effect was of comfort, and of excellent taste. Despite his wealth, Kit was not an ostentatious man. His extravagances were all for public consummation—the horses, the mistresses, the gaming. In private he was obviously much more restrained.

Her thoughts were interrupted by a gentle tap on the door, preceding the entrance of a maidservant. 'If you please, ma'am, it's close on six o'clock. Would you like to bathe now?' At Clarissa's nod, a flurry of activity saw a large copper hip bath placed before the fire and filled with bucket after bucket of steaming water. Several screens placed strategically ensured that no draughts would intrude. Towels were placed on a rail to heat, and rose oil added to the water to give the final touch of complete comfort.

Clarissa had never bathed in such opulence, and luxuriated in the heat and steam, allowing it to ease her tense muscles. She emerged in a rosy glow, feeling much better. Her underclothes had been miraculously laundered, and the creases in her dress ironed out. There was a supply of brushes and combs on the dressing table, allowing her to tame her unruly curls into a simple but fresh style. Checking her *toilette* in the glass, she was pleased with the result. A nod, a deep breath, and she was ready to be shown downstairs, ready to face Kit, though how to deal with him, she had no idea. Trusting to her instincts and her sense of self-preservation, trusting also that Kit would have had time to reconsider his actions in the light of her story and his injured arm, Clarissa followed the maidservant with her head held high and a sparkle in her eyes.

She was shown into a small dining room on the first floor. It was brightly lit and, as she had come to expect, showed impeccable, if restrained, taste. The table was set for two, the white damask cloth laid with gleaming silver cutlery and delicate Spode. On the walls, the paintings were more modern than those in the parlour and on the staircase, obviously Kit's own purchases rather than those of his ancestors. Clarissa recognised a small seascape very much in the style of Mr Turner, whose work she had seen and admired earlier that year in the Royal Academy. There were others, portraits and landscapes that were unfamiliar to her, but all unmistakably of the new, naturalist school.

Kit was standing by the fire, resplendent in a dark, tightly fitting cutaway coat, tan pantaloons replacing his buckskins. His cravat was intricately tied and adorned with a small diamond pin, his black hair brushed forward. He appeared to be in good humour, but Clarissa noted immediately the smile was his satanic one, his lips curled in that mocking way she knew so well.

'I trust my servants looked after you? You found everything sufficient to your needs?'

'Even a toothbrush, thank you. I feel much better.'

'You look much better too. Quite charming, in fact.'

'And you, my lord? How is your arm? I notice you have decided against a sling?'

'Yes, I'm sorry to disappoint you, but really I had no need of it. Now, I expect you are hungry. I know I am.' As he spoke, Kit pulled out a chair for her, at right angles to his own at the head of the table. Almost immediately, the door opened and dinner was served.

The food was delicious. There were stewed oysters, woodcock roasted on the spit, a broiled turbot, and side dishes of artichokes, a delicate soup, and braised chicory. A Rhenish cream and a fruit jelly followed. Both Clarissa and Kit ate with appetite, warmed by the excellent burgundy, confining conversation to general subjects. In the relaxed atmosphere, they discovered anew a delight in each other's company, and shared opinions on many things, from a hearty dislike of Mr Pitt who, they both believed, had been in office much too long, and a liking for the plays of Mr Shakespeare.

Clarissa asked Kit more about his childhood in Thornwood Manor, and in turn shared some of her memories. The days when her father had been alive, his habit of turning up, after an absence of days, with presents, full of laughter, brushing aside her mama's remonstrations to hug them both, swinging Clarrie high over his head. 'Now, of course, I realise he must have been on a gambling spree. He would bet on almost anything, and I suspect that he won less often than he lost. The times he came back with his pockets to let, drunk and in a foul temper, pushing me aside rather than picking me up and throwing me into the air—well, there were more of those.'

Clarissa paused, deep in the memories of those past childhood days. Papa, in his evening clothes even though it was always morning when he returned, his breath stale, his wig askew, pushing aside a small Clarissa, anxiously tugging for attention at the skirt of his coat. Mama, so pretty and so young, pulling at his other side, tugging his sleeve, demanding to know where he had been. Papa intent on his bed, swatting at them both, calling for a servant, demanding to know why breakfast was not on the table for him. Mama handing Clarissa over to the servant, pulling her father up the stairs, her father shouting, waving his hands in the air, but allowing himself to be pulled.

Looking up to find Kit watching her closely, Clarissa blinked, and smiled. 'I haven't thought of these things in years. I'm sorry, I didn't mean to give the conversation such a depressing turn.'

He shrugged. 'So, dear papa was a gambler. I take it that explains the poverty?'

'Yes, he left us with nothing. And by the time he died, you know, he had been cast off completely by his family. They did nothing for Mama, she was left almost penniless. Except my aunt. It was she who provided for my schooling. She would have done the same for Amelia, had she wanted it—but Amelia, I'm sorry to say, was inclined to frivolity from an early age.'

'Leaving you to be the dependable one?'

'Yes, I suppose so.' She was surprised at his perception.

'Well, from what you've said, you could hardly have relied on your mother.'

She laughed at that. 'No, you're right. Mama's idea of economy is to buy only the best, most expensive wax candles because they burn more slowly than tallow. Or to place another order with a merchant when the bills come in on quarter day, rather than to pay what we owe.'

'My own experience of parents isn't so far from your own, despite the differences in our financial circumstances.'

'I find that difficult to believe.'

'My father was a gambler too, prone to disappear for days on end. We all learned to dread seeing him on settling day, and Newmarket was worse—he never seemed to win. As to my mother, she is just as air-headed as yours in her turn. Her latest idea of saving money is to buy new curtains for every room in the house at once, on the assumption that the bigger order will get her a bigger discount. The only difference is that my father added womanising to his vices, and my mother can well afford to indulge her extravagances, having my purse to turn to when her own runs dry.'

The deep cynicism in his voice betrayed his

feelings. Like Clarissa, Kit was the provider. She suspected that like her, too, the role was not one that garnered much by way of thanks or loving appreciation. Looking at him, she realised he was as surprised at the comparison as she. Knowing him well though, she thought the better of dwelling on it, merely reaching over to squeeze his hand, before turning to a less personal subject.

The meal was a success. After the covers were removed, they left the table to sit opposite each other in the cosy downstairs parlour, Kit sipping contemplatively on a brandy, Clarissa merely watching, relishing his presence, desperate to make the moment last for ever, yet knowing that she must bring it to a close.

'I think I should retire. Thank you for a most pleasant evening. I take it we start early for London in the morning?'

Placing his glass to one side, Kit raised an eyebrow in surprise, having expected another show of resistance. 'Very well. I'll join you when I've finished my brandy.'

'Join me?'

'In your bedchamber, of course. Or if you prefer, we can use mine?'

'Yours?'

'If you prefer.'

'But I thought…'

'What, my fair Clarissa, did you think?'

'I thought that you had—had—I thought you realised—now you know I was telling the truth—I thought you realised I cannot go through with this. I thought you had accepted my reasons, understood my reasons. I thought that…'

'That I would forgo payment?'

'Yes.'

'Did I say so?'

'No, but…'

'But you thought I would let you off anyway, after your touching tale of rescuing your sister? And just to make sure, your touching revelations about your papa and mama over dinner to arouse my sympathy.'

'No, that's not true. You make it sound as if I had planned to tell you those things. I've never talked to anyone about those things before, I was just—I thought we were becoming friends.'

'Friends!' The astonishment in his voice was genuine. 'Don't be ridiculous. There can be no friendship between men and women. What we were doing, Clarissa, was simply foreplay. Mental stimulation, a prelude to physical stimulation. We are not, nor ever will be, friends. Tonight we will be lovers. After tomorrow we will be strangers. And for now, we will stop talking, lest we lose the benefits of all this mental foreplay and I remember what a lying, scheming, double-crossing wretch you are.'

'Please, Kit, I beg you this one last time, won't you believe me? I am not the woman you insist on thinking me. I'm simply a foolish sister whose plan to save her sibling from ruin has gone awry. I have done you no real harm. We've enjoyed each other's company when we've not been at odds. I give you my word that I will never attempt to blackmail you, nor even to recognise you, should we meet again. Please, let me go.'

Almost, he did. Despite her lies, despite her scheming, she was right. He had enjoyed her company, more than he could have believed. He found her challenging, brave, surprising. Friendship was not the word—it was *affinity*. In many ways, they were kindred spirits. The thought gave him pause, Clarissa's fate hanging in the balance, the scales tipping slightly, very slightly in her favour for the first time.

But then he remembered the rest, and the scales swung heavily against her finally and for ever. She had lied to him from the first. Despite all her protestations, he believed her intention was entrapment. All the evidence was against her. But most of all, it was her body that had betrayed her. Her kisses, those kisses, which roused in him a passion more intense than any he had felt before. The way she knew just where to touch, how to hold, to caress, to stroke. The depth of her arousal when they kissed matching his own. None of this came from inexperience. These were not the actions of a virgin. And tonight he would have them all, her full repertoire. Nothing would stop him.

The decision was there in his eyes for her to interpret, as clearly as if it had been writ. There would be no last-minute reprieve. He would show no mercy. Wordlessly, Clarissa turned and left the room.

Alone in her bedchamber, she sat by the fire and thought deep. She was curiously calm, resigned to her fate, certain that there was nothing more she could do to fight it. She had gambled, and she would pay the price with the loss of her virtue. Now that the decision had been taken out of her hands, she felt something almost akin to relief that she would not have to resist him further.

Raising her cold fingers to the flames, Clarissa sighed. There was no point in fooling herself. A large part of her was glad this was happening. She had fought and lost. To the victor would come the spoils. Kit would have her body. But she would also have his.

Stop fooling yourself, Clarrie, you want this as

much as he does. It was true. She had always tried to be ruthlessly honest with herself. She would not have chosen this fate, but since it had chosen her she would take everything from it that she could. She would relish tonight. It was like to be her only experience of passion, for she knew she was designed to love like this only once in her lifetime. There would never be another to replace Kit in her affections. So, she would have Kit in the flesh tonight, and she would have the memories of it to savour for the remainder of her years.

A shiver ran through her body at the thought, which had nothing to do with the cold. With a defiant toss of her curls, Clarrie rose to prepare. She would not present herself as a sacrifice. She would not let Kit think this was a seduction. She would do her best to meet him on his own terms, as an equal in passion, if not in experience.

The vision that met Kit when he opened the door some fifteen minutes later made him pause on the threshold in amazement. Clarrie stood by the fire, her back to the flames. Dressed only in her chemise, her arms and neck were bare, her breasts gleaming white and taut against the restraining lace. The full glory of her bright auburn hair tumbled in curls down her back, the only additional colour her soft lips and her bright emerald eyes. Quite literally, she took his breath away.

'Won't you come in, my lord?' Clarrie extended a welcoming hand, her voice husky. Only the rapid rising and falling of her breasts gave away her excitement. Her stance, her commanding invitation, the direct look from those intelligent eyes, showed her to be a woman secure in her own attractions, sure of herself, and equally sure of the man she was waiting for. It was an intoxicating mix.

Walking slowly over to take the outstretched hand, Kit pressed a long, lingering kiss in the palm. His tongue caressed the pad of her thumb, and he licked the tip of each finger in turn, causing tiny ripples of feeling to run down Clarrie's arm. Kit pressed his lips to the thin skin on her wrist, his tongue on her pulse, which fluttered like a bird against a cage, betraying her excitement. But still Clarrie stood, unmoving, content to let him take the initiative, resisting the urge to run the fingers of her other hand through the crisp dark hair on the tender nape of his neck as he bent over her arm.

Kit worked his way to the skin on the inside of her elbow, his tongue circling hot erotic circles, stirring that pulse deep within her to throbbing, insistent life. She could restrain herself no longer. With a sigh that expelled all final doubts, all cares of the future, allowed for no thoughts other than this moment, this man, these feelings, Clarrie surrendered. 'Kit, kiss me. Please.'

The words were whispered, but they were enough. She had submitted. Admitted to her own desire. With a harsh moan, Kit swept Clarrie into his arms, pulling her close against him, enveloping her yielding mouth, kissing her with a deep, encompassing intensity that threatened to consume them. He was on fire, but the flames licked at them both.

Wrapping her arms around his neck, pulling his head closer, his mouth harder against her own, Clarrie matched move for move, passion with passion. She arched against him, feeling the lean length of his body against hers through the thin cotton of her chemise, but it still wasn't close enough. She wanted flesh on flesh. His tongue entered her mouth, thrusting, a foretaste of the more intimate thrusting to come, and his hands roamed over her back, through her silken hair, spanned her waist, clutched at the soft, round flesh of her bottom, pulling her tighter, closer, all the time kissing her harder, more insistently.

Breathing heavily, Kit pulled back. 'Clarrie, slow down, for God's sake.' Grasping her hands and holding them in a clasp in front of her, Kit looked into the flushed face before him. Never had he felt so aroused. Never had his passion been matched like this. She was fighting him every step, demanding as much from him as he was demanding from her. She was not submitting to him, he was not extracting payment—she was giving it. But he wanted to savour every second. And he had waited too long for this to be over quickly.

Shrugging out of his dressing gown, clothed only in his shirt and pantaloons, Kit picked Clarrie up in his arms and deposited her on the bed, where she lay sprawled, her hair streaming out in a fan of colour on the pillows, a tempting, wanton picture that he could happily dive into and drown. Struggling to remove the rest of his clothes, he watched her, as she watched him, her eyes roaming his body as he revealed it to her, drinking in the hard, muscular flesh of his torso, the black, crisp hair that curled over his chest, arrowing down to the line of his breeches. Widening when he removed the rest of his clothes to stand naked in front of her, gasping slightly as she took in the full extent of his proud, erect manhood, but refusing to look away.

The hot feel of his tongue sucking on her toe, flicking on the tender skin of her ankle, moving slowly up to circle the back of her knee, was more erotic than she could have imagined. She moaned, and tried to find purchase on the soft feather mattress to raise herself up to return the contact more freely.

'No. Relax. Enjoy it. Let me pleasure you, I want to.' Kit pushed her gently back, and she was like jelly, unable to resist. He undid the fastenings of her undergarments, and removed them. His fingers gently caressed her soft, perfectly rounded bottom, the thumbs running tantalisingly down the insides of her thighs as he pulled her clothing free.

The throbbing within her centred, focused between her legs. Clarrie moaned low in her throat and twisted restlessly on the sheet, her body making demands she had no idea it possessed.

Still Kit forced himself to go slowly, drinking in the beauty of the body revealed before him. The long, shapely legs, the delicate ankles, the gentle arch of her feet. He ran his fingers over each part, familiarising himself with the curves, the delicate bones, taking note of which touch made her shiver, anticipating the moment when those legs would be wrapped around him, the muscles flexed, holding him close. Yet he was content to wait, postpone the ecstasy.

He moved onto the bed beside her. Spreading her legs to allow him to kneel between them, he pulled

Clarrie slightly upright to remove her chemise, to free the rest of that delectable body for his ministrations. Lifting her arms above her head, he pulled the last piece of fabric between them free, taking in the high, full breasts, thrust upwards by her raised arms, the dark nipples proud evidence of her desire. He licked each one slowly, lazily, then sucked on them, running his tongue across the valley of her breasts to alternate between them, pinching one between his fingers as he tended the other with his mouth. When they were pebble hard, he allowed himself the brief pleasure of pulling her naked body close against his.

Clarrie moaned his name, her breathing rapid and shallow, her lids heavy on eyes dark with a passion reflecting his own. Mindlessly she wrapped her arms around his neck. Sinuously she rubbed herself against his skin, her nipples responding to the abrasion of the dark crisp curls of hair on his chest, warm, hot, wet, with desire as she felt the hard silkiness of his erection against the soft skin of her belly. Their kiss was swift and hard, their skin hot, heating, the need for fulfilment becoming almost unbearable.

Clarrie reached round to pull Kit more fully against her, grasping his firm muscled buttocks, pushing against him, into him, revelling in the contrast of all this male hardness against all her feminine softness. But she wanted more. She wanted—she wanted—oh!

She was on her back, splayed out before him, thrust away from him, but before she could object his mouth was there, right at the very centre of her desire, and she lost all ability to think. His tongue circled, lapped, licked. His fingers dipped, stroked, flicked, plunged slowly, tortuously slowly, making her pant, lifting her ever higher to a place she had never been, didn't know existed. She felt swollen with desire, soaked with desire, bursting with desire, and still Kit's tongue and fingers drove her on, questing, taking her to dizzying heights higher, higher until at last, with one long, slow, pulsing caress, she plunged down, down, swirling headlong, rushing towards the depths, then soaring high through a stunning climax that jerked her up from the bed.

He could contain himself no longer. Raising himself over Clarrie's hot, wet, body, Kit thrust into her depths with one hard stroke, feeling her heat clenching around him. And meeting an unexpected resistance.

My God, she hadn't lied. He couldn't believe it. Looking down into her face, the question on his lips, he felt her move beneath him, her head shaking from side to side in denial.

'No, no, don't stop. Please.' She reached up her arms to pull his head down, fastened her mouth on his, and thrust upwards underneath him, urging him on. Suddenly the resistance was gone.

He had no option but to respond. Shifting to take his weight on his elbows, Kit moved gently inside her, slowly, praying that he could withstand the ripples of pleasure which each tiny movement gave him.

'Kit, Kit,' Clarrie whispered his name, a whisper of pleasure, not pain. 'Please.'

He needed no more urging, and as she wrapped her legs around him, the movement opening her up inside, all worries about hurting her, all conscience at taking her virginity, were quelled, lost, forgotten, in the urge only to thrust harder, deeper, longer, responding to the moans of encouragement, feeling her muscles tighten against him, feeling the responding ripples of her own climax as he finally reached his own, pouring himself, hot, endlessly, possessively, deep into her molten core.

Chapter Nine

They lay enfolded in each other's arms without speaking, basking in the warm, rosy afterglow of their tumultuous love-making. With nothing to compare it to, Clarrie knew only that it had been everything she had ever dreamed, all she had ever desired it might be, and more. She had not thought she was capable of giving way to such an intensity of emotion, had no idea she could abandon all restraint without a trace of modesty, had not believed that instinct could lead her so surely down the path to fulfilment. As her body slowed to a steady thrum of satisfaction she smiled, completely content in this moment, certain only that she didn't want to move, that she wanted to feel the heavy, rough, solid weight of Kit holding her safe, possessively like this for ever.

For some time Kit was also beyond thought,

caught up in the wholly new experience, for him, of feeling such profound passion, unable to believe the intensity of what had just passed between them. His sated body curled possessively round the fragile, wanton, deliciously beautiful woman beneath him, giving in to the instinct to protect, hold on, prolong the perfect intimacy of the moment.

Clarrie sighed and opened her eyes to look into the face of her beloved. So strong and starkly handsome. So passionate and giving. How had she come to feel so much for this wonderful, complex enigma of a man, in just a few short days? She had no idea, and no intention of questioning anything for the remainder of the night. She had only this one time and she intended to savour it.

When Kit kissed her tenderly, his mouth framing the question uppermost in his mind, Clarrie reached out to sooth his brow, whispering 'Shh, this is no time for words' in his ear. Turning to him in a deliberate echo of his own confident and dominant possession of her body, she pushed him back on to the sheets and began a slow, sensuous exploration of her own with her tongue. She might not have the experience of his other mistresses, but she knew enough by now to be certain that the same things which gave her pleasure would pleasure Kit, so she set out to prove it. And she was right. He was lying back, his eyes clenched shut, the question forgotten, and she could see quite clearly that he was enjoying what she was doing— very much. So she carried on, down, and further down, until she knew he could think of nothing, nothing in the world, save her ministrations.

Kit awoke to bright sunlight streaming through the gap in the heavy curtains, and blinked. Rubbing a hand over his forehead, shaking his hair from his eyes, he stretched luxuriously, wondering idly why the slight ache in his muscles felt so good. Opening his eyes properly, he realised he wasn't in his own bedchamber, but the adjoining one. Then it all came flooding back to him, a vivid montage of tangled limbs and blissful love-making.

'Clarrie?' There was no response. The other side of the bed felt cold, though there was an indent on the pillow where her head had been. The bruise on his shoulder where she had bitten him showed her tiny teeth marks. His lips felt rough, tender, and the bed was in complete disarray. She was no figment of his imagination. That night of passion—exquisite, never-before-experienced passion—was no dream. So where was she?

Kit sat up, examining the room properly. His

clothes had been picked up and folded neatly on a chair, but of Clarissa's attire there was no sign. Perhaps she had gone for a walk? Kit got out of bed and donned his dressing gown, striding through the connecting door to ring the bell and summon his valet. He was being foolish, he knew he was, but he couldn't help the feeling of panic rising inside him.

The blank look on Fanshaw's face only added to his concern. 'The young lady, my lord? But she left for London early this morning.'

'Are you sure? I gave very specific orders to the stables yesterday. My coach was to be ready at noon. I can't believe they would leave without checking any change of plan with me first.'

'Oh, she didn't go in your coach my lord, naturally,' the valet said reassuringly. 'No, no. No need to worry about that.'

'Damn the coach, man. I am not worried about my coach. In case it had escaped your notice, I am more concerned for the lady. If she didn't go in the coach, how does she intend to get to London. Walk?' Actually, Kit realised ruefully, he wouldn't put that past her.

Fanshaw, with all the consummate professionalism of his calling, remained impassive, one eyebrow raised quizzically skyward the only sign that he was somewhat taken aback by his master's agitated behaviour. He had been Kit's valet for a number of years, and had never seen him anything other than pleased to be rid of whatever female was currently gracing his bed. Come to think of it, mind you, he could not recall Lord Rasenby ever having allowed a female to stay in his bed overnight before. Preferred to stable them in their own quarters.

Kit was pacing the room anxiously, trying to work out what Clarissa had done. 'Did anyone see her leave?'

'I shall make enquiries of the staff immediately, my lord. It was very early, but perhaps one of the maids knows something. Will you require your shaving water now?'

'Just go and find out where she is, will you? No, wait. I need to get dressed, so bring the water. But make enquiries first.'

Fanshaw left, returning a short time later with a steaming jug of water and a letter on a silver salver. 'It seems the young lady left a short time after seven, my lord. She asked for the nearest inn, and young Jem, the stable hand, took it upon himself to drop her off at the Green Man, since he was on his way out to fetch some sacks of horse feed. I believe the mail coach passes through at about nine; no doubt she obtained a seat on that. Although Jem, of course, did not wait to wave her off.' Fanshaw permitted himself a small smile at this witticism, but, seeing Kit to be in no mood for joking, quickly suppressed it. 'She left this for you, my lord.' He proffered the salver.

'For God's sake, could you not have said that in the first place? Go away, I will shave myself, and I'll call if I need you.'

Dismissed, Fanshaw left the room with slow, dignified grace. Kit, ripping the wafer from the letter, was already intent on the contents and did not look up.

Dear Kit, it started prosaically enough, *I have decided to return to London immediately. Having fulfilled my part of our bargain, our adventure is concluded, and we must never see each other again.* Exactly as he had specified it should be. Kit sat down abruptly, a feeling of emptiness sweeping over him. Last night had changed everything for him. For Clarissa to leave without any forwarding address, with no goodbye even, giving him no chance to suggest—whatever it was he was thinking of suggesting—beggared belief. *Bereft*: that is what he felt. And very, very lonely.

Kit returned to the letter. It was brief enough and to the purpose, giving him no clue as to her feelings. She thanked him for her adventure and assured him of her discretion. *I will not seek you out, for there can be no relationship of any nature between us in the future.* Even had he wanted her as his mistress, the message was quite unmistakable. She would not accept. The plea beseeching him to refrain from renewing his pursuit of Amelia was, after the events of last night, rather unnecessary, but it was the final words that really hurt. *I want you to know that you took nothing from me that I did not want to give, and give freely. We had a bargain and I agreed to the terms. You have nothing to feel guilty about, nor to blame yourself for.* The words pierced his conscience more deeply than any recriminations could have done. *You have nothing to feel guilty about!* God Almighty, what had he done?

The reality of the situation was as clear as the bright light of day streaming through the window. Clarissa was a virgin—or she had been until last night. She had told him she was untouched, had in fact told him so repeatedly from the first, but he had ignored her, refusing to believe what did not suit his purposes. He had not stopped when he realised the truth. And even afterwards, lying sated on top of her, he had not tried—not very hard, anyway— to apologise, even to find out if he had hurt her.

Worse. There had been little respite from their ardour the whole night long. Carried away with lust, he had given no thought, after her gentle *don't*, to calling a halt or soothing her hurt.

Kit clutched his head in his hands, clenching his eyes shut in an effort to rid himself of the visions his mocking conscience was running through his mind. He groaned in despair. What kind of man was he? He had seduced an innocent girl, and now she was gone from him, ruined but refusing even to blame him, dismissing him from her life and taking all the responsibility for the consequences on her own slim shoulders.

Thinking of those possible consequences, Kit groaned again. Who would she turn to if, in addition to taking her virtue, he had left her with child? He had been careless, had given the matter no thought last night. So unlike him, but then in all his dealings with Clarissa he was unlike himself.

A child. Kit tried to picture what the product of their union would look like. A girl, he decided, with her mother's eyes and his own colouring. What a temper she would have. How much he would love her. She would wrap him around her little finger.

Enough, damn it! Reminding himself that he had no desire for children, legitimate or natural,

Kit dismissed the vision of his imaginary daughter, ruthlessly brushing aside the pang it caused him, and returned to the problem in hand.

What in the devil's name was he going to do? Go after her? And offer her what exactly? he asked his reflection as he shaved. A *carte blanche*? Money, recompense? She was likely to throw it back in his face, and who could blame her. Tying his cravat in a simple knot, paying it so little attention that Fanshaw would have tutted disapprovingly had he witnessed it, Kit decided he must return to London and seek Clarissa out. He ignored the tight feeling around his heart as he considered the possibility that she meant what she said, and would never see him again. He would find her, if only to ensure she knew she could rely on him if ever she was in need.

A breakfast of ham and eggs washed down with a tankard of ale brewed from his own hops did nothing to lighten Kit's mood nor break his thoughts of last night. Their love-making had been beyond anything in his previous—plentiful—experience. Clarissa matched him step by step in everything, her own desires seeming as strong as his. She had come to him readily enough in the end. It had been no ravishment, he had not taken her against her will, had not forced himself on her. The passion between them was real. No, he could not doubt her consent.

But he could not deny to himself that he had ensured Clarissa had no option but to consent. That was the nub of it. Kit's conscience, which had lain dormant for the vast part of his thirty-five years, was making up for lost time now. He might not have seduced her, but he had made sure she couldn't say no.

As soon as the coach was ready Kit set out impatiently on the journey to London, aware of a growing need just to see Clarissa. He missed her in truth, even after such a few short hours' absence. They had spent almost three days constantly in each other's company, and he had come to depend on her being there—if not indefinitely, then at least for some time to come. To be without her made him feel as if some part of him he'd never known he'd had was missing.

You took nothing from me that I did not want to give, and give freely. The words ran in circles round his head, but he was no nearer to a course of action than when he had first read them. Clarissa could not have made him feel more guilty had she accused him to his face.

This thought gave Kit pause. Could the letter be

a very clever ruse? Not a salve to his conscience, but a deliberate twist of the knife to ensure that he came after her? True enough, she had come to him a virgin, but did innocence of all other crimes follow automatically? Had she given him the prize of her virtue hoping for recompense in the form of marriage? Had he been duped after all?

Kit stopped at an inn *en route* to London for a change of horses. It took but a moment to swallow a cup of hot, strong coffee before he re-entered his chaise, anxious to be on his way. When he arrived later that afternoon at his house in Grosvenor Square, he was no closer to finding any answers to the questions dogging his thoughts.

Clarissa's journey had been slow and tedious. She reached London not much in advance of Kit. She had not had sufficient money to purchase a seat on the mail coach at the Green Man, and had been forced instead to buy a ticket on the stage. For much of the journey she was squashed between a large fat woman on a visit to her sister who, she informed Clarissa proudly, was expecting her eighth child, and a prim, elderly vicar, who clutched his bible as if afraid it would be wrested from him, and who smelled unmistakably of strong spirits. Emerging shaken and nauseous, she thought

how apt was the term *rattler* for such public con-
veyances, realising in retrospect just how well
sprung had been Kit's own equipage in contrast.

Completing the journey in a hired cab exhausted
her meagre funds. As the hack turned into the
familiar street and she caught the first welcoming
glimpse of home, Clarissa emitted a long, low
sigh of relief. The last three days had been tumultuous ones, by turn thrilling and terrifying. She felt
as if her whole world had been shaken to its foundations and turned on its axis. She had a splitting
headache and craved only the restful sanctuary of
her own bedroom, to safely return to the welcome
predictability of her life where no more dramas lay
in wait for her.

Clarissa stripped off her gloves and was about
to mount the stairs to her chamber when Lady
Maria's trembling voice called to her from the
small parlour. 'Clarissa? Is that you back at last?
Oh, thank the Lord.'

Turning, Clarissa noted with surprise that her
mother was actually standing in the doorway, her
lace cap askew, obviously just arisen from her
couch in order to greet her. 'Mama, dearest. Did
you miss me so much?' Stooping to press a light
kiss on her mother's soft cheek, Clarissa noticed
traces of tears. 'Mama, what's wrong? What has

upset you? Come into the parlour and tell me what's amiss.'

'Oh, Clarrie! I have been so stupid. And I am so sorry, but I simply did not know what to do, and you were not here to advise me.' A sob stopped Lady Maria from further speech, and her tears flowed afresh. Clarissa sighed wearily, placed an arm around her mother's shoulder and guided her towards the sofa. All thoughts of her own problems were effectively driven from her head.

It took a little effort to stop the flow of Lady Maria's tears, and even more patience still to extract the cause of them from the garbled, inarticulate story recounted to her, accompanied as it was by sobs, apologies for being so silly, and countless accusations of villainy against some unknown figure who preyed on poor widow women. 'Oh, Clarissa, I knew you would have advised me against it. I am sorry for being so foolish, but you were not here—what was I to do? With Amelia clamouring for a new dress, and that money-grabbing *modiste* Madame Clothilde refusing to provide it until we paid at least part of her last bill, I was at my wits' end. I even tried to reach you at Constance's, but your aunt refused to tell me where you were.'

'You spoke to Aunt Constance?' That Mama

would do such a thing had not occurred to Clarissa when she had written the note from the inn to explain her absence. She had said that her aunt had need of her and explained no further, sure that Mama would not enquire.

'Yes, I did, for you left me no choice. I needed to talk to you, and your note said you were staying with her. But Constance just said you were engaged on some errand and could not be disturbed and could she help instead. As if I would let myself be beholden to *her.* Nor would she understand—what knows that woman of the trials of being poor? So you see I had no one to turn to, and, oh, Clarissa, I wish you had not needed to be away at such an inopportune time for me.'

Overcome by sobs once more, Lady Maria searched fruitlessly for her handkerchief amongst the plethora of shawls and wraps that lay strewn over the sofa on which they were seated. Clarissa wondered fleetingly why her aunt had not given her away. No doubt she had not wanted to alarm Mama, but she would demand answers from Clarissa, and she was not a woman who could be lied to. Dreadful as this prospect was, however, Mama's needs were rather more pressing.

Pouring a few drops of sal volatile into a glass, Clarissa helped Lady Maria to sit back and waited on the calming effect of the medication to take effect. 'There, dearest, that's better. Now tell me what happened after you spoke to Aunt Constance?'

'Well, I know I promised you I wouldn't borrow any more money, but I felt so bad leaving my problems to you, and then Mrs Barrington—you know, Chloe's mama—said that she would fix it for me to borrow just a little more from the same nice man as before—the one who was dunning me. And I thought, you see, that my luck at the tables was simply bound to turn on account of it's been so very bad until now. So I borrowed just enough for one more night at the tables, and I planned to use my winnings to pay it straight back and pay Madame Clothilde too, and then be able to buy Amelia her dress. It would have worked, I know it would have worked, if only I had not played faro, which is not my game as you know. Mrs Barrington said it would be a quicker way to win a bigger sum. But, oh, she was very wrong. And if I had but ignored her and stuck to my usual game of ombre we would not be in this situation. But I did, and there we have it. And really, it is all your fault for not being here to stop me, Clarrie dear. Now we are in such a fix, for soon this gentle-man—though really he cannot be a gentleman to be treating me like this—will be dunning me for payment and if I cannot pay I cannot imagine what we will do and it is such a mess. But you will fix it, won't you, Clarrie?'

Clarissa's head whirled at the attempt to sort out the salient points from this tangled tale. 'Let me understand this, Mama. You borrowed more money from the man who was already dunning you after I told you, and you promised, not to?'

'Yes, but it was all perfectly above board, for I signed a document when he gave me the money. Then this morning I received a letter from a different gentleman saying he had acquired my debt from the first gentleman and I do not understand it all, for I have no head for business.'

'Mama, may I see the letter? And the one you signed?'

'Oh, Clarrie, dearest Clarrie, do you think you'll be able to make things right?' Lady Maria said, clasping her hands.

'I have no idea until I have sight of the letters. Does Amelia know about any of this?'

'No, no, how could I burden the poor child with my worries when she is so taken up with her own plans.'

That her mama had no qualms about burdening Clarissa with her worries did not surprise her elder daughter. With a worried frown, she read through the two documents Mama had retrieved from the desk. The first, the original loan, to be paid back at a rate of interest that made her brows rise in consternation, was signed by a Mr Dalton. This must be Mrs Barrington's friend—a loan shark, no doubt. No doubt either that Mrs Barrington had been paid a healthy retainer for putting the business his way. Clarissa would have words with Mrs Barrington later. She looked forward to that.

The second letter was from a lawyer acting on behalf of an unnamed client. The paper was heavy and expensive, the letter brief and to the point. The unnamed client had acquired Lady Maria's debt by unspecified methods. The letter informed Clarissa's mama that she had a new creditor and confirmed that for the present the agreed interest rate would stand, but the schedule of repayment had been reduced, so that the full amount became due not within six, but three months. Should this be unacceptable to Lady Maria, the writer would be pleased to put any alternative proposal to his client, but felt it prudent to advise her that an extension of the loan period was unlikely to be granted.

A cold fear clutched at Clarissa as she re-read the epistle. Whoever the creditor turned out to be, Lady

Maria could expect no sympathy from him. The plain fact was that they were now in debt to the tune of thousands of guineas to a complete stranger who was likely to be ruthless in extracting payment. They had no security. They had nothing left to sell, no means of raising the capital, never mind the outrageous amount of interest that was growing almost by the hour. Mama would be clapped in irons and taken to the Fleet prison. It did not bear thinking of. Reminding herself that panic never did anyone any good, Clarissa folded the letters carefully and tucked them into her reticule.

'Well, dearest? Can it be fixed?' Lady Maria's voice was tremulous, her words pleading.

'I need to think about it, Mama. For now, the best thing you can do is to put it from your mind and try for some rest. You look exhausted.'

'Oh, Clarrie, it's so good to have you back. You will make all well now, I know you will. I missed you, child. Tell me you won't go off to live with Constance when I have sore need of you here.'

'I won't go and stay with Aunt Constance, Mama, you may put that thought out of your mind. Now, why don't you try to rest for a while? Here, let me tuck this shawl around you. There, that's better, is it not? Best to say nothing to Amelia about all of this, we don't want her worried.'

'Oh, no, no, Clarrie, I won't say a thing. Except—what about her new dress?'

'I'm afraid that will have to wait,' Clarissa said drily. 'It is hardly a priority in the grand scheme of things.'

'Oh, but it might prove to be so, Clarrie. Only think, if she gets a new dress and Lord Rasenby sees her in it, he will like as not be so taken with her that he will propose, and then all of our troubles will be at an end. You would not want to spoil that for the want of a new dress now, would you dear?'

'Mama, I beg of you, you must put all thoughts of Amelia marrying Lord Rasenby out of your head. It is simply not going to happen.'

'But, Clarrie, Amelia assures me he is on the very brink of asking. She has seen him the last two nights at balls, and he has been most pressing.'

'She saw Lord Rasenby last night?'

'Yes, and the night before. He was most attentive, apparently, and would not leave her alone. Begged three whole dances and would not take her nay. So you see Clarissa, she simply *must* have a new dress.'

The only thing Clarissa saw clearly was that Amelia had been lying to their mama. Well, she would not get off so lightly when Clarissa spoke to her, that was for sure. 'Leave Amelia to me,

Mama, think no more of it. But you must promise me one thing.'

'Anything, dearest, for you always know best, and I feel so much happier now. When you came in I was quite sunk in despair, what with the letter, and Amelia's dress, and the cook demanding to know what was for dinner. I am very glad you are home; we don't get by nearly so well without you.'

'Well, Mama, and I am glad to be home too. But you must give me your solemn promise that you will not play cards with Mrs Barrington or any of her cronies again. And you must on no account, under any circumstances, borrow any more money.'

'No, dearest, I won't, I promise.' Thus unburdened of all her cares, oblivious to the turmoil she had stirred up in her daughter's mind, Lady Maria composed herself for sleep.

Rest was not a luxury Clarissa could afford, much as she was in need of it. Thrusting thoughts of her mother's debts to one side for the time being, she went in search of her sister. She did not have to look far. Amelia was waiting in her bedchamber, a vision in pale green printed calico.

'I was sure I heard you come in. Mama has been in a tizzy about something, I've barely been able to get a word of sense out of her. I thought I should have to give her a James's powder to calm her, she was so upset, and you know I can't be doing with quacking her. I trust you've calmed her down?'

Amelia's breathtakingly selfish attitude made Clarissa grit her teeth in order to keep a clamp on her temper. She needed to find out what her sister had been up to. Upsetting her would only make her defensive, much as she yearned to give Amelia a sound slap about the cheeks. 'Mama is sleeping now,' she said merely, sitting down at her dressing table to remove the pins from her hair. Her head was thumping.

'You look tired, Clarrie. Did Aunt Constance have you run ragged? When Mama tried to get her to send you back, she was quite rude. She told Mama that it was time she stood on her own two feet and stopped relying on you to resolve every petty domestic crisis. Mama was really quite upset.'

'She's not such an ogre, you know, our aunt. She just has different ideas from Mama, but we shouldn't forget that she is the only one of Papa's family who stands by us.'

'Much good it does us. It's all very well for you, she likes you, and you can talk for hours to her about boring politics and books and things. It's different for me. I'm too pretty, for one thing, and she's always so nit-picky, I really can't abide it. You should do this, Amelia, or think about that,

Amelia, or consider this, Amelia. What she really means is that I should be more like you. Well, I'm not like you.'

A sharp pang of guilt shot through Clarissa as she thought bitterly of her behaviour over the past three days. 'Maybe we are more alike than you realise,' she said ironically. 'Anyway, never mind Aunt Constance or Mama for the moment. Sit down and tell me about you. Have you seen much of Edward?'

'Too much! He has become almost as tedious as Aunt Constance, prosing on and on about what I may do, and what I may not do. I'm fed up with Edward.' With a flounce Amelia sat down on Clarissa's bed, her rosebud mouth in a pout, and burst into sudden loud sobs. 'Oh, Clarrie, I'm so unhappy. You can have no idea.'

Clarissa eyed her in astonishment. 'Calm down, Amelia, try not to talk until you are more composed. Let me get you a glass of water.' Much to her relief, Amelia's sobs quieted. She sat up, the threatened tantrum averted. 'Now, tell me what's bothering you. You'll feel better when you've got it out in the open.'

'It's Edward. He's—he's—he wants to marry me.'

Clarissa struggled to contain the mixture of relief and euphoria that swept over her at this much-hoped-for development. 'Well now, that's surely something to be very happy about.'

'No, it's not, Clarissa, for he has no money and no prospects, only his stupid job, and I won't marry him and live without money, I *can't*. He says that if we are happy it shouldn't matter. He says that I don't need new gowns and balls and parties and—and such, if I have him. He says that if we have each other, I won't notice our modest means. But Clarrie, he's *wrong*. I *need* money, but I don't want to lose Edward, so I need to find a way to have both. But every time I suggest what seems to me a perfectly simple solution, he threatens to leave me and never see me again.'

With a sinking heart, Clarissa posed the question. 'And what is your simple solution, Amelia, that Edward is so set against?'

'Well, it's obvious. I'll accept Lord Rasenby's *carte blanche*, then he'll be obliged to buy me lots of dresses and jewellery and a carriage and maybe even set me up in my own establishment. I'll save every penny of the allowance he gives me, and then I can marry Edward.'

Even for Amelia, this was breathtaking. Clarissa could find nothing to say, and sat staring at her sister in open-mouthed amazement.

'Why are you looking like that? You look like Edward did. I thought you'd be pleased.'

'Pleased?'

'Yes, for I have quite given up my plan to trap Lord Rasenby into marriage, you know.'

The smug satisfaction in Amelia's voice was too much. Clarissa was tired and heartsore. Instead of the sanctuary of her own room, she had been greeted with her mother's gambling debts and impending imprisonment. And now her sister was gaily recounting a plan to become the mistress of one man in order that she might marry another. That the man she intended to extract payment from was the man Clarissa was in love with was the final straw.

'You thought I'd be pleased to hear that you're proposing to sell yourself to Lord Rasenby in order to fund marriage to Edward?'

'Well, I thought at least you'd be pleased that I'd given up my idea of tricking Kit Rasenby to the altar. And pleased to find that you're right—I do love Edward after all. And I want to marry him.'

'But you're still willing to let another man take you to bed?'

'Well, but it might not come to that.' Amelia's pout was back, her posture defensive.

'You expect to persuade Lord Rasenby to take

you as his mistress, to fork out a fantastic sum on kitting you out in style, setting you up in a house, and not expect anything in return?'

'Well, I thought I could string him along for a while without having to—you know, without actually letting it come to that. There are ways, Clarissa, of keeping a man in suspense, without—'

'Do tell me, Amelia, what are these ways, exactly?'

Taken aback at the martial light in her sister's eyes, and unused to having her bluff called quite so directly, Amelia faltered. 'Well, I don't know exactly, but I'm sure I could—at least I... You know, I don't think we should be discussing this, Clarissa, Mama would be shocked.'

'And you think it would shock her less if you told her what you intended? Don't be ridiculous. You clearly haven't thought this through, you've just got carried away with wanting to have your own way as usual. And so long as you get your own way, you don't care who pays for it, whether it's Edward, or Kit Rasenby, or Mama or me! You're a selfish, stupid, inconsiderate little girl, and you don't deserve Edward. In fact, if I were him I'd wash my hands of you. All I can think is that he must be so madly in love with you as to be beyond reason himself, for you are nothing more than a—a—trollop! Kit certainly deserves to be protected from the likes of you.'

Amelia watched her normally placid sister's outburst in astonishment. Clarrie didn't seem at all concerned about poor Amelia. Didn't seem to want to help her, hadn't even put her first, as she always usually did. Had seemed more worried about Edward, in fact, not to mention Lord Rasenby. And—but that was it! 'Why are you suddenly so concerned with protecting Kit Rasenby?'

'I don't know what you mean,' Clarissa replied defensively. 'I don't want anyone hurt by your stupid behaviour. I'm just as worried about poor Edward.'

'No, you're not. And now I come to think of it, I haven't seen Kit Rasenby for a few days. No one knows where he's been.'

'Yes, but that's not what you told Mama, is it? You told her you'd been dancing with Kit—Lord Rasenby—at two different parties.'

Amelia waved her hand dismissively. 'Well, what did you expect, I had to find an excuse for seeing Edward, and I didn't want Mama to worry. And anyway, that's not important right now. What I want to know is where was Lord Rasenby—or Kit, as you now seem to be calling him—over the last few days? The same few days, dearest sister, when you were also absent? I think there's something you're not telling me, isn't there?'

Clarissa could not think of a reply, and only shook her head in silent rebuttal.

'Goodness, I'm right, aren't I?' Amelia said gleefully. 'There *is* something you're not telling me. Look at you, you're all red. You can't lie to me, Clarissa, what's going on?'

'Nothing! Nothing's *going on*, as you put it. I'm tired. I need to be on my own. Let's leave this discussion until later.'

'No, you don't, Clarissa Warrington. I know you, you're going to lie in here on your own and make up some clever story to tell me later. I'm not going to leave you on your own. Whatever was going on between Kit Rasenby and you, I'm going to find out right now, so you might as well tell me and get it over with.'

Amelia's eyes sparkled at the confusion on Clarissa's face. She had never seen her normally unflappable sister so distressed. Leaping from the bed, all trace of her own upset vanished, she pulled Clarissa towards a chair and pushed her into it. 'Talk, Clarrie. I won't leave until you do.'

'I—Amelia, if I do, you must promise not to say a word to anyone?'

'Yes, yes, just go on.'

'Very well. But no matter what you think of my behaviour, you must believe me, I meant it only for the best.'

'Clarrie, will you just tell me what on earth you've been up to?'

Thus was Clarissa persuaded to provide an open-mouthed and increasingly incredulous Amelia with a highly censored version of the events of the last three days.

Chapter Ten

Once Amelia had fully recovered from the shock of discovering her sister capable of such wantonly reckless behaviour, she predictably took Clarissa's interventions on her behalf sorely amiss. 'You spiteful cat, you couldn't bear to see me happy, could you? You've gone and spoiled everything, ruined my only chance of ever being rich. How could you? What am I to do now?'

'But, Amelia don't you see, I did it for you, I saved you.'

'*Saved me!* Saved me for what, pray tell? For a life with Edward in a horrible little cottage with a dozen brats running round my feet? I'd rather go on the streets!'

'*Amelia!* How can you talk so? You don't know what you're saying.' Taking a deep breath, almost relieved to have the confession over with, Clarissa tried to turn her full attention on her sister. 'My actions have come as a shock to you, I can understand that. But when you've had time to reflect, you'll see it's for the best. You love Edward, for goodness' sake, and now there is no real obstacle in the way of your marriage.'

Unfortunately for her peace of mind, this phrase served only to remind Clarissa of the many and insurmountable obstacles she herself had placed in the path of her own, never-to-happen marriage. It took an effort to focus on the problem in hand. 'You cannot seriously think that wealth is so important, Amelia? It's not as if Edward will have no money at all—in fact, you'll probably find that as a married lady you'll have at least as much to spend as you do at present.'

'But I don't have *anything* to spend at present. I'm sick of eating the poorest cuts of meat. I'm tired of having to make do with only three or four pairs of evening gloves, and living in terror of getting stains on them. I'm fed up having to beg and plead for every new dress I need. And if I have to fashion one more hat from the trimmings of an old one, I'll scream.'

Clarissa smiled in what she hoped was a winning and reassuring manner. 'But when you're married, you won't need so many clothes, for you won't be going to so many parties and the like, will you?'

'Oh, Clarrie, don't you understand? That's exactly the point! If I marry Edward, we'll be cooped up together in our hovel because we won't be able to afford to go out. I do love him, but I'm neither stupid nor entirely blind to my own character. How long do you think I could endure such a life? How long before I get bored and start to blame poor Edward for it? How long before I start to look for entertainment elsewhere, no matter how dear he is to me?'

Taken aback by Amelia's unexpected insight, Clarissa could only shake her head sadly.

'And as for Edward,' her sister continued despairingly, 'well, it wouldn't exactly be a bed of roses for him either. I'd be sure to make his life a misery with my constant nagging about our lack of money. He'd soon get tired of coming home to ruined dinners and a disgruntled wife. I have no idea about cooking, I've never placed an order at a butcher or a grocer, I don't even know which coals to burn or anything at all about running a house. Don't you see, Clarissa, it would be a disaster?'

Clarissa did see, but she wasn't about to give up so easily. 'Surely Edward has some prospects?'

'He works hard and he seems to be well respected by his employer, but without backing he has little prospect of rapid advancement. Mr Fortescue said that there's a good opportunity coming up soon for a partnership, but without money to assist him, the post will go elsewhere.'

'Mr Fortescue?'

'He's a partner in Edward's firm, Fortescue and Browne. Their offices are in the city—Lombard Street, I think. They're a very prestigious law firm, Edward says, with any number of clients from the *ton*.'

Fortescue and Browne. That had been the heading on the letter Mama received this morning, now safely tucked away in Clarissa's reticule. And Edward worked for them. An idea began to form in Clarissa's mind. Perhaps Edward could be persuaded to find out the name of the man who held Mama's debt? It wouldn't be ideal, having to involve a stranger—well, almost a stranger—in their affairs. Edward might prove reluctant to compromise his position too, but since he clearly loved and intended to marry Amelia, surely these were not insurmountable obstacles. What she would do when she had the information she had no idea, but at least it was a step forward.

'Amelia, do you think you could give Edward a note from me when you see him next?'

Amelia looked suspiciously at her elder sister. After her recent revelations, who knew what subterfuge she was capable of? 'Why? A note about what?'

'I need some advice about a trifling legal matter on Mama's behalf, and he may be able to help, that's all. Nothing for you to be worried about, I promise. Well, will you do it for me?'

'I suppose so, I'm seeing him later this evening. Although we had such a disagreeable conversation last night, he may have already decided that he doesn't love me after all.' Amelia's lip trembled. 'Oh, Clarrie, I do love him. I must marry him, for I can't marry anyone else. And now you've spoiled it all. If you hadn't gone off with Lord Rasenby, I could have accepted his *carte blanche*, and maybe by as early as next month I could have been Mrs Edward Brompton. And now you've ruined any chance of that. Oh, I do hate you.'

'Don't be silly. I'm sure things may still work out for the best, if only you will have patience.'

'And pray, what difference will patience make?' Amelia demanded with a stamp of her foot. 'I need money! Kit Rasenby has plenty of it, and he's famed as a generous provider into the bargain. Now I'll be forced to accept an offer from someone else, who like as not won't be as rich or as generous. So I'll have to stay with them for longer, and then Edward might not wait for me. Oh, why did you have to meddle in my affairs?'

Once more Clarissa could think of nothing to say. In truth, from Amelia's point of view, she could see that she had ruined things. It was clear that her dream of Amelia and Edward disappearing into a future of unclouded marital bliss without the funds to provide Amelia with a decent lifestyle was just that, a ridiculous fantasy. Now she faced the prospect of a future with Mama in prison, Amelia on the streets, and herself a ruined relic teaching someone else's children their letters. Always assuming she hadn't already conceived a child of her own—then she really would be ruined. That thought she refused to give house room, having more than enough worries without it!

'You're very quiet all of a sudden, Clarrie. What are you thinking?' Amelia had regained control of her temper. Having mentally reviewed Clarissa's tale, she was beginning to sense some glaring gaps in her sister's story. As an accomplished liar herself, she prided herself on having a finely tuned nose for such things, and there were some aspects of the story that just didn't quite add up. 'Remind me again, Clarrie, just exactly how you left things with Kit Rasenby.'

'As I said, he told me he had no intention of

getting married and that he had been aware of your plot to entrap him all along,' Clarissa replied. 'He also agreed not to offer you a *carte blanche* since you are in love with someone else.' It was close enough to the truth, and all Amelia needed to know.

'And how did you persuade him, in the end? You must have had to work exceeding hard at it, for you were away nigh on three days.'

'Yes, but I explained that to you. He was not happy at first with my interfering, and insisted that I accompany him to France. While we were on board the *Sea Wolf*, there was little time for discussion.'

'So you didn't really get a chance to persuade him until you returned and spent the night at Thornwood Manor?'

'Yes, that's right. Then when I talked to him properly over dinner, he finally saw sense.' Repeating the story only served to make it seem even more flimsy and unlikely. Clarissa tried to change the subject. 'There's no point in going over it again. I'm tired. You're upset. Come, let's leave matters until tomorrow.'

'No, let's discuss it now, sister dear, while it's still fresh in your mind,' Amelia said remorselessly. 'You admit you were alone with Kit Rasenby for three days?'

'Not alone, precisely. There were servants and the *émigrés* and—'

'But you spent last night alone with him, did you not? And then he gave in to your demands without asking for any sort of recompense? Nothing at all, no payment of any sort?'

Amelia's use of the term payment made Clarissa flush deeply, a fact her sister spotted immediately. 'He did want something in return, didn't he? And knowing Kit Rasenby, I bet I know exactly what it was. I've said before, you're really quite pretty, Clarissa, although you pale beside me, of course. Did he kiss you?'

A blush and a shake of the head were not convincing denials but they were all Clarissa could muster.

'He did kiss you. Well, well, Clarrie. Tell me, did you find it to your liking?'

Again, a blush, deeper this time. 'Amelia, please, I—'

Amelia continued relentlessly. 'But what you were asking was really quite a big favour. Giving me up when he was really very taken with me was no small demand, Clarrie, was it? So a kiss probably wouldn't have sufficed. What else did you give in return for saving me, my virtuous sister? It must have been more than a few kisses?'

'Amelia, you must not ask. Suffice to say it was

not—it was not—well, it was not Kit's fault in the end, but mine.'

'Not Kit's fault in the end? Lord, Clarissa, you make no sense. Why would you—good God!' Realisation dawned on Amelia just as Clarissa covered her face with her hands and burst into tears. For a few seconds, Amelia was too astonished at the sight of her sister crying to take in the full extent of her confession—but only for a few seconds.

'He bedded you! Clarissa Warrington, I can't believe it. Goodness, my holier-than-thou sister deflowered by the most notorious rake in town. Well, well, well!'

Speechless at the full import of what she had learned, Amelia sat down and stared at her sister in a completely new light. A thousand questions came to mind, but for the present she was simply fascinated by the fact that Clarissa had experience of something she hadn't. A malicious smile marring her beautiful face, Amelia pulled her chair closer. 'Come then, Clarrie, you must tell me all. Was it as nice as they say? Did he give you pleasure? Was he gentle? Did it hurt? Did *he* enjoy it?'

'Amelia, I have no intention of discussing this with you, so you can stop your questions right now. It's a private matter between Kit and myself.'

Head tilted to one side, Amelia looked closely

at Clarissa's flushed face. She was deeply embarrassed at the revelations, of that there was no
doubt. But there was something else. She was different in some way. Despite being so tired, she
looked prettier than before. And sort of—glowing.
Realising that nothing was to be gained by threats,
Amelia tried a different tack. 'Clarrie, even if you
won't talk about it, won't you at least tell me—
since I'm going to get married soon—did you
enjoy the act?'

'Oh yes. It was wonderful.' The blush, and the
look of sublime fulfillment, took Amelia aback.
The final flaw in the story became clear. 'You're in
love with him, aren't you? It's the only explanation.
Poor Clarrie, to fall for a rake. It's true, isn't it?'

Clarissa's silence was answer enough.

'I knew it! In fact, now I come to think of it,
you've probably been in love with him from the
start. You just used me as an excuse, you wanted
him for yourself all along. Well, am I right?'

'No, no,' Clarissa said hurriedly. 'I had no such
intention, you must believe me. I wanted to save
you. My only aim was to buy you some time so
that you would realise the depth of your true
feelings for Edward. I had no other thought.'

'Rubbish, I don't believe you. In any event, you
are in love with him now, aren't you?'

'I—I—oh, what does it matter, for nothing can become of it Amelia. He cares naught for me and I must live with that, and what I have done. But he won't be making you an offer now, and no matter what you feel at present, I'm still glad of that outcome, at least. We'll find a way for you to marry Edward, if only you will have some patience and a little faith. Kit Rasenby has no place in either of our lives. I don't want to talk about him, or this, or anything any more. I have the most awful headache. Please, Amelia, I need to be alone.'

Clarissa got abruptly to her feet, grabbed Amelia by the hand, and shunted her unceremoniously out of the room with a final reminder, on pain of death, not to breathe a word to anyone. Locking the door, she threw herself dejectedly on the bed and sobbed as though her heart was breaking. And indeed, indeed, it felt as if it was.

Dinner that evening in the Warrington residence was a very subdued affair, each of the three ladies being preoccupied with their own thoughts. Lady Maria fretted over her gambling debts. Clarissa was trying very hard—and failing—not to think about Kit. She dared not imagine how he had reacted to her sudden flight. She wondered where he was, what he was doing, who he was with. The stab of jealousy at the endless possibilities such speculation led to felt like a physical pain.

The truth, if she but knew it, was that across London Kit was enduring a similarly miserable dinner with his sister and her husband, absorbed in almost identical thoughts.

And Amelia? Had her sister been privy to the plots she was hatching as she chewed her way indifferently through her Hogg's pudding, she would have thrown up her hands in horror.

After dinner, Clarissa wrote a note to Edward, beseeching him, for Amelia's sake, to find out the name of her mama's creditor if he could do so without compromising himself. She sealed it and gave it to Amelia with strict instructions to pass it straight on without reading it herself. Needless to say, the strictures merely served to arouse her sister's already inflamed curiosity further. Amelia opened the letter as soon as she was out of the house.

When Clarissa finally retreated to the sanctuary of her bedchamber she could scarcely believe she had been home for less than a day. The rescue mission to France and the events at Thornwood House seemed like a lifetime ago, and yet only this very morning she had been lying in another bed encircled by Kit's strong arms, his warm muscular body pressed against her own receptive flesh. Clarissa tried desperately to conjure the sensations of that moment, the feel of Kit's skin, the scent of his body, but she was exhausted. Frustrated and lonely, she drifted into a troubled sleep.

The next morning, while Clarissa slept unusually late into the morning, her sister and mama sat together in Lady Maria's bedchamber, discussing Amelia's latest scheme to solve all their troubles. Having broken the seal of Clarissa's letter to Edward, Amelia had made sense enough of it to realise her mama was in dire need of an enormous sum of money. Since she was still determined to find the means of laying her hands on an equivalent sum for her own purposes, she had formulated a plan that would resolve both issues in one fell swoop.

Deciding that the need to enlist Mama's help in solving their monetary difficulties was of much more import than keeping Clarissa's confidences, Amelia had no hesitation in disclosing all. 'Mama, I'm afraid I must tell you something shocking.' Her version of Clarissa's story was brief and to the point.

Lady Maria was deeply shocked. 'Are you saying that your sister, my daughter—our Clarrie—was *compromised* by Lord Rasenby,' she uttered shakily.

Amelia impatiently handed her the vinaigrette she had had the foresight to bring along. 'Yes, Mama, but please don't go off into one of your swoons at the moment, for I need you to pay attention.'

Taking a sniff strong enough to make her recoil, Lady Maria blinked owlishly. 'No, no, Amelia, your sister was with Constance, her letter said so.'

'Mama! For the last time, I tell you she was not. She was with Rasenby. He abducted her and took her to France on his yacht. Then he took her back to his house. And he ravished her!'

It took burnt feathers and a tisane to revive Lady Maria from her swoon, and when she came to, Amelia had to repeat the entire story. 'So you see, Mama, he seduced her. And now she is in love with him. Do you not think that he should pay for such a dastardly crime?'

'Pay? What payment can there be to recompense my poor girl for the loss of her innocence?' demanded Lady Maria, frantically tugging at the strings of her cap, which had become entangled in the chicken-skin gloves she wore to keep her hands soft. 'The monster! There is nothing too bad for such a man. Nothing! If I were not a poor widow woman, with no one to defend me, he would not have taken such an advantage.'

'Yes, yes, Mama, indeed he is very wicked. But never mind all that, I have an excellent idea. Lord Rasenby shall pay, but not with his blood. He shall give us something much more useful. Money!'

'Well, to be sure dear, that would be much more useful, but why would he?'

'We shall threaten him, of course. And demand recompense for the loss of my sister's virtue. Then you can pay your gambling debts and I can marry Edward.'

'How do you know about my gambling debts? And who is Edward?'

'Edward. I *have* mentioned him to you, Mama. I'm in love with him.'

'In love with Edward,' Lady Maria exclaimed, momentarily distracted. 'But you barely know the man. Don't be foolish, Amelia, my head is spinning as it is.'

'Well, you might as well get used to it, for I'm marrying him, no matter what you say. Once I lay my hands on enough funds to do so, that is. Let us not discuss Edward just now, we have much more pressing matters to see to. We must write a letter to Lord Rasenby. And we must on no account tell Clarissa any of this, for she would be sure to try to stop us.'

'No, no, dear. Clarrie knows how important it is

to settle my debts, though I wish she had not told you about them—she said she would not.'

'No, Mama, she must know nothing, for she will put an end to it all, and then we won't get any money, and she will be ruined, and you will be in prison or the poor house, and I won't be able to marry Edward and—so you see, you must promise.'

'Well, when you put it that way…' Lady Maria remained doubtful, but she was a woman used to being told what to do, and was no match for Amelia in this determined mood.

The letter was duly written and dispatched within the hour. When Clarissa finally emerged from her room dressed for walking, Lady Maria and Amelia were huddled innocently together over a pattern book in the parlour. Calling a subdued good morning, Clarissa left the house for a brisk walk around the park. Her head was still aching.

Kit had also taken to the fresh air to clear his head. One minute he was missing Clarissa desperately and castigating himself with having taken her innocence. The next minute he was sure his suspicions had been right all along, and congratulating himself on having been rid of the baggage. The next again, he was trying to persuade himself that to take Clarissa as his mistress would be a compromise well worth attempting, even if it did mean humbling his pride a little. At least he would have her delectable body at his disposal long enough to sate this consuming passion, which was overthrowing the normal order of his mind.

On his return, the arrival of Lady Maria's letter put an end to the torture. Kit did not recognise the hand, and the name signed at the end was unfamiliar. Skimming through the note with difficulty, for Lady Maria's writing was spidery and had a tendency to slope dramatically at an angle on the page, Clarissa's name leapt out at him. Kit repaired to his favourite chair in the large, oak-panelled library and read through the epistle carefully. By the end of it his temper was as white hot as the flame in a blacksmith's forge—Clarissa's duplicity was the bellows which fanned it.

He had been right from the first. She was a scheming wretch. She had not lied when she reassured him she would not be getting in touch. Had not lied when she said she would not blame him for taking her innocence. *Oh, no, she had not lied.* Clarissa had done none of these things. She got her mother to do her dirty work instead!

My God, it was beyond the pale. Screwing the letter into a tiny ball, Kit hurled it into the grate. That it missed and lay intact on the hearth added fuel to his anger. How could he have been so duped? He had been so close to believing her. So racked with guilt for most of the last twenty-four hours. So afraid that Clarissa was hurt, upset, sobbing her heart out somewhere, alone and facing an uncertain future. And all the time, the plotting, scheming doxy was waiting to launch her attack on him. He was beginning to wonder if it was possible somehow that she had faked her innocence in the first place. For a woman who could lie so very convincingly, pretending virginity would be simple enough trickery. She was a witch, and she had come so close to bewitching him that he was overcome with rage at how gullible he had been.

Kit groaned. He prided himself on being up to snuff. He was so sure he knew every trick in the book. Yet here was a variation on the very oldest trick, and he had almost fallen for it, hook, line and sinker. Almost convinced himself that he cared. Almost decided to seek her out, to offer her his protection. Almost believed he had true feelings for her. My God, he had almost come to believe that they might have a future together, one based on—damn it, one based on genuine affection!

Almost, but not quite. And certainly not now. Revenge would be his. Nothing would prevent him from putting Clarissa at his mercy. He would see to it that her suffering was slow and drawn out, preferably something that would ensure that she and that entrancing, delightful body of hers were at his disposal night and day. Until he tired of her, that is. Until his desire for her was sated and his need for her exorcised.

It was a relief to Kit to be able to think ill of Clarissa, having spent the last twenty-four hours thinking so ill of himself. He was well and truly vindicated. She spoke the truth in that damned letter of hers. He had taken nothing she had not freely given! And no doubt had freely given to any number of others in the past, too. He did not relish the idea of Clarissa in any other arms than his own, however. She was a doxy, but she should be his doxy, and his alone!

Bitterly, Kit tried to repress the feelings that, despite all Clarissa's perfidy, were determinedly calling to his conscience in her favour. She had courage and integrity. She was witty and intelligent. Surely there was some mistake in all this? Alas, the facts combined with this dastardly letter did not lie. And yet he still wanted her.

There can be nothing without trust, nothing worth while based on deceit. Clarissa's own words mocked him. Her face, those expressive green eyes, that slumberous, quirky smile. The voluptuous curves of her body. She haunted him, filling his mind, leaving little room for aught else. There was no escaping the hurt and disappointment that were his overriding emotions as the full depths of her betrayal sank in.

Kit retrieved the letter from the hearth and unravelled it. Lady Maria demanded *suitable recompense* for the loss of her daughter's innocence. There was no indication of how much this sum would be, but he had no doubt that it would be enormous. After some garbled threats and recriminations over Kit's *cruel and callous treatment* of her *pure and innocent child*, Lady Maria's epistle launched, confusingly, into a catalogue of Clarissa's charms. Clarissa was *very fair*—Amelia had baulked at *beautiful*—her brain *above ordinary*, her wit *very clever.* She could manage a house efficiently, was well versed in *books and the like*, and was generally considered to be an asset that any gentleman would relish the opportunity to *have at his side.*

Kit wondered idly if Clarissa herself had been privy to compiling this list of accomplishments. He doubted it. He wished he could have watched her face if she had. How she would laugh. Her eyes would sparkle, that kissable little top lip of hers would quirk up at the corner, and that delicious gurgle of hers, like a brook in full flow, would escape, as she read her way down the eulogy. She would look up at him, a brow raised in question, and ask if he thought her merely *very fair*, knowing full well he thought her the most beautiful woman he had ever seen. Had he not told her so during their night of passion? Had he not shown her so as he worshipped her body? And she would smile, content.

Damn it! He had to stop this. Returning to the letter, the point of Lady Maria's eulogy became clear. Not only did she revile Kit and demand compensation for the taking of her child's innocence, she was offering to assist him in persuading that same innocent child to become his mistress. One thing Clarissa had not lied about— her mother was singularly lacking any trace of intelligence. Clarissa might be at the root of this plot, but of a certainty she had no part in this bird's nest of a letter.

He would not demean himself by writing back to the mother, Kit decided. His dealings would be with Clarissa, and Clarissa alone. He would be happy to cross swords with her again. She would very soon realise she had underestimated him as an adversary. She might have outwitted him, but retribution was nigh. He was looking forward to it.

Kit's reply on hot-pressed paper was brief and to the point. He was pleased to have received *your mother's charming blackmail letter sent on your behalf*, but he preferred, in matters of business, to deal with the *puppet master and not the puppet*. Unless Clarissa would correspond with him direct, all contact between them *of any nature* would be at an end. He congratulated her on her *effortless and skilled deceit*. Kit would not be threatened, nor would he negotiate. He would be happy to make her an offer of a nature *suitable and appropriate to her station*, and he anticipated to *compensate her more than adequately for her services*.

With grim humour Kit pictured Clarissa's response to these well-turned and carefully considered phrases. She would not misunderstand him. *He was hers, etc.*, the letter ended, and was signed with a flourish. A last-minute postscript assured her that he took issue with her mother's rather harsh description of her in her *bill of fare* and that he considered her not just *very fair* but *quite beautiful*. Satisfied, he sent a footman off to deliver the letter by hand.

It was too late in the day to expect a response. Kit poured himself a brandy, trying to ignore the flat depression that threatened to overtake him at the thought of Clarissa's betrayal. Some male company, cards, and a good deal more brandy were what he needed right now. He set off for White's in St James's Street at a cracking pace, and passed the following hours losing such a satisfactorily enormous sum as would have met the demands of Lady Maria and Amelia more than sufficiently. He also became systematically and resolutely drunk.

Chapter Eleven

Kit awoke the following morning with a splitting headache as his valet drew back the heavy curtains with a flourish. The weak morning sunlight struck the bed, making Kit squint wearily at the unwelcome intrusion. With difficulty he resisted the urge to burrow back under the pillows.

'The young lady is waiting to see you, my lord.' Fanshaw spoke in hushed tones. 'She has been here some time, but I was reluctant to disturb your rest since you returned in such—er—obviously high spirits last evening.'

Kit tried to sit up, but groaned at the effect the sudden movement had on his already delicate constitution. He ran a hand through his tousled hair, looking puzzled. 'What young lady? What o'clock is it? This is no time for morning callers—get rid of her, whoever she is, for pity's sake.'

'It's the young lady from Thornwood Manor, my lord, the one who left so precipitously the other day. I thought, since you were so animated by her departure, that you would wish to see her.'

'Clarissa is here?' Kit could not stop the quiver of anticipation at the thought of seeing her again. 'How long has she been waiting? What does she want? Never mind, never mind. Make sure she is looked after, and have Hodges inform her that I'll join her in fifteen minutes—no, better make that twenty. Come on man, what are you waiting for?'

'Twenty minutes, my lord? But you are not shaved. I have not laid out your dress. I require an hour at least to make you presentable. Please, my lord, I beg of you—'

'Fanshaw, shut up and do as you are told. And bring me a draught of porter before you bring my shaving water, I have sore need of a hair of the dog that so savagely bit me.'

Clarissa was pacing the floor of the small withdrawing room anxiously, becoming less and less confident as time went on. Kit's letter had come as a complete shock, and in those first numbing moments after reading and re-reading it in disbelief, she had thought it must be some sort of monstrous practical joke. Reality quickly set in, however, as she realised, with growing dismay, that there could only be one possible explanation for this extraordinary turn of events, and that the answer, unfortunately, lay very close to home. Her confrontation with Mama and Amelia had been far from pleasant.

Tears there had been aplenty. And drumming of heels—Amelia—and lamenting on the trials of life imprisonment—Mama. Remonstrations and threats alternated with an attempt to paint a picture of the bright and comfortable future that awaited all three of them, would Clarissa but comply with their plan and take Kit for a protector. Throughout, Clarissa remained intractable and implacable, determined to ensure that their interference ended once and for all. A threat to tell Edward the whole sorry tale put a stop to Amelia's resistance. And from there, it was not much to persuade Mama to keep quiet and reassure her that all would be well without Kit Rasenby's help.

Clarissa had then spent a torrid night haunted by what Kit must think of her, for her mama and sister had unwittingly ensured that she appeared every bit the scheming wench he had accused her of being. There was nothing she could write in return that he would believe. Nothing she could say in a letter to make amends for the one he had received from Mama. She must see him in the flesh and apologise, try to convince him that she had naught to do with the letter. But it would be the most difficult thing she had ever had to do, and she dreaded it.

She dressed for the task with care in a walking dress of palest blue wool and a three-quarter pelisse of dark blue merino. The hack deposited her at Grosvenor Square just before noon, but it was now nearly one and she had been waiting for almost an hour, having been informed, rather snootily, she thought, that his lordship was currently indisposed. Resisting all the butler's attempts to persuade her to return at another time more convenient to his lordship, eventually the determined tilt to Clarissa's chin and the mulish look in her green eyes had gained her the interview. Taking another turn around the room, unable to sit still, she wondered if he would keep her waiting for ever.

Finally, the door opened. In the time it took him to become presentable, the effects of last night's brandy had added to Kit's already-worn temper. He surveyed her coldly.

Clarissa's heart leapt at the sight of him, so tall, so handsome, so *exactly* right. But the frown was firmly in place, the dark brows almost meeting, the eyes almost black, unforgiving pools, glittering as brightly as his polished Hessian boots. His mouth was fixed in a firm line, not even a trace of the normal mocking smile.

'So much, then, Clarissa, for your promise never to see me again.' Kit closed the door behind him and walked slowly into the room, not once taking his eyes from her face.

As he approached she could see faint lines of tiredness, and had to put her hands firmly behind her back in order to prevent them from reaching up to sooth away the harsh frown on his brow. 'Good morning, my lord. I beg your pardon for intruding, I assure you I had no intention of breaking my promise not to see you again. I came merely to clear up the grave misunderstanding that has arisen between us from my mother's misguided letter. A letter whose contents I knew nothing of, and condemn with all my heart.'

More denials. He was not in the mood for her games. 'For God's sake, woman, have done with your lies.' The ice-cold voice was gone, replaced by a hot rage that made her tremble. 'I don't think I've heard one word of truth from those treacherous lips of yours since we met. You have schemed and plotted your way into my life. You have bewitched me with that body of yours. And when you've found yourself bested, instead of giving in and admitting defeat, you simply twist and turn until you find another way to gain your devious ends.'

Kit paced around the room, breathing deeply in an effort to control the rage that was consuming him. A rage that was fuelled by the sight of Clarrie standing in front of him looking so vulnerable. Those big green eyes were gazing up at him full of hurt. That full bottom lip was clenched between her little white teeth to stop her from crying. He would not, *would absolutely not* be taken in by her wiles again.

'I thought you understood enough of me, after the days we spent in each other's company, to see that plain dealing would get you what you wanted. I thought there was enough truth between us for you to realise that an honest request direct from you—not through the medium of your mama— would have gained my attention. I thought you would at least grant me that.'

Fleetingly, the hurt her behaviour had caused showed on Kit's face, but the mask was back in place before Clarissa could be sure. She could find no words at present, could only watch in dismay the results of her own reckless actions, of Amelia's and Mama's idiotic attempts at blackmail. The damage was well and truly done. With each word Kit uttered, she felt her heart shrivel and grow colder, felt herself retreating a little more into that dark place deep inside where she would have to learn to live.

'Well I was wrong, obviously,' Kit continued. 'You have played me for a fool Clarissa, but you have mistaken your man. Now, if you've said your piece you can go, and this will indeed be the last of our acquaintance. No, wait,' he added urgently as she turned to obey him. '"Let us kiss and part," Clarrie, we should end on a more pleasant note. You must realise by now that you will "…get no more of me."'

For the first time that morning he smiled, that lopsided, harsh, malicious, mocking smile which made her go weak at the knees with desire.

'"And I am glad, glad with all my heart, that thus so cleanly I myself free."' Clarrie recited the next line of the poem bleakly. 'Oh, Kit, don't let it end like this. Won't you believe me? I'd do anything to have you believe me.' Clarissa laid a beseeching hand on the cloth of his dark blue coat, her eyes wide with unshed tears as she looked up at him.

'Anything, Clarrie? But what is there left that you have not already given me?' Kit lifted the hand from his arm and held it, trapped and fluttering between his own, like a small bird.

I would give you my heart, Kit, if you would but take it. But the words could not, would not, ever be uttered. Instead, a watery smile and a shake of the head were all she could summon. She turned to go, overcome with weariness and despair, realising how useless it would be to try to persuade him of her honesty after all that had transpired. But he held tight to her hand, perversely refusing to let her leave.

'Surely, Clarissa, you don't want to go without extracting something from me? All that effort, all that work to charm me. All the trickery you employed to entice me. Surely you want some form of return for such a very time-consuming investment?'

Clarissa's face was burning with shame and embarrassment, but she was as cold inside as if sculpted of ice. His scorn at her behaviour, his callous dismissal of all the passion they had shared, were clear evidence of how little it had all meant to him. He had taken her to bed once, and obviously had no desire to do so again. As for the rest? Well, he would never trust her, never believe her. What future could they possibly ever have? Best that she walk away now with some shred of dignity and spend the rest of her life trying to forget him.

Clarissa blinked away a tear and tugged her hand free. 'I want nothing from you, my lord, except perhaps your forgiveness. Since that is unlikely to be forthcoming, I can only apologise once more for any pain I have caused you, and assure you that you will not see me again. I bid you good morning.' A small curtsy, a last look into that beloved face, and Clarissa made for the door.

She had the handle in her hand when he reached her. Grasping her by the shoulders, Kit turned her round to face him and, ruthlessly pushing her bonnet back, kissed her. A hard, long, vengeful kiss, his lips devouring hers, his tongue seeking entry to her mouth, determined not to be gainsaid.

'No, Clarrie, don't go. Not yet. I've missed you.'

The words were growled low, drawn unwillingly from him, but they were enough. Clarrie melted into his arms, throwing her own around him, clutching desperately at him to pull herself into his hard, achingly familiar body, feeling as if she was coming home. 'Kit.' She opened her mouth, her soft lips giving against his hard demands, the fire of passion igniting instantly as the tip of his tongue touched hers, the heat starting low down in her belly and rising quickly to engulf her as Kit's kisses became passionate, hungry, commanding.

His hands roamed restlessly over her body, frustrated by the thick wool of her clothing. Her cloak was cast off, her bonnet hung down her back by its ribbons, but it wasn't enough. Kit licked the corners of her mouth, then traced a pattern of kisses down her neck, pulling at the fichu of her gown to reveal the white mounds of her breasts underneath. He kissed the valley between them, and circled her nipples with his thumbs through her clothing, the cotton of her chemise causing a delicious friction that added to the sensation of pleasure.

Casting off her gloves, Clarrie pulled him closer in, pulling his lips to hers once more, meeting his demands with her own, threatening to overpower his control with her passion. It was this, Kit thought hazily, this matching of needs and wants, that was at the root of his obsession. A woman who was his equal in desires, who challenged and commanded and was unafraid of expressing her own needs—this is what made Clarrie so very necessary to him.

Necessary? The word startled Kit back to reality. Forcing himself to let her go, slowly unfastening his lips from hers, he shook his head in disbelief. So near she had been to leaving. So quickly had passion overtaken them. Looking at her, flushed and dishevelled, her green eyes dark with desire, he knew that what she was feeling, for now at least, was no pretence. She wanted him every bit as much as he wanted her.

He could not let her go. The stark truth stared Kit in the face. He could not let her go. Not until he was over her. Not until he could face a future without her. No matter what kind of scheming trollop she was, she needed to be *his* until he had cured himself of this strange addiction. He could not contemplate any alternative.

Taken up with the attempt to put her clothing into some sort of order and to control her breathing, Clarissa noticed none of the thoughts flitting over Kit's face. *I've missed you.* That was all it had taken from him to destroy her resolution, to turn her into this strange, wild, Clarrie she didn't recognise. A Clarrie with no control over her passions. A Clarrie with no thought other than the fulfilment of those passions. A Clarrie so far from the upright, staid, practical Clarissa that she seemed like quite another person.

I've missed you. Did she imagine it? Did it matter, when ultimately it would make no difference between them? He wanted her body, that was all. He would take her and use her and dispose of her, and she would be left with an empty shell. Nothing had changed. Dejectedly, she retied her bonnet, thrusting the curls that had escaped their pins under the brim any old how, afraid to see the evidence of their passion should she look in the mirror. She had to get out of here before she made an even bigger fool of herself.

A vice-like grip on her arm made any move impossible, however. 'You're not going anywhere until we've talked.'

'We have nothing more to say to each other. I must go; Mama does not know where I am.'

'I suspect your mama knows exactly where you are right now, my dear, and moreover heartily approves.'

'You have her wrong, Kit. She is merely a foolish woman in desperate need of funds. She did not really intend to bribe you, nor to sell me.'

'No? I'm afraid it is you who are mistaken. But I'm already bored with discussing your sainted mama. I am much more interested in what happens next between us.'

'Nothing. Nothing more can happen, Kit, you know that as well as I.'

'Don't insult me. We have unfinished business between us. As well it were settled now while we are alone.'

'I don't understand.'

'Come, Clarissa, don't pretend. We are extremely compatible. You must admit that, for you are obviously experienced. I have not met such a passion in a woman before. Together, we are well matched.'

The burning flush that covered her face was a mixture of anger and disappointment. To discuss what they had shared seemed so wrong. To denigrate what for Clarrie had been love-making, into something that was mere bodily pleasure, made her furious. And for him to deny, despite the evidence, that he had been her first, her only lover, was the final straw. 'You do me a grievous disservice, my lord. If your intention is to hurt me, then let me assure you that you have been more than successful. I have not your lordship's experience in such matters, despite what you think of me. And I find it distasteful to discuss our love-making—' she could not bring herself to give it another name '—in such cold terms. I was an innocent until two nights ago, you know it yourself, though you choose to deny it. I gave you my body in payment, as I promised—I am no longer in debt to you, nor you to me. I am pleased that our union was not distasteful to you, but it is over. Now let me go.'

Completely taken aback at her anger, Kit's grip on her arm did not relax. The tiny voice deep inside him that had been on Clarissa's side from the start, supporting her claims, telling him to trust her, gained volume. One truth he would allow her. He knew she had been innocent, had been mad or desperate to think otherwise. But still, he could not reconcile this fact with his experience. She might have been unpractised, but she had definitely been tutored. Innocence was not, after all, the same as virtue.

It did not matter. None of it mattered. Allowing himself to accept that he had been the first, the only lover she had ever had, gave Kit a glow of satisfaction, making him realise how necessary it was that he continued to be so. She was, must be, exclusively his. 'Clarrie, we can deal better than this. I'm sorry for disbelieving you, I'm not thinking straight. I beg your pardon. Please, let us sit down and talk properly.'

'There's nothing to talk about, Kit. Please let me go.' But she allowed herself to be led over to a sofa, and sat down nevertheless.

Kit sat down beside her. 'There, that's more like it. I awoke with such a headache,' he said apologetically, 'I was a trifle foxed, a touch too much brandy last night, for which I must blame your mama and her letter. I confess I am not at my best, and my temper is ragged as a consequence. But I am feeling better by the minute.'

'Really, Kit, blaming my mama for your headache is a trifle unfair.'

Clarissa looked up, the tilt of her determined little chin, the challenging lift of her brow, so exactly as he remembered that for a moment he forgot all that had gone before and laughed, his rare, genuine laugh. 'Fair enough, I must accept some of the blame. You allow me no quarter, do you, Clarissa fair?'

'Nor you I, my lord and in that we are certainly well matched.'

'Clarissa, I want you to listen to me, and not to interrupt.' Seizing her hand, Kit gazed into her eyes, urging her compliance. He would do it, he had to ask her, he didn't care what damage it did to his ego. What use was it to have his pride intact when what he really wanted was right here in front of him? He could nurse his injured pride at length when his more pressing needs had been satisfied. 'Please, listen. I don't want an answer now, I want you to think carefully about it.'

'Very well. But I think you should know that—'

'Clarissa, be quiet.'

This time his smile lit up his eyes, making him so incredibly handsome that Clarissa gulped in an effort not to lean over and kiss him once more.

'We started out our liaison, both of us, under false pretences. No matter your real motives, whether to rescue your sister or to entrap me for yourself, you lied to me from the start. And I was not so honest with you either, for I led you on, knowing full well that you were scheming, yet so bored with my life that I chose to indulge you in your pretence.'

A brief silence greeted this, as both reviewed the last few days, acknowledging the truth. Neither could claim to be blameless.

'Yet much good has flowed from such inauspicious beginnings, Clarissa,' Kit continued, 'you must see that now. I have never met a woman whose courage I have so admired. You took everything I threw at you and coped without tears or tantrums. You showed such a lust for life on board the *Sea Wolf*, such an empathy towards Monsieur and Mademoiselle Renaud. I came to honour your judgement, to enjoy testing your intelligence. In short, despite your scheming, I enjoy your company, Clarissa, in a way I have never liked the company of any woman before.'

Her heart was beating faster with every word, for she could not quite believe what Kit was saying to her. She dared not speak, dared not hope, merely gestured for him to continue.

'The consummation of our relationship was— well, I will not cause you to blush further. Let me just say that it was all I had hoped and beyond all my previous experience. I want more of it, I cannot think straight until I have more of it. I think we will deal well together. What do you say, Clarrie. Is it yes?'

She could not quite believe it. He had proposed. He had not mentioned love but it was there surely, clearly implied. 'Are you sure it's what you want, Kit?'

'I never offer anything unless I'm completely sure.'

'Oh Kit, yes, yes, yes.' Clarrie threw her arms around him, almost knocking him flat back on the sofa, her body lying on top of his, pressing against him with abandon. Their kiss was slow and languorous. Tasting, renewing, hot, yet restrained. Clarrie pressed tiny kisses onto Kit's eyes, his cheeks, his ears, kissed her way across his mouth, licking the tender skin inside his lips, and licked back again. She ran her fingers through his locks, feeling the fine silk of his hair run through them, contrasting with the crisp dark hair on his nape— the feeling awakening a vivid memory of the crisp curls on his chest.

Kit made to sit up, but she pushed him back down, arching into his arousal, rubbing herself against him, the friction of their bodies and their clothes sending shivers of raw desire through her. Cautiously, she rubbed herself against him again, cat-like, sinuously, testing his control, revelling in the feeling of power this ability to arouse him gave her. All thought of restraint left her as she heard his groan of surrender and wild Clarrie took over from staid Clarissa, heedless of their surroundings, intent only on giving pleasure and receiving it in return.

She kissed him again, a hard, passionate kiss, holding his face in her hands, refusing to let him move from underneath her. Clumsily at first, but with growing confidence, she fumbled for the fastenings of his breeches and released him from their constraints. His arousal was a hard silken length in her hand, hers to hold, to caress, to rub, to tease, and she did all of this, all the time watching Kit's face, flushed like her own with passion, his eyes closed, his breathing heavy. *She* was causing this, *she* was doing this to him—he was hers. A thrill of possession ran through her, causing her hands to tighten, threatening to upset the delicate balance of control. Just in time, she released him, twisting away to stand upright.

Clarissa quickly disposed of her own undergarments, discarded the fichu at her neck, and untied the strings of her chemise. Kit needed no encouragement, but sat up, pulling her back down astride him, freeing her breasts with urgent hands, enveloping first one, then the other, nipple with his soft mouth, sweeping circles on each with his clever, tantalising, teasing tongue. Clarrie panted, wet with desire, and pulled her dress up around her waist. Bracing herself with her hands on the back of the sofa behind Kit's neck, she began, slowly, delicately, to draw him inside her, slowly to engulf his hard length with her own silken heat. Kit's hands held her waist to guide her, support her, but she needed no encouragement. She held them both still for a heart-stopping instant, her muscles clenched around him, then moved, tilted up, then slowly down, twisting herself against him to heighten her own pleasure, feeling him pulse inside her. Slowly, resolutely resisting the urge to quicken the pace, she repeated the motion, rising up and thrusting down, hearing Kit's gasping, growled pleasure in her ear, feeling his grip on her waist tighten, feeling her own climax climbing to its peak with each downwards motion, until suddenly she was soaring, released, flying in ecstasy. As she lost herself in the feeling, Kit's grasp became demanding, and she instinctively thrust more urgently, hard and fast, relishing the feeling of still being in control even as she floated in the afterglow of her climax, moaning as Kit's own climax came in a final powerful thrust that pulsed through her, ripples of pleasure ebbing out from a whirlpool of passion.

They lay limp and panting, a tangle of clothing

around hot, damp, satisfied bodies. Clarrie raised her head from where it rested in the nook between Kit's neck and shoulder to look into his eyes, still dark with passion behind hooded lids. A crooked, exhausted smile met her own slightly trembling, slightly questioning look. Holding her tight against him, their bodies still joined, Kit reached up to curl a bright auburn lock around his finger. Pressing a slow, sated kiss to her mouth, he finally moved to separate them, brushing her skirts down, adjusting his breeches, holding out her undergarments to her with a rueful smile.

Retreating behind a small screen by the fire to compose herself, Clarissa felt a hot flush of embarrassment. What had come over her? She could not blame Kit this time for becoming carried away, it had been all her own doing. What if the servants had come in? She doubted she would even have noticed.

'I think we had better confine such activity to our bedchamber when we are married, do not you, Kit?' Clarissa emerged from the screen, tying her fichu into place, and saw the smile on his face freeze at her words.

'Married? Whatever gave you that idea?'

'Why, you did. You proposed to me—and I said yes.' Her confidence faltered. Looking back on the conversation, she realised that he had not specifically mentioned marriage at all.

'You are mistaken, Clarissa. My proposal was of a nature much more appropriate to our relationship, as I believe I indicated it would be in my letter.'

'But I thought you had changed your mind. You said you couldn't do without me. You said you missed me. You said you wanted me.'

'All true—for the present, at least. But none of those words imply marriage, my dear. You don't bring me up to scratch so easily.'

Clarissa slumped down in an armchair, her legs too weak to support her. He was right. She had been so carried away just being with him, with his avowal of need, of desire, she had not questioned the nature of the proposal. In a small voice she determined once and for all to clarify the situation. 'You were not offering marriage?'

Kit's raised brow and mocking smile were the only answer, but they were sufficient.

'What, then? I don't understand.'

'A temporary but exclusive liaison.'

'You mean I would be yours and only yours?' *He had that already, and for ever, if he were but interested.*

'Yes, but I would be yours too, exclusively, for

the duration. I have never offered a woman that before, Clarrie, you should be honoured.'

'Yes? Well, then, thank you, my lord, I must be honoured if you say I should be.'

She glanced up at him, hurt and confusion writ large on her face, causing that nagging voice in his head to speak in her support. His instinct to hold her close, to promise never to leave her, was quelled with extreme difficulty. Defiantly, he reminded himself that she would do anything to have her way, to trap him, even into marriage. He would not be a victim. He would take her, he had to have her, but on his own terms, and those terms alone, no matter how urgently he wished it could be otherwise.

'Come now, Clarrie, there's no point in tears. We have something out of the common way together. Let us make the most of it while it lasts. For it will end, as these things always do, so it's best to make arrangements now, to make that ending as painless as possible. Then we can enjoy to the full the precious time we have together. I am a generous protector. You will find you want for nothing, I promise. And when we part, as part we must, you will be more than adequately recompensed. I think that is a bargain neither of us can carp at.'

She continued to look up at him, the hurt reflected deep in her emerald eyes, but the tears were held defiantly in check. Reminding himself that she was an astonishingly good actress, Kit leaned over to pull her to her feet, pressing a swift, gentle kiss on her yielding lips.

'I asked you to think carefully about my proposal, you may remember. Don't say no, Clarrie, it would be a mistake. Go home and think about what we have. Think about the alternatives. Then give me a yes that you will honour. I'll meet you tomorrow, when you've had time to reflect. But bear this in mind. Though I offer you something I have never offered before, I will not offer more, nor will I offer it twice. If you say no, it will be final, and we will see no more of each other. And much as I wish and hope that will not be so, I won't be blackmailed, nor held to ransom. This is my final offer, Clarissa, so think carefully before you turn it down.'

Shaking her head, Clarissa could still find no words, silenced as she was by the deep hurt inside her, the determination not to show Kit how much she cared. Submissively, she stood while he re-tied her bonnet and draped her cloak around her. Wordlessly, she allowed him to kiss her cheek, permitting herself only one brief, final embrace before she left without looking back, and the door to Grosvenor Square closed firmly behind her for ever.

A small boy in dark green livery stepped aside into a doorway as Clarissa exited the house and hailed a hack. When the carriage pulled away, the boy launched himself on to the back of it, unbeknownst to either the jarvey or his passenger. As the hack pulled up to deposit Clarissa at her home, the boy leapt off and hid round the corner, taking careful note of her address. With a satisfied whistle, he waited to make sure she went through the door, before running off to inform his master of his findings.

Robert, Marquis of Alchester, was partaking of a late luncheon in the sunny breakfast parlour when his servant returned. Lowering the *Morning Post*, to listen carefully to the boy as he recounted his morning's observations, he smiled with satisfaction. The coin he handed over was larger than the lad had anticipated, and the boy bowed low, thanking his master with assurances of his continued service, and a rather gappy, cocky smile. Alchester dismissed him with an imperious wave, and returned to the table.

The address the boy had given him was the same as the one he had received from his lawyer. Lady Maria Warrington's gambling debts had been acquired almost by accident, payment from another of Mrs Barrington's innocent victims in the gambling hell to which she had introduced Lady Maria. Alchester had not made the connection with Kit Rasenby until last night, when Kit, in his cups, had let slip Clarissa's name after a deal too much of White's brandy.

Robert Alchester had waited a long time for revenge. For years, he had watched as Kit's reputation as a rake increased as surely as the richness of his lands, as abundantly as his wealth. Robert looked on in bitter resentment as Kit flourished, as his callous treatment of women was rewarded with devotion, as his reckless gaming was rewarded with winnings beyond anything Robert could dream of. The *Sea Wolf* had seemed to offer the first chink in Rasenby's armour, but he had somehow escaped from the excise men. As Kit's lucky star continued in the ascent, so Robert Alchester's plummeted. He was known to be in debt, reduced to extorting money from acquired gambling debts such as Lady Maria's in order to keep his many voracious creditors at bay. And as the vultures circled closer, so the ladies moved further away.

Now surely the tide was turning his way. The innocent Miss Clarissa Warrington would prove to be Rasenby's Achilles' heel and Robert Alchester's salvation. Rasenby would be crushed once and for all. The Marquis of Alchester cut himself another slice of bloody beef. He was suddenly ravenous.

Chapter Twelve

Clarissa returned home for the second day in a row in desperate need of the solace of her bed-chamber. She wearily opened the door, feeling that everything which could possibly go wrong with her life already had. For the second time in two days she was summoned urgently into the parlour before she even had time to remove her hat. This time, the voice belonged not to Lady Maria, but to Aunt Constance. Her heart sank. This was an encounter she had been dreading and could well do without.

'Child, what on earth have you been up to?' Aunt Constance got to her feet as Clarissa entered the room. Dressed neatly as ever, in a plain but elegant dress of brown silk with matching ribbons in her cap, she was clearly upset. A frown darkened her pale countenance as she anxiously assessed her niece. 'Come and let me look at you properly. I have asked your mother to afford us some privacy. Your mama has already given me some muddled story about your escapades, but I confess I would much rather have it direct from you. Why don't you sit down and tell your aunt exactly what's been happening, there's a good girl.'

The gentle voice and the obvious note of concern in her voice, when she was entitled to anger, were quite oversetting. Clarissa cast herself into her aunt's arms and gave way to another unaccustomed fit of tears.

Lady Constance held her close, patting her back and whispering soothing platitudes while patiently letting her have her cry. When Clarissa finally looked up, gulping down the last of her sobs, Lady Constance handed her a fine linen handkerchief, but continued in her silence, concern for her normally placid niece having the upper hand over curiosity.

Eventually Clarissa sat up properly, and with a sigh turned to her aunt, her face resolute. 'I don't know exactly what Mama will have told you, for it was Amelia who broke my confidence and told a version of the tale to her. I have yet not apprised Mama of the true facts myself. I'm afraid I put you in a difficult position, forcing you to lie to Mama, and no doubt making you worry about my whereabouts. I am so sorry, Aunt Constance, but you must believe me when I say that I did it only because I thought it for the best.'

'Silly child, of course I realise that. I am only sorry that you felt the need to act without first consulting me. I thought you trusted me, Clarissa. I thought you knew you could always turn to me if you were in need of help.'

'Indeed, dearest Aunt Constance, I thought of it, I assure you. Only, knowing what you think of Amelia, I was not sure you would *want* to help. And so I did such a stupid thing, and now we are all reaping the consequences of it, myself as much as Mama and Amelia. And, oh, Aunt Constance, if ever any of this gets out, I will have brought such shame and disgrace to your good name, too, as you truly don't deserve.'

'Clarissa, my dear, I cannot believe you would ever deliberately do anything to shame me, you must not be worrying your head about that. Whatever has happened, I'm sure that if we put our heads together we can fix it. But first you must tell me exactly what has transpired, for I could get no sense out of your mama, and Amelia would only say I must talk to you, and that you had ruined her life.'

'Well, that's true enough, Aunt, I think I have. And mine too, for I am ruined, and it is all my own fault.'

'Ruined? Do not tell me, Clarissa, that your mother spoke the truth? Is it—no, I cannot believe it. She told me you had been seduced. Please tell me that she is mistaken.'

'No, I wasn't seduced.'

Aunt Constance clapped her hands together in relief. 'I knew it, I knew that muddle-headed mother of yours must have managed to get the story amiss.'

'No, you don't understand. I was not seduced, but I am no longer innocent. I was not coerced, nor was I ravished. I was—I was compliant. It's not Kit's fault, no matter what Mama says, but I am ruined none the less. Oh, Aunt Constance, the truly wicked thing is, I cannot bring myself to regret it.'

Her aunt struggled to absorb the import of Clarissa's words. 'My dear, please tell me you are not deluded into thinking you are in love with this man?'

'Oh, but I am, I am, I am. I cannot help it, I can't, I love him so much, and I have made such a mull of it, and now there is no future for it. But still, I cannot regret it. You will hate me for it, but I won't lie to you, Aunt. I do love him.'

Slowly, determinedly, Lady Constance extracted the round tale, her face becoming grimmer with each admission from her niece. Of Amelia and Lady Maria's part in the whole thing Clarissa made little, but Lady Constance heard enough to make up her own mind. Heard enough to have a pretty clear picture of Lady Maria's stupidity and Amelia's selfishness.

At the end, she held Clarissa close, assuring her that all would be well, that she was on her side and would never think ill of her. Inside she was cold and furious, already planning the best way of raining retribution down on Kit Rasenby's arrogant, selfish head. His sister, Lady Marlborough, was long overdue a visit. Lady Constance would start there. If nothing else came out of this, Kit Rasenby's conscience would certainly take a battering from which it would never recover.

Allowing her niece no hint of these thoughts, Lady Constance turned to practicalities. The letter from Fortescue and Brown detailing Lady Maria's debts was pursued with a deep frown, and Amelia was summoned. 'I understand that you opened your sister's letter to Edward Brompton, Amelia. I trust that you are aware that you should not have done so? To pry into another's private correspondence is the kind of behaviour one would expect from servants.'

Amelia, who had never been able to stand up to Aunt Constance, hung her head in shame.

'Well, have you nothing to say?'

'I'm sorry, Aunt Constance, I only did it to help Clarissa out.'

'And in what way did you imagine you would be helping her, Amelia?'

'I just thought if I knew why she was writing to Edward, I might be able to give her some advice.'

'That is a ridiculous lie, and you know it. I can only hope that this Edward fellow was as shocked as I to find his correspondence tampered with.'

Amelia blushed at the memory of Edward's reaction. He had indeed lectured her, and it had quite spoiled the evening.

'Well, I can see from your face that Edward does have some sense then. And did he also have a reply for Clarissa's query?'

'No, not immediately, Aunt. He said he would look into the matter, and would give Clarissa the information she wanted if he could do so without any breach of confidence.'

'Hmm. Obviously a much more sensible young man than you deserve. I am told you love each other and wish to marry, but his meagre prospects are a barrier. In that case I would like to meet this young man. You may inform him that he can call on me tomorrow at eleven. If I am happy with him, I will see what I can do. Despite what you think, Amelia, I have no desire to see you unhappy, and every wish to see you happily settled, even if you scarcely deserve it. If there is anything I can do to further Edward's position, I will look into it—if, and only if, I have your promise that you will interfere no further in your sister's concerns.'

'But, Aunt, what about—'

Lady Constance continued inexorably. 'I will hear no more from you on any subject, Amelia. You will leave Clarissa alone and refrain from any discussion at all of the events that have taken place over the last three days. If I hear that you have made any attempt to open negotiations of any sort with any gentleman other than Edward Brompton, I will disown you. Am I absolutely clear?'

'Yes, Aunt Constance.'

'You may leave us now.' Lady Constance waved an imperious hand. Amelia left with relief, casting a backwards sympathetic glance at her sister, looking extremely subdued on the sofa.

'I must go now, Clarissa,' Lady Constance said, drawing on her gloves. 'I have a lot to do, and a lot to think about. You must get some rest, child, and try not to worry for the present. We must wait and see if there are any other consequences of your liaison with Lord Rasenby, and pray for your sake that there are not. In the meantime, you must naturally have no further contact with him. As to your mother's debts, you may trust me to investigate the matter fully. It may be possible to negotiate repayment on easier terms, I will know more when I have spoken to this Edward person and learned who your mother's creditor is.'

'Aunt, I'm so sorry that you've been put through all this. I hadn't meant you to become involved. I've made such a mess and caused you all this worry when I thought I could deal with it myself.'

'Clarissa, once and for all I assure you, dear child, that my only regret is that you didn't feel you could turn to me in the first place. Perhaps this could have been avoided if you had.' Seeing Clarissa's lip tremble, Lady Constance hastened to hug her reassuringly. 'There, you are a good child, you deserve better than this. Now try to put all of this out of your head, you really must get some rest. This whole episode has been traumatic for you, more than you realise yourself at present. But time, you know, is a great healer. One final thing before I go. I want your assurance that you have told me everything. I would rather know the worst if there is aught else.'

Of Kit's latest proposal and their meeting this morning, Clarissa had not spoken, and she found that she could not bring herself to now. So she shook her head in denial, hugging her aunt close, promising to retire at once to her bed and to worry no more.

Lady Constance left in her waiting town coach, already planning her next steps with something akin to relish. It was nice to feel she could be of use. She was looking forward to getting one over on Lord Rasenby. He would find she was no mean adversary.

Deciding to act immediately, while her anger still fuelled her thoughts, Lady Constance directed her coachman to take her to Lady Letitia Marlborough's house. She was fortunate enough to find Kit's sister at home alone. The interview gave her some satisfaction, providing, as it did, a relief for her pent-up emotions. When Lady Constance departed she left her old friend shocked, upset, and in a state of high dudgeon. Lady Constance had every expectation that all this pent-up ire would soon be raining down on Kit Rasenby.

It was late in the day and she was tired but reasonably satisfied with her efforts. Her only regret was that she would not be present to witness the confrontation between Letitia and Kit.

Having spent the remainder of the evening, despite her promise to her aunt, ruminating on events, Clarissa went to bed clear in her own mind that there was only one possible answer to Kit's proposal. She loved him, that much was beyond dispute. His offer was therefore tempting from a purely selfish point of view, scarcely impossible as it was to contemplate life without him. Tempting too since she could, if she chose, conveniently assuage her guilt by convincing herself she was making a selfless sacrifice to secure Mama's and Amelia's future. But it was wrong and she knew it. She could be nobody's mistress, it was marriage or nothing, and even then, only if she was truly loved. Since Kit was offering neither marriage nor true love, it could not be.

Clarissa realised that there was something else even more important. Kit cared for her more than he knew, or would admit, but eventually he would grow tired of her and bring their liaison to a conclusion. Knowing that the ending was coming, inevitably, surely, on some yet-to-be-decided date, would be intolerable to Clarissa. No, she could not settle for anything less than perfect. She knew in her heart what she must do. It was precisely because she loved him so deeply that she must turn him down.

A night's rest saw Clarissa full of renewed determination. She arose early, but her note to Kit, brief as it was, took her some time and many sheets of paper before the final version was ready to be delivered. Clarissa thanked him *profusely* for his *very generous offer*, was most flattered by it, but found that, alas, she must *in all conscience, refuse it*. She reminded him of his promise to make her no other offers, and assured him that she had no regrets. While their time together had been *enlightening and for the most part enjoyable*, it was time to end it. She trusted Kit would respect her wishes and cease all communications between them. There was no need to reply to this letter. Clarissa wished him well.

Refusing steadfastly to give in to the tears that seemed to be taking over her life these days, Clarissa next turned her attentions to the future. Aunt Constance seemed confident that something could be done about Mama's debts, and perhaps even Amelia's marriage, if Edward came up to scratch, but she could do nothing for a ruined niece. Forcing herself to face up to harsh reality, hoping that it would eventually dull the pain in her heart that threatened to overcome her with each thought of Kit, Clarissa turned her mind to obtaining a position. It would not be easy, but a governess or lady's companion she must be. With a heavy heart she pursued the advertisements in the *Tatler*.

* * *

Kit slept soundly, confident that the morrow would bring Clarissa's consent to his proposition. Waking at his usual time he smiled, embracing the day with a sense of pleasurable anticipation that surprised him, until he traced the feeling of well-being to Clarrie, and thoughts of what today would bring. He looked forward to spending his money on her, looked forward to looking after her—for the present, in any case. They could travel, she would like that, and he could teach her to sail. They would spend some time at Thornwood. She would not like to mix with the *ton* as his mistress, and he did not in any case wish to share her.

With irritation, he dismissed the voice in his head that asked him just how long he expected their liaison to last, his record to date of a mere two months being hardly sufficient for these plans. There was no need to put a timescale to it, no need to think of life after Clarissa. She was different. Two months—that was paltry.

The familiar writing on the letter proffered by his valet caused Kit's heart to skip a beat. Assuring himself that she was merely writing to confirm their arrangement to meet later, Kit opened the short note and quickly scanned the contents, anger warring with disbelief and enormous disappointment. What was her game? Surely she did not think she could up the stakes now?

Swearing softly, he became aware that Fanshaw was hovering by the bed. 'Well?'

'I am sorry to have to tell you that Lady Marlborough awaits your lordship's pleasure. She apologises for calling at such an early hour, but says that the matter is of such import it will not wait. Hodges has placed her in the breakfast parlour, my lord.'

'God damn it, what the hell does she want? Did she say what it was about?'

'No, my lord, when Hodges inquired further she merely repeated that the matter was urgent.'

'No doubt that brat of a nephew of mine has been trying out his blasted gaming system again. Oh, very well, then, tell her I'll be down as soon as I can.'

'And the letter, my lord—is there a reply?'

'No, there is not. And you can take your interfering nose out of my business and get on with shaving me.'

'Yes, my lord.' With injured innocence, Fanshaw traipsed to the dressing room to gather together the necessary component's of Kit's riding dress. There was definitely something afoot with the master, and if Fanshaw knew anything about it, it had to do with that young woman from Thornwood

Manor. He'd give a lot to see the letter, but it was already locked away safely in Kit's writing table.

'Well, Letty, what is so urgent that you must needs call before breakfast? It's not like you to be up so betimes.' Kit strode into the breakfast parlour an hour later, planting a brief kiss on his sister's cheek before pouring himself a draught of ale. 'Have you eaten? Did Hodges bring you coffee?'

'I am in no mood for sustenance, Kit, and neither will you be when you've heard what I've got to say. I have a very busy day ahead of me, I can scarcely afford the time for this matter, you know. I am engaged to take the girls to see the illuminations at Vauxhall tonight, and I have a host of errands to attend to before then.'

'Well, make it quick then, Letitia,' Kit said, 'I have pressing business to see to myself. Has Jeremy been out on the tiles again? How much is it this time?'

'It is nothing to do with Jeremy. You may say what you want of my son, Kit, but at least he is not a seducer of innocent virgins!'

Kit grinned distractedly. 'No? Well, he's young yet, I suppose there's still time. So what is this pressing matter then?'

Kit sat down at the table, addressing himself to

a plate of ham, his thoughts on what he should do in reply to Clarissa's letter, only half-aware of his sister fuming silently beside him.

'It is you, Kit. You really have gone too far this time. I am appalled, absolutely appalled at what I hear. You have placed me in a dreadful position; I have never been so embarrassed. And poor Constance—well, needless to say she is up in arms at your behaviour.'

Kit's attention finally secured, Letty sat back in satisfaction, watching her brother carefully putting his knife down on his plate before speaking. His voice was measured, but she knew that look of old. He was angry. 'Who is this Constance that I have so unwittingly offended?'

'Lady Constance Denby. You must have heard me mention her, Kit, she's one of my oldest friends.'

'I remember her vaguely now—a widow, isn't she? Her husband was that rare thing, an honest politician. What of her?'

'She called on me yesterday. You are obviously not aware that she has a niece. Two nieces, to be precise.'

'And,' Kit said cautiously, 'what of them?'

'I am led to believe you've had dealings with both of them recently. Amelia, Constance informs me, you intended to offer a *carte blanche*, but were induced to change your mind. Not content with trying to ruin one who, Constance admits, was at least colluding in her own downfall, you then proceeded to ravish the other, Clarissa—a complete innocent—who is now apparently heart-broken in love with you.'

'Clarissa Warrington is Constance Denby's niece?'

'Yes, and not just her niece, but very much her aunt's favourite. Constance thinks highly of her, paid for her schooling, had hoped to have Clarissa as her companion. But she is unwilling to abandon her mother and sister even though, from what I can gather, they live in rather straitened circumstances. Honestly, Kit,' Letitia said exasperatedly, 'the girl is respectable through and through; it's not like you to make such a mistake.'

'I had no idea she was so well connected, Letty, nor such an innocent, I promise you.'

'So I informed Constance must be the case. A rake you are, Kit, and no mistake, but I know that seducing innocents is not in your usual line.'

Kit smiled grimly. 'Thank you for the tribute, sister.'

Letty's face softened. 'I am not going to deny, brother, that you have *some* good points. I am par-ticularly grateful for the unwavering support you provide to my poor weak, foolish Jeremy, you know I am. But really, Kit, you have gone too far this time. What possessed you?'

'God, Letty, I'm sore pressed to understand that myself.' Kit shook his head in an effort to assemble his thoughts. Clarissa, it would seem, had been telling him the truth all along, and was every bit the innocent she claimed to be. He could not for the moment reconcile this with his own knowledge of her. If she was the person her aunt claimed, why had she behaved so recklessly? It would certainly explain her letter this morning— she would never accept a *carte blanche* from him.

'Is it true that you abducted her and took her to France on the *Sea Wolf*?' Letitia enquired incredulously. 'I told Constance that part must be a lie, for no woman has ever been on board that yacht of yours, even me!'

'Letty, you'd be sick before we left harbour, as well you know. That part is true, actually, although she came willingly—or so I believed.' Kit ran his hand distractedly through his hair, causing one lock to fall forward into his eyes. He brushed it away angrily. What had he done?

His conscience, dormant since yesterday, launched itself with renewed vigour, castigating him so thoroughly that his voice, when he recovered enough to speak, was clipped and grim. 'I

thought she was lying. She protested her innocence, but I chose not to believe her. I wanted to
take her with me, you see, I was—I don't know,
Letty, I was bored, she was different, I was
enjoying myself. She must have been terrified,
though she gave no outward sign of it. I didn't
realise what I was doing to her.'

'Well, according to Constance, there was
precious little you *didn't* do to her.' Letty's reply
was tart, the stinging dressing down she had borne
from her friend still fresh in her ears.

Kit looked up at the sharp words, seeing the hurt
on his sister's face. 'I'm sorry that you have been
embroiled in this. I take it that Lady Constance
vented her spleen on you in my absence?'

'It was awful! Constance has an extremely sharp
tongue—I did not at all relish being on the receiving end of it, I assure you. But that is nothing to
what you must have put that girl through, Kit.
Why, it is a very ravishment, for goodness' sake.'

'No, no, it's not that simple, I assure you, Letty.
But never mind that, did Lady Constance say how
she does, my poor Clarissa?'

'Much you care.'

Seeing Kit wince, Letitia softened. At least he
wasn't wholly indifferent to the damage he had
done. 'Clarissa apparently knew nothing of her

aunt's visit to me. She is upset and hurt, but she is obviously a girl of some strength and backbone, I must say, for Constance told me she would hear nothing against you, and despite all the evidence, insisted that she had consented to everything. She makes no accusations against you and wants merely to forget the whole episode. And that, let me tell you, Kit, is far more than you deserve.'

Some vestige of self-preservation made him cling to the idea that he had been the victim of a plot. That somehow, despite the overwhelming evidence to the contrary, he had not behaved completely abominably. 'Why did Lady Constance seek you out? She must have known you would come straight to me.'

'Naturally, I assume that was her intention. Sometimes, Kit, you can be quite dim-witted.' It was not often that Letitia felt superior to her brother, and it had to be admitted that in spite of the circumstances she was enjoying it for now. 'Regardless of her niece's wishes to the contrary, Constance felt that you should understand the extent of your—perfidy, she called it. It's obvious, Kit, she wants you to suffer.'

'So she wasn't asking you to intervene in any way?'

'Intervene? In what way? Oh, you mean with

you?' A trill of laughter greeted this idea. 'Quite the contrary, Kit. She was immensely relieved Clarissa wanted no more to do with you, for the last thing on earth she would wish on her niece was marriage with a rake like yourself.'

'Are you sure she said that? This was definitely no plot to entrap me in some way?' The voice in Kit's head that had always been Clarissa's supporter scented the winning post, with just this one obstacle to clear.

Letty stared at her brother open-mouthed. 'You actually think that Lady Constance Denby would plot with her niece to trap you into marriage? You have windmills in the head, Kit, I declare.' Letitia continued in full sail. 'Do you have any idea, my dear brother, just how very respectable that family are? I mean, I know the mother and the other daughter are plainly not the brightest buttons in the box, but the family pedigree is impeccable, and Constance is probably better connected than you or I. No, Kit, there is no plot. Face it, the poor deluded girl must be in love with you, there can be no other explanation.'

'She never said a word of her feelings towards me.' *Not a word, but what about her actions?* The seed of doubt Letitia had planted in his mind was taking firm root. What else explained Clarissa's behaviour? The way she had accepted him yester-day with hardly a moment to consider when she thought he was offering marriage? Could it have been love and not avarice? His past experiences made him assume the worst of everyone. But, then, did not Clarissa turn all those things on their head? 'Letty, are you sure you are right? I find it hard to believe Clarissa would keep such a thing from me.'

'Do you? Well, perhaps this chit understands you better than you think. How would you have reacted had she declared her love for you in the circumstances? Would you have believed her?'

No, of course he wouldn't have. He would have thought it yet another ploy. Yet it was the one thing, the only thing that made sense of her be-haviour. Despite the shock of Letitia's revelations, following hot on the heels as they did of Clarissa's letter refusing his *carte blanche*, Kit began to feel a sense of rising excitement.

But Letitia had not finished with him yet. 'You have done a very stupid thing, Kit. I can only pray you have not left the girl with child—although, to give you credit that is not, to my knowledge, something you make a habit of. The best thing for everyone involved in this dreadful affair is to forget it ever happened. And as for you Kit, I rec-ommend you repent for the first time in your life, and look to the future. Put the girl out of your mind. Constance is the best person to deal with her. She will find her a position as a governess or some such thing, and we can all get on with our lives. But let this be a lesson to you.'

Letitia rose to go, well satisfied with the visit. Her brother was looking thoughtful, his initial anger long since dissipated. Well and good—perhaps now was the time to give his mind something else to think about. 'You know, Louisa Haysham is not yet betrothed. I've mentioned before, she would make a biddable bride for you. It's time you settled and mended your ways, Kit. Think about it.'

Kit had been thinking hard on his sister's words. His conclusions, only just now reached, were not likely to make Letitia happy. In truth, he found them quite shocking himself. How could he have been so blind? It was as if a fog had been lifted from his mind, allowing him to see with frightening clarity. Now that the situation was for the first time crystal clear, he was determined on a rash course that made him feel quite light-headed. He stood to usher his sister towards the door. 'Put Louisa Haysham from your mind, I am not interested in her. The woman I am going to marry is a fiery, feisty, green-eyed temptress who goes by the name of Clarrie.'

'Clarrie?' Looking at him, Letitia saw a strange light in his eyes, a small smile quirked at the corner of his mouth. 'Kit, you're not going to do anything foolish, are you? I'm sorry I spoke so harshly, even if you did deserve it. You are not all bad, you know. Sometimes I think you act the part because you enjoy it.'

'Do you Letty? You are not the first to tell me so, strangely. Clarrie said something similar almost the first time she met me.'

'Kit, listen to me. That will not do, you know, Constance will not hear of it. Kit, tell me you're not going to… Oh, if I had known you would do this, I would not have come.'

'But I am very glad you did come, for you have put it all in perspective for me. You were right, Clarissa would not have behaved the way she did unless she loved me. I was just too stupid to see it. Thank you, and say thank you to Lady Constance, although I intend to do that myself when everything is settled.'

'Oh Kit, please don't do it. She'll not have you. Kit, you can't marry a ruined girl—think of your good name.'

'Letty, you have assured me all too many times that I don't have a good name to think of, and you are right. I am thinking only of Clarissa's good name. She is not ruined, we merely anticipated our vows, and that is hardly an uncommon thing. And if I find that one word of this story escapes, I will know who to blame, I warn you. Do not be the cause of an estrangement between us.'

'But I don't understand. Why are you doing this? You don't have to marry her.'

'Oh, but, Letty, I do. Don't you see? I love her. There, I've said it! Don't look so astonished. No, do, because it is quite the most astonishing and extraordinary thing ever to happen to me. Now you must pick your chin up from the floor and go, for I have important things to attend to.'

Finding herself deposited in the hallway, a frankly flabbergasted Letitia had no option but to leave, which she did reluctantly, directing her coachman to drive to the Royal Exchange where she intended to purchase several unnecessary pairs of kid evening gloves. The afternoon would be more profitably spent in indulging an unwonted fit of the vapours.

Before Letitia had even mounted the steps of her barouche, Kit had already ordered his carriage and bounded up the stairs calling for his valet. Fifteen minutes later he was negotiating the streets with care, perched high on the seat of his phaeton.

He felt he was seeing the world with a clarity of vision never before granted to him. Clarissa, the embodiment of all his desires, who overturned everything he believed in, was in love with him. It seemed so obvious now—how could he have deluded himself so? Challenging, brave, lovely Clarissa. His other half.

For he could deny it no longer, he was every bit as much in love with her. Had been in love with her for who knows how long, but was too stupid to recognise it. Calling it lust, desire, bewitchment, refusing to recognise that this need to see her, be with her, was anything other than love. He had been too afraid to admit it, but he was afraid no longer. If only it wasn't too late. If she would only forgive him.

Impatiently, Kit urged his horses forward to overtake a cumbersome gig loaded high with bales of hay. Recklessly he took a corner at breakneck speed, narrowly missing a crossing sweeper standing idly in the middle of the road, barely noticing the string of expletives that trailed in the air behind him. A mere half-hour after saying goodbye to Letitia, Kit pulled up in front of the Warrington household.

A maid in a mobbed cap showed him in to a small parlour where a faded woman much resembling Amelia was waiting. 'Lady Maria, I presume. Lord Rasenby, at your service, ma'am. I am come to see Clarissa, if I may.'

'I am surprised at your temerity, my lord. I cannot believe that you have the nerve to intrude on our privacy like this. Vile seducer.' With this, Lady Maria sank back on to the sofa, clutching a small vial to her nose, and dissolved into wild sobs.

The noise brought the maid back. Kit watched, appalled and intrigued, for he had never seen such a determined display of distress. Forgetting that Lady Maria had quite legitimate grounds for being upset, he stood to one side as first, feathers were burnt under her nose, then her wrists were chaffed, a cordial was poured, and when this had no effect, the bell was rung. Lady Maria continued to sob, and still Kit stood, becoming bored and more than a little anxious as time passed and Clarissa did not appear.

The door opened and finally Clarissa entered the room. Seeing Kit, she stopped abruptly and blushed a deep, fiery red. Her voice, however, was cold. 'I have no idea what you are doing here, Lord Rasenby, but as you can see you have upset Mama greatly. Please go, and let me tend to my mother.'

'My God, Clarissa, how do you stand it? I'm extremely glad that you take after your father's side of the family. Is she always this operatic?'

She couldn't help it; she smiled reluctantly. 'No, no, not always quite this bad. Please leave, I beg you, Kit. I wrote you a letter, which you have obviously not yet received. When you have read it you'll understand that you have no need to visit me again.'

'I've already seen the letter, Clarissa. That's not why I am here.'

She looked up at this, temporarily arresting her ministrations. Lady Maria lay quieter, but still incoherent, on the sofa at her side. 'If you've read it, you'll know that you have no need, nor any right to be here.' Clarissa turned back to her mama, after some time succeeding in making her comfortable enough to summon the maid to take over.

Lady Maria sat up. 'Clarissa! Do not, I beseech you, sit alone with that—that monster!'

Clarissa walked purposefully towards the door. 'It's all right, Mama, Lord Rasenby is just leaving.'

Kit followed her out into the hall, but when she made to open the door to show him out, placed a restraining hand on her arm. 'Clarrie, I must speak with you. Is there a room where we may be private?'

'I have nothing further to say, Kit. All is at an end, I said so clearly in my letter. And you promised, Kit, you were quite specific, in fact, that you would make no more offers if I turned you down. My answer is no, and it is final. Now please, let me alone.' She was pale where she had been flushed earlier, determined not to break down, nor to show him how much this was costing her.

'Please, allow me just a few moments. It's very important, Clarissa. Please? I promise not to touch you. I want only to talk.'

'Can I trust you?'

'Please, Clarrie.'

It was the edge of desperation in his voice that swayed her. Without another word she directed him into a small, dark room at the back of the house where she was wont to do the household accounts. She closed the door behind them, but stood with her back to it, as if poised for flight. 'I'm listening, but you must be swift. It's cold in here, and I must go back to tend to Mama.'

Having never in his life thought to make a proposal of marriage, Kit had not considered how to phrase it. He therefore plunged into words without any of the finesse he prided himself on when making a proposal of a less permanent nature. 'I'm sorry. I was wrong. I didn't listen to you. I didn't believe you. I've made a big mistake, thinking all the time that you were lying to me when you spoke the truth about yourself. I got it wrong, and now I want to make it right between us.'

'I've told you, Kit, you have nothing to apologise for. I consented to everything we did together. You neither abducted nor seduced me. And in any case, both are beside the point. I won't become your mistress. I won't spend every day wondering if it's going to be our last together. I won't go to sleep at night wondering if you will decide you've had enough of me on the morrow. I can't live like that, Kit, I won't do it. Now, if that is all, I must go and see Mama.'

'Clarrie. I'm not asking you to be my mistress.' As she turned to open the door, Kit grabbed her wrists, only to drop them as Clarissa stared haughtily at him.

'You said you wouldn't touch me.'

He flushed and loosed his hold. 'I'm sorry. Don't go. God, I'm making such a mess of this. Clarissa, I'm trying to ask you to marry me.'

'Don't be silly, Kit, it's the last thing you want, and there's really no need.'

'There's every need. I want you. I don't want you to go off and be a governess somewhere.'

'How did you know that was my plan?'

'What? I don't know. My sister may have mentioned it this morning, I don't know. Does it matter, for God's sake?'

'What has your sister to do with all of this?'

Too late, Kit remembered that Clarissa knew

nothing of Lady Constance's visit to Letitia. Too late, he realised just how Clarissa would interpret his proposal in the light of this knowledge. Foolishly, for almost the first time in his life allowing his emotions to get in the way of his logic, Kit tried to brush aside the facts. 'My sister has nothing to do with this. I just—she called on me this morning.'

'Why? Why should your sister take an interest in my affairs? She knows nothing of me. What is going on, Kit?'

'Your aunt and my sister are good friends,' Kit blurted out. 'Your aunt confided some of our affairs to my sister. My sister was mightily displeased with my behaviour. She came this morning to inform me of such.'

'My aunt is acquainted with your sister? Yes, now I remember, she mentioned it; I had forgotten. But I swore my aunt to secrecy. I thought Aunt Constance of all people would have wanted to keep the whole thing as quiet as possible. This is dreadful.'

'Clarissa, your aunt quite naturally wanted to make me, through the medium of my sister, feel a little of the guilt I sorely deserve for the grievous hurt I inflicted on you. She is angry at me on your behalf, and wants me to suffer. Do not blame her for that.'

'But I told her it was not your fault. I told her I did nothing I didn't want to. I told her to keep it to herself.' Clarissa left the doorway to take a quick turn about the room, her brain in a turmoil. 'And what has any of this to do with you asking me to marry you? You were certainly not of that inclination yesterday, as I know only too well. Tell me, Kit, what has changed your mind today?'

'Yesterday I was not myself. I didn't see things as clearly. I want you more than anything in the world, I see that now. I know you want me.'

'You said yourself, Kit, that passion fades.'

'I was wrong, Clarrie. What exists between us, I've never felt that before, never.'

'Well, but that doesn't mean you'll feel the same thing in a month, a year, ten years hence, does it? And your track record, you know, is not in your favour—two months, I believe, is the longest period you have ever managed to remain faithful.' She felt as though the pain would prevent her speaking, but she was determined to finish things while she retained some dignity. So easy it would be to give in. But so painful it would be to watch Kit spend his life regretting.

'You're different, Clarrie,' Kit said desperately. '*I'm* different now, you've changed me. And I know the truth about you. I'm so sorry I didn't believe you.'

'That's just it, Kit, you didn't believe me yesterday, you wouldn't believe me today, or tomorrow either. It's your sister you believe, your sister who enlightened you, and it is due to your sister that you are here now. In fact, were it not for your sister, you would still be at home, and no thought of marriage would have crossed your mind.'

'No, that's not it—well, not precisely. I would have realised, sooner or later, Clarrie. Surely the only thing that matters is that I have come to my senses now?' Kit could see her retreating inside herself with every word, and felt helpless to stop it. This was all going horribly wrong. 'Clarissa, I want you to marry me. I've never offered that to anyone before, I've never wanted to. But I want to offer it to you now. Say yes, say you will be my wife.'

'You asked me to say yes yesterday, and I did. But I was sadly mistaken, wasn't I? I don't think I'll make the same mistake again, Kit. Thank you for the honour, but I'm afraid I can't accept.' Clarissa blinked back the tears as she spoke, biting her lip to stop the words *yes, yes, yes* come screaming out. He did not love her. He was driven to propose by guilt, coerced by her aunt and his sister. She didn't want him on those terms. In the end, wife or mistress, she'd still wake up every morning with that same feeling of impending gloom, wondering when he would tire of her. She would not let him grow to hate her.

'But I thought you loved me.'

'My aunt again? So I can add pity to your motivations now, as if I did not feel bad enough.' Clarissa looked up at Kit, her eyes full of unshed tears. It was so difficult not to run to him, not to soothe away his pain, no matter how temporarily, with avowals of her eternal devotion. 'What I feel is of no import, Kit. You don't really want to marry me. You are merely trying to do the right thing by me, and there is no need. You say you believe me now you realise that I tell the truth. Well, if that is the case, remember what I said in the letter I left you. You did not take what I was not happy to give. You have no need to feel guilt.'

'Clarrie darling, please. I know I hurt you, forced you, frightened you. And I'm sorry. I'll spend the rest of my life feeling sorry. But I can make amends. Please, just listen to me. You *must* listen.' Kit reached for her hand, but she wrenched free.

'No! No, I won't. I don't want your pity or your apologies, I won't listen any more, for you say nothing that I want to hear. Now please leave me alone, for I can't take any more. I will deal with my aunt, and your sister will no doubt forgive you in time. It was a lovely adventure, Kit, truly it was, and I enjoyed every minute of it. But it is over.'

'I see.' His voice was cool, his mouth a grim line of anger and hurt. Bewildered and confused as he was by her rejection, he could think of nothing else to say, nothing else to persuade her. Letitia must have misunderstood Lady Constance. He had been too quick to make assumptions himself. She didn't really love him. And it was no wonder, after the way he had treated her. He could not blame her. 'Very well, I will relieve you of my company. Please be assured, however, that you can count on me in the future if you ever need anything—anything at all.'

The touch of his lips on her hand was cool. He did not meet her eyes, but turned and left. It was almost too much to bear, knowing that she had caused such hurt. But it would be harder, so much harder, to see him repenting for his behaviour every day of their lives together, bound to her through obligation, tied to her side when all she wanted was for him to be free to be himself.

Clarissa swallowed the protest that rose to her lips as he closed the door, and tottered into a nearby chair, her legs unable to support her. This time it was final. There would be no more Kit. She should be pleased that she had not given in, pleased she had not humiliated herself with an admission of love.

Desperately reviewing his proposal, seeking some trace of emotion, some hint that he felt for her even a tiny part of the love that she felt for him, Clarissa had to admit defeat. He had asked her from a sense of duty, bullied into it by his family, no doubt relieved to have been refused. She could not build a future on such flimsy foundations. The thought was cold comfort. Distressed far beyond tears, Clarissa sat alone in the cold room, unable to move, lost in a world without Kit.

Chapter Thirteen

Robert, Marquis of Alchester, was also contemplating life without Kit Rasenby, but in his case it was a state of affairs much to be desired. In fact, he had been extremely busy making arrangements over the last twenty-four hours to bring about exactly that outcome. Envy of his childhood friend had turned over the years, like milk gone sour, into bitter hatred. Plotting Rasenby's downfall consumed almost every waking moment. Not everything that was afoot was absolutely clear, but Alchester was satisfied none the less that at last he had enough information to put his plan into action. His network of spies and outlay on bribes was finally starting to pay dividends.

The exact nature of Clarissa Warrington's place in Kit Rasenby's life still taxed him. The visits to his house in Grosvenor Square and the sojourn at

Thornwood Manor, on each occasion without an escort, were not the actions of a respectable female. On the other hand, Rasenby was not in the way of asking his mistresses into his homes. There could be no doubt in Alchester's mind that the pair were lovers, but what intrigued him was Kit's intentions towards the wench. She was Constance Denby's niece, not one of his common flirts. Rasenby had called on her today, leaving those showy chestnuts of his to be walked in the cold for more than an hour. It was not like him to be so careless of his horses. Whatever Rasenby's ultimate intentions, Alchester had seen enough to know that Clarissa was important to him, and that would suffice. In Clarissa he now had a tool with which to extract his revenge.

Faith, it was satisfying, the thought that he'd finally be taking something away from his enemy. Something so obviously highly prized. Something whose loss would definitely pain him deeply. Someone whose disappearance would cause him to suffer agonies. Alchester almost rubbed his hands together with glee at the thought, his weak mouth set in a malicious grin. When Rasenby found the chit had been abducted and seduced it would pay in some part for all the humiliations Robert had suffered at his hands over the years. It was perfect. With profound satisfaction, Alchester set about making his final preparations.

Clarissa received his letter later that day. The Marquis of Alchester requested her presence at a meeting to discuss the settlement of her mother's debts. An office in the city was named, and the time of the appointment given for early the following morning. Exhausted and heavy hearted from her interview with Kit, Clarissa looked at the contents dully, convinced that it meant her mother was doomed to an early death in prison. This terrible thought failed to shock—Clarissa was numb—and she merely noted the address and time and thought no more of it. So clouded was her mind that it did not even occur to her to wonder why the letter was not addressed to Lady Maria direct.

She spent a listless day and could only toy with her dinner, scarcely aware of her sister's unusually animated prattling to Mama beside her. The meeting between Lady Constance and Edward had gone well, it seemed, and Lady Constance had intimated that she would not be averse to pulling the strings necessary for Edward's promotion. Amelia was transformed by happiness—although oblivious as ever to the cares of others.

'And I must have a decent trousseau, Mama, for I am like to mix with many of Edward's new clients, to say nothing of having to give my own parties as a married lady. Edward says that I must not expect too much, but with Aunt Constance behind him, I know it won't be long before we are rich. Oh, Mama, I am so happy. Edward says—'

'I am going to bed.' Clarissa rose abruptly from the table, scarcely glancing at the two faces staring at her in consternation.

'Yes, dear, but we were discussing Amelia's trousseau. We would welcome your views.'

'Your time would be better spent discussing how we are to pay the butcher's bill, Mama. And as to Amelia's trousseau—perhaps we should wait to see if Edward will actually propose before buying anything.'

'Clarrie dear, that is most cruel and very unlike you. Are you quite well, dear?'

'Oh, never mind her, Mama, she's just jealous because I have a beau who wants to marry me and hers doesn't. Even though she has tried quite *everything* to persuade him—is that not so, sister?'

As she watched Clarissa turn pale at the remark, even Amelia realised she'd gone too far. 'Clarrie, you mustn't worry, must she, Mama? We don't need Kit Rasenby or any of his sort now, do we?

Perhaps once I'm married I'll be able to help find someone for you.'

'It doesn't matter. I don't care. I'm going to bed.' With a shrug, Clarissa left. Almost nothing touched her. She felt as if she was seeing the world through a thick wall of glass, which naught could penetrate. Nothing mattered, save that she would never see Kit again. Blinking away a single lonely tear, she took to her bed and fell into a deep, haunted sleep.

Awaking the next day, the future seemed bleaker than ever. Listlessly, she got ready for her trip to the city, barely glancing in the mirror as she thrust her hair into a simple knot and donned a cloak over her plain cambric gown, dressing rather for the weather than the vogue. Expecting to return before either Lady Maria or Amelia rose from their bedchambers, Clarissa decided against leaving any word of her whereabouts, for Mama would only get into a state. She left the house for her meeting with the Marquis of Alchester unnoticed even by the maid.

Twenty minutes later the hackney cab deposited her in the busy animated bustle of the streets of the Fleet in the heart of the City. Clarissa stood, bewildered by the multitude of cries from the streetmongers offering up pint pots of ink, bundles of faggots or pecks of oysters for sale. Directly above her she spotted the sign of Coutts Bank, and remembered her father had once mentioned doing business there. She wondered if they served Kit, and reminded herself that it was none of her business who he banked with. All these people going about their business, making money, drawing up contracts, with hardly a glance at her. To the world, it's as if I neither exist nor matter, she thought with unaccustomed bitterness. For one mad moment Clarissa felt an overwhelming urge to scream aloud, *Does no one know or care that my heart is torn asunder!* Repressing the thought, however, she instead stepped into the address she had been given, to be shown into a dingy office by a clerk.

As she sat opposite a desk, alone in the stuffy room, Clarissa grew ill at ease, realising for the first time that the requested interview was rather unorthodox. Why had the letter been addressed to herself and not Mama? Why was the Marquis of Alchester meeting her here, in this run-down office? And what could they have to discuss when the debt was not yet due? A slight tremor of fear ran through her. Something was amiss here. No one knew where she was. She should leave now and go home. But even as she rose to go the door opened and a man appeared, closing it firmly behind him as he entered.

He was slight of build, seeming neither young nor old. His face showed signs of dissipation, his eyes hooded, the lids pulled downwards by an intricate network of lines. His nose was long and thin and his gaze darted this way and that even though there was no one else in the room. His skin was pale, the colour of one who does not often see the sun. His movements were nervous and fidgety. The Marquis of Alchester reminded Clarissa of nothing so much as a small rodent.

But he was impeccably dressed and smiling, a tight smile, thinning his already narrow lips into a straight line. 'Miss Warrington? Robert, Marquis of Alchester, your servant, madam.'

The touch of his hand was cold as a corpse, his lips barely grazed her glove. Clarissa shivered, her fear taking shape as he bent over her. Whatever this man's intentions, they were not noble. She must escape.

'I am afraid there has been a mistake, my lord. I should not have come. Forgive me for wasting your time, but my mother is waiting for me outside. I came only to inform you to write to me with your terms that I may consider them on my mother's behalf. Now, I must bid you good day.' Clarissa gave a small bow and moved towards the door.

'I'm afraid I must ask you to stay for a moment, Miss Warrington. I'm sure your mama can spare you.'

'I'm afraid not, my lord. We have a morning call to make, we are expected, and I am late already.' Her voice trembled, but she stood her ground.

'Sit down, Clarissa. You are not going anywhere. You may spare me your pathetic attempts at lies. Your mama is not waiting for you outside. You are quite alone. You don't think your arrival went unnoticed, do you?'

His voice was cold, like a breath from a cadaver. Fear clutched her insides. She sat down, silent, unable to trust her voice, cursing her stupidity for not having informed anyone of her intentions.

'Your mama owes me quite a little sum, doesn't she? And I doubt she has the means to pay it, am I right?' Robert Alchester looked at the woman before him. She was terrified, he had no doubt about that, though determined not to show it. He liked a bit of spirit in a woman—that augured well for later. She was not beautiful in the common way, but there was something about her, a challenging look, a tilt to her face, and a curvaceous body despite her slenderness—yes, he could see why Kit Rasenby found her to his liking.

Clarissa cleared her throat to speak. Her voice

was quiet, but resolute, despite the shaking that was threatening to prevent her from moving. 'The debt is not due for some time. There is nothing to discuss at present. I must leave now.'

'You are going nowhere, my dear. At least, not home in any event.'

'What do you mean?' Clarissa got quickly to her feet and tried to push past the Marquis, but he caught her arm in a firm grip, his bony fingers showing surprising strength. She stood without struggling, repulsed by his proximity, her breath coming in shallow, sharp gasps. 'Unhand me at once, sir!'

Robert Alchester merely laughed, a soft, low, vicious growl that made her skin prickle. 'Very good, but you will learn to be more—accommodating—unless you wish to be harmed. I have no wish to hurt you Clarissa, but I will do so if I need to.'

His face was close to hers, those cold, icy eyes watching her like a hawk, his mouth a thin sneering line. She had no difficulty in believing him. He looked like the type to inflict pain for pleasure, would no doubt enjoy seeing her suffer. The mixture of distaste and disgust showed clearly on her expressive face.

'Yes, I can see you believe me. Now sit down and I'll explain all.'

Clarissa thought it prudent to obey and sat back down without a word.

'Directly, we will leave this building. My carriage is waiting, you will accompany me into it without a struggle. If you do struggle, I have the means to overpower you—thus.' He held up a small brown vial. 'You will not like to be unconscious, will you? No, I thought not. We are going on a short journey to one of my estates—you will be familiar with the terrain, for you have already visited my neighbour, Lord Rasenby, at Thornwood Manor.'

'How do you know that?'

'There's little I don't know, Clarissa. I know you've been to France with him, and I know you are lovers.'

Her gasp of surprise and her blush confirmed this. 'This doesn't make sense. Wait a minute.' Suddenly she remembered. 'It was you, wasn't it? You who informed the customs men that night. But I still don't understand. What have my mother's debts to do with all this?'

'A lucky chance only, my dear. I took them in lieu of payment from a less fortunate opponent at hazard. I confess, at the time I would much rather have had the money. But when I realised what they were I decided that after all fate was smiling on me. For they brought you to me. And when Lord Rasenby knows I have you, I will have my satisfaction at last.'

'So, you have some sort of grudge against Kit—Lord Rasenby—is that it? But that still doesn't make sense. I am nothing to him, cannot influence him, you can achieve nothing by kidnapping me.'

'You underestimate your charms, Clarissa. I am sure that Kit Rasenby will be extremely upset to find you have decided to keep company with me, rather than him—for that is what I shall tell him, you know. It will give me immense satisfaction, knowing I have taken something he treasures. To say nothing of the pleasure that your company will afford me too, of course.'

The lascivious smile that accompanied this remark left Clarissa in no doubt about his ultimate intentions. She had to act quickly if she was to save herself—but how? Of a certain to be unconscious would be fatal, she could not risk it. Her best chance would be during the journey, for they must change horses at some point. He would not ravish her in a coach, surely? 'Very well, I'll come with you, my lord. But I warn you I am expected at home, and will be looked for soon, if I do not return.'

'Yes? Now, why do I not believe you? It is of no matter—we will be gone from here and no one knows our direction. If you are ready, madam, we will leave.'

Her knees were shaking so much she could barely stand, but Clarissa brushed Alchester's arm away angrily. 'I can walk, my lord, I have no need of your support.'

Slowly, unable to quite believe what was happening, Clarissa descended the steps from the building and climbed into the waiting coach. The Marquis of Alchester followed, close enough to ensure she could not make a run for safety, pausing only to hand a sealed note to the small boy waiting with the postillion. Once inside the coach however, he took the seat opposite, making no attempt to touch her. Deciding to feign sleep, Clarissa closed her eyes and focused all her thoughts and energy on escape.

Kit woke late. He had fallen asleep as dawn broke, having spent most of the night going over and over that final interview with Clarissa in his mind. It had all gone so horribly wrong, nothing he said had come out right. He could not believe she didn't care. Could not believe how miserable he felt at the thought of a future without her. Could not see the attraction of a world without Clarissa by his side. The image of her as he left her house yesterday haunted him—her beautiful little face set like stone, her eyes brimming with unshed tears, her luscious mouth held in a stern line, the words she was biting back lost to him for ever.

He had done this to her. The only person in the world whom he loved beyond words. He had been so overwrought yesterday he hadn't even told her so. But she knew, she must know, it had been implicit in all he said. Still, the actual words had not been spoken. He would go back today to try again, do it properly this time. And if she didn't listen today, then tomorrow. And the day after that. And every after that, if it took a lifetime to win her back. With this invigorating thought, Kit got out of bed.

He was breaking his fast when his butler came in, looking apologetic. 'Forgive the intrusion my lord, but there is a visitor demanding to see you urgently. A Lady Maria Warrington.'

Assuming that she had come to berate him again, Kit rose from the table wearily. 'Faith, Hodges, I am weary of these women and their early morning tirades. Can you not be more effective at keeping them at bay, man?'

Kit read the reproachful look on Hodges's face only too well. 'Oh, very well, I take your point. It would take a platoon of the dragoon guards to dissuade the unholy triumvirate of my sister, Miss Warrington or her mother from their stated course. You had better show her in, then.'

Lady Maria entered the room in a breathless state, her hat askew, her scarf, which had come loose, trailing on the floor, threatening to trip her over. 'Where is she, my lord? I demand to know, what have you done with my daughter.'

Firmly closing the door on his fascinated butler, Kit hastened over to Lady Maria. His experience of her was limited, but it was suffice to know that a fainting fit was imminent.

'Won't you sit down, madam, and take a moment to calm yourself.' A firm hand on her back guided her to a chair, into which she tottered gratefully.

Looking up at Kit, her mouth trembling, Lady Maria heaved a great sob and waved an accusing finger in his direction. 'Where is she? Where is my Clarissa? Oh, say you have not murdered her, you assassin! My poor dear, she does not deserve such a fate as this.'

Realising that there was actually something more drastically amiss with Lady Maria than a need to vent her spleen, Kit bit firmly down on his temper. 'Madam, I can see that you are distressed, but there is no need for histrionics. I haven't seen

Clarissa since yesterday. Do you mean to tell me she has gone missing?'

'Missing! Likely dead of a broken heart and hidden in your attics, if nothing else. You blackguard! I know you have her here. Let me see her. Oh, was ever a poor widow more badly treated. First it is the butcher, demanding settlement before I have even had my chocolate. Then it is Amelia, demanding money for a trousseau when she has not yet received a proposal, although I am sure that Edward *will* propose, for he is not the type to be leading innocent girls astray—unlike *some* people, my Lord Rasenby.' A black look accompanied this remark. 'And now my darling, my sensible, my poor ruined Clarissa has disappeared, and you stand there denying responsibility when it is all your fault, and what am I to tell Lady Constance, when I promised I would look after her?' Breaking into sobs, Lady Maria leaned back into the chair and for some minutes cried heartily, oblivious of Kit's attempts to revive her.

'Madam, I need to understand your meaning fully. I beg of you, tell me what is wrong that I may help. Where is Clarissa?' Kit was becoming increasingly angry, concerned and frustrated in equal measures.

'You cannot fool me. I know she's here. I've come

to fetch her. My poor lamb, strayed from the fold under such a vile influence as you. You monster!'

'For God's sake, will you be calm and tell me what is going on.' Looking up to see his butler had entered the room, Kit let go of Lady Maria's hands, which he had been chafing. 'Hodges, fetch some brandy. This lady is not well.'

'Yes, my lord. This note came for you just now, my lord. I thought it may be important.'

'Yes, thank you. Now go and get me some help before this—this lady becomes hysterical.' Abandoning Lady Maria to her tears, Kit snatched the note from the salver. He broke the seal and glanced at the contents, then sat down abruptly. Robert, Marquis of Alchester, sent his compliments. He felt it only fair that Kit should be informed, in the light of *his previous relationship*, that Clarissa Warrington had agreed to submit to Robert's *protection*. Miss Warrington wished Kit to understand that he should withdraw *forthwith* from any attempt at future contact with her *in the light of her new circumstances*. The Marquis and Miss Warrington were leaving town for a short period away from the distractions of society in order to *enjoy the fruits of their liaison.*

Kit looked at the note, completely dumbfounded. The words leapt out from the page, taunting him. His first coherent thought was that he had not known Clarissa and Robert Alchester to be acquainted. His next was closer to the truth, and he felt a cold fear clutch at him as he took in the import of what had been written. Alchester was using Clarissa in revenge against him. She would not have gone willingly. Kit's emotions were everything that the Marquis had hoped for when he had so gleefully penned the note a few hours previously.

Clarissa was in danger. And he didn't know where she was. And she was in danger only because of him. My God, could he do any more damage if he tried? He was finally paying for his years of raking, that was for sure—and paying a price beyond anything he had thought possible. Kit clutched at his hair and groaned, tempted for an instant to join with Lady Maria in hysterics.

The despair was short-lived. He would find his Clarissa, he would rescue her—he had to. The situation could not possibly be as hopeless as it appeared. He would not allow it to be.

A racking sob reminded Kit of Lady Maria's presence. Grabbing the tray of brandy that Hodges proffered and thrusting his butler from the room again, he decided that extreme measures were needed. Bracing himself, he administered a ringing slap to Lady Maria's face.

The effect was immediate. She stopped crying and gasped, staring up at him in astonishment. Forestalling any speech, he held a glass of brandy to her mouth and forced her to take two large gulps.

'Before you accuse me of either assault or making you drunk, madam, listen closely,' Kit said, as Lady Maria gasped, fish-like, in her chair. 'This letter is from the Marquis of Alchester. He has kidnapped Clarissa. Can you think of any reason why she would have gone to meet him, for I cannot understand it? Were they acquainted in any way?'

Subdued by the harsh treatment and stirred by the genuine concern in Kit's voice, Lady Maria sat up. 'Alchester, you say? Alchester? No, she has never mentioned that name before. Unless—no, it's not possible. But stay, let me think. Alchester? Yet the name is familiar. Why—oh, I have it. Oh my goodness. But surely… No, no, he would not. But then he might—and of course, Clarissa would—'

'For the love of God, madam,' Kit said through gritted teeth, 'speak slowly and clearly, I have no wish to strike you again. What is the connection between them?'

'Well, there is no need to be so harsh, my lord.'

'Madam, your daughter has been kidnapped. Do you not wish to find her?'

'Well, of course I do, my lord. I am just as keen to find her this time as I was the last time she was kidnapped. By yourself, in case you need reminding.'

'I can't waste time on discussion, madam, Clarrie is in danger. Alchester is not a man to be trifled with. I need to know why she was persuaded to meet him.'

'Oh dear, what have I done? If it is indeed the same Alchester, I owe him a terrible amount of money. I borrowed some money, and then the nice man I borrowed it from passed on the debt to another man at the hazard table. And he wanted to be paid much sooner. And I thought I should have to go to prison. Except Clarissa said not to worry because she would take care of it. And since she always *does* take care of things, I didn't worry. Except that Constance—Clarissa's aunt, you know—Constance told me only yesterday that the man who is dunning me is the Marquis of Alchester. So perhaps she also told Clarissa, and Clarissa has gone to meet him because of me. And, oh dear, it is all my fault—what am I to do?'

Kit struggled to make sense of Lady Maria's confession before dismissing it as irrelevant. 'You should go home madam, and await word from me.

I think I know where he might have taken her. Don't worry.'

'Don't worry? What do you intend to do?'

'I am going to fetch her back and I am going to marry her, madam. But I cannot stay to discuss this with you. Every moment is precious.' As he left the room, calling to Hodges to summon his groom, Kit heard Lady Maria give way again to tears. He made a mental note to inform Clarissa that he very much regretted her mama could not form part of their future household. He would buy her a house of her own. In the country. As far away from him as possible.

Rapping out a stream of orders, Kit pulled on his hat and picked up his riding crop. He had no doubt as to Alchester's destination, his estate next to Thornwood Manor being the only one within a day's journey of London, but he had no idea how much of a head start they had. Knowing the state of Alchester's finances, it was unlikely that they would make the journey with more than two horses, however, so Kit reckoned he had a good chance of catching them if he went on horseback. And knowing his Clarissa, he had no doubt she would do everything in her power to delay the Marquis in the hope of rescue. He would not allow himself to consider the possibility that he might be too late.

* * *

Urging his horse into a gallop as soon as they were free from the traffic of the town, Kit reviewed Lady Maria's revelations. That she had been so foolish as to get into debt beyond her means did not surprise him, for Clarissa's mama was as stupid a woman as he had yet come across. She had uttered but one thing of interest, that she thought her daughter likely to die of a broken heart. Clarissa *did* love him. *Of course she loved him.*

How very foolishly he had behaved yesterday, Kit realised. He hadn't once said the only important thing—that he loved her. He had attempted explanations when he should have swept her into his arms and kissed her. He had assumed Clarissa knew how he felt, had been so devastated at her refusal as to leave without telling her. Promising himself he would tell her every day for the rest of their lives together if only he could reach her in time, Kit spurred his horse on, their fast pace eating up the miles from the town and south into the open countryside in record time.

Fortunately for him, Alchester was in no hurry. As Kit had correctly deduced, his coach was driven by a team of just two horses. Inside, Clarissa continued to pretend sleep as she racked her brains for a plan to escape. She had come up with no idea other than to make a break from her abductor at the first posting inn, and had been occupying her mind this past half-hour in wondering how long it would be before Mama would miss her, and what, if anything, she would do when she did. They had been on the road about two hours when the blast of horns warned her that they were pulling up for a change.

Clarissa yawned, as if just awakened. Alchester watched from the seat opposite, a lazy smile on his cold face.

'Where are we, my lord?'

'We are stopped for a change of horses. You may descend, madam, if you wish, and partake of some refreshment. But don't, I beg of you, try to escape. The landlord is known to me, and will ensure that we are private with no interference. Any noise or fuss will lead only to embarrassment.'

'I'll be discovered eventually, my lord. You had as well stop now, before it is too late. Let me return home and I will say no more of this outrage.'

His soft laugh made her shiver. 'You have a deal of courage my dear; it will be a positive pleasure to tame you. I pay you the compliment, even, that I would enjoy it without the spice of knowing I am taking Rasenby's property.'

They descended from the coach. Alchester urged Clarissa towards the ramshackle inn and directly into a parlour at the back. The ostlers, busy with the change of horses, had their backs turned—deliberately, Clarissa could not but think—and there was no sign of anyone else. Coffee and brandy awaited them in the parlour.

Clarissa took her time, stripping off her gloves, sitting down, pouring herself some coffee with an almost-steady hand. 'I repeat my lord, you have mistaken your mark. I am nothing to Lord Rasenby, he cares naught for my fate. Whatever your plan is, to rouse him by kidnapping me is bound to fail.'

Alchester kissed the tips of his fingers and bowed. 'Bravo my dear. Really, with every minute of your delightful company you make me happier to have found you. But I know you are lying, you see. You have set far too many precedents with Rasenby for me to believe you mean nothing to him. Any fool can see that. And I am not, I assure you, a fool.'

'What do you mean?'

'Dining alone with you in Grosvenor Square. Taking you to Thornwood Park. The trip on the *Sea Wolf*, of course. Your visit to him the other day. His visit to your home yesterday.'

Alchester smiled contentedly at Clarissa's shocked expression. 'Yes, you have been watched every step of the way. Maybe now you will take me seriously. You see now why I cannot believe, my dear Clarissa, that the gentleman could spend so much time with you and have no feelings. You make too little of yourself. But this discussion is become tedious. Let us turn our minds to more pleasant topics.'

'I have no wish for conversation, sir. You've kidnapped me, and my mother will be searching for me. Please, I beseech you, let me go. Let me go at once.'

She was frightened. This couldn't be happening. Forcing herself to calm down, thinking only to delay the moment when they had to go back into the coach, Clarissa tried a different tack. 'Why do you hate Kit—Lord Rasenby so, my lord? How can he have so wronged you so as to drive you to such desperate acts?'

Alchester's voice was bitter, the venom in his words clear. 'You wouldn't understand. I've known him all my life. All my life he's taken everything I've ever wanted, been everything I've ever wanted to be. He's bested me at everything, at every turn. But this time I'm victorious. This time I've won.'

'Not necessarily, Robert.' Kit stood in the doorway,

mud splattered, his hair in disarray, his riding crop clutched in one hand and a grim look of controlled fury darkening his handsome countenance.

'Kit!'

'Rasenby!' Before she could move, Alchester had Clarissa in a firm grasp, one hand clasped around her waist, the other at her throat. 'She's mine, Rasenby. You are too late.'

'No, Kit, no. It's not true.'

But Clarissa's words fell on deaf ears. With a snarl of rage, Kit crossed the room. In one fluid movement he wrenched Alchester's hands from Clarissa, pushed her to the side, and landed a punch so hard on Alchester's jaw that he staggered back against the settle by the fire, knocking over a set of irons. It was a blow of which even the champion, Gentleman Jackson, would have been proud.

Recovering quickly, Alchester pushed himself upright, at the same time grabbing a poker with his left hand. As Kit moved in to land another blow, Alchester raised the poker. Clarissa screamed and ran at him, pushing with all her might. Her attack deflected his aim. The poker missed Kit's head, but hit him a glancing blow on the shoulder, causing him to fall back, the punch he was aiming finding only air.

The poker clattered to the floor. Alchester searched for it with one hand, keeping an eye on his opponent. He knew that he was no match for Kit without a weapon. As his fingers felt the edge of the fire iron, Kit recovered his balance and moved forward, kicking it out of Alchester's reach. This time Kit's punch hit Alchester's nose, drawing a spurt of blood. Giving him no time to hit back, Kit planted a second punch square on Alchester's jaw. He went down heavily, almost without a sound, and lay on the wooden floor with his eyes closed.

'Oh God, you've killed him.' Clarissa went to kneel at Alchester's side, grasping his wrist to feel for a pulse.

'Don't be ridiculous, Clarrie, you can no more die of a punch to the jaw than you can of a scratch on the arm, more's the pity. Let him be and come here. Are you safe?'

She looked up, taken aback at the raw edge in his voice, and saw the worry reflected in his strained face. Kit's dark blue eyes searched her countenance anxiously, his mouth a grim line. He was concerned for her. A flicker of hope sprang to life in the darkness of Clarrie's heart. What if Alchester was right? What if she really did mean more to Kit than she realised?

But she had been here too many times before. 'I'm fine. I promise you I took no harm from him, save fright and embarrassment at my own stupidity for falling into such a simple trap. Give me a hand-kerchief, Kit, I must staunch some of this blood.'

'He can look after himself. Come here, Clarrie.' Kit leaned down to grasp her hand, and pulled her to her feet. 'I was worried. Really worried. You wouldn't believe just how worried, you stupid girl. You really must break this habit you have of allowing yourself to be abducted.'

'Were you, Kit, really worried?' Clarissa smiled wanly, looking up into his eyes. She blinked at the blaze of emotion she saw in their dark depths. 'Kit?'

'Clarrie. Clarrie, I…'

Alchester groaned, startling them both, and tried to sit up. Reluctantly, Kit pulled back from Clarissa's gaze, turning to view his adversary. 'Get up,' he said grimly. 'Get to your feet and get out of my sight. You are lucky to escape so lightly. Take heed, Alchester, you get just this one chance. If I ever hear of anything, any rumours, any word at all, of your doings today, or if you breathe one word of scandal concerning Miss Warrington, I will ruin you, I swear. I have the means, I know you're in debt up to your scrawny neck. So get out, and crawl back into whatever hole you came from.'

Alchester stood, clutching Kit's bloodied handkerchief to his face, his eyes burning with hatred and impotent rage at his ignoble defeat. Reluctantly, he realised he had no choice but to obey. A brief bow to Clarissa and he left the room, cursing under his breath. Not only had his plan failed, he had been revealed in the cold light of day as Kit's enemy. He knew Rasenby too well to argue. He had no wish to be ruined or ostracised.

Kit shut the door firmly behind him. 'Now, Clarissa fair, we can be sure of no further interruptions.'

'Kit, take me home. Mama will be worried.'

A brief smile crossed his face at that. 'You have no idea how worried. She accused me first of murder, then of hiding your body in my attics.'

'Oh, please tell me she did not. I will die of embarrassment.'

'She called me a blackguard too.'

A small gurgle of laughter escaped from Clarissa. 'Oh, no, surely not.'

'I assure you. And that was on top of vile seducer from yesterday. Oh yes, and monster. I don't think I stand in very good stead with your mama, although even she could not find a way to blame me when she realised you must have been tricked into meeting Alchester in order to discuss her debts. What can you have been thinking of, you foolish child, it's not like you to be so easily taken in?'

'I know, I realised it was a trick, but it was too late. I don't suppose Alchester will be dunning Mama now, after today. It doesn't matter though, they are gaming debts and must be paid somehow.'

'As your husband, it will be my responsibility to sort that out.'

'Kit, don't let us go through all that again. You don't want to marry me. And I don't want you to hate me.'

'So that's it, my absurd, darling Clarrie. I wondered what prevented you from saying yes when I had been assured, first by your Aunt Constance and then by your dear mama, that you were dying of love for me.'

'Oh!' Clarissa flushed. 'I am *so sorry*. What you must think of us all. Please believe me, I told them again and again that it wasn't your fault, but they wouldn't listen.'

'I know you did. And I was so stupid I didn't listen to you either. But when I did finally come to my senses, I realised the truth. You would only have behaved the way you did, my darling love, for one reason. But it was the one thing that I didn't think possible. Forgive me.'

'No, there's *nothing* to forgive. We must go back. I must go home. And you must forget about me.'

'But don't you see, I can never forget about you. You silly girl, I'm not proposing to you because I feel guilty or because I'm worried what my sister might think. I don't even care much about what your precious Aunt Constance thinks. I'm proposing for very, very selfish reasons. I need you. There will never be a time when I wake up feeling anything other than glad that you're by my side. In my bed. In my head. And in my heart. Darling, dearest, Clarrie, how could I ever hate you when I'm so in love with you I can't imagine life without you. I got it all wrong yesterday, said all the wrong things, didn't say the most important thing. But I won't ever get it wrong again with you by my side to keep me right. I love you, Clarrie. Please, Clarissa, don't turn me down again.'

Giving her no time to respond at all with words, Kit pulled Clarrie towards him and kissed her ruthlessly, devouring her mouth like a man drowning, clinging to the rock of their love like a man saved. Crushing her to him, and pushing her bonnet back, he looked into her beloved green eyes, eyes so honest they could never lie, eyes that told him everything he needed to know. 'I love you. I love you.

Clarrie, say yes. Say yes now, or I swear I'll wear you down with the asking.'

The tiny flame of hope in her heart ignited, but still her mind urged caution. She wanted to believe him. *She so wanted to believe him.* But how could she be certain?

It was as if he read her mind. 'You're wondering if this is just some sort of temporary infatuation, aren't you? You're thinking I'll grow bored with you, regret this one day, aren't you, Clarrie?'

She could manage only a nod.

Kit looked down at her pale face, the strain of the past few days showing in the dark lines under her beautiful green eyes, eyes that were looking at him with hope, with doubt, seeking reassurance. He wanted to kiss it all away, to hold her, make love to her.

But she deserved an answer. Their whole lives depended upon this moment. 'If I had a magic wand, I'd cast a spell and you'd never doubt again. But in truth, my own darling Clarissa, I don't know what it is that makes me so sure. I can't put into words, not properly, what it is that's so different about how I feel for you. I just know that it is. In the same way as I just know, with deep and unshakeable certainty, that I need you by my side to make me complete.'

Pulling her closer, Kit wound a finger round one of her curls, then tucked it behind her ear. Giving in to the temptation of those soft lips, that beloved face, he kissed her softly, tenderly, pouring all his love, channelling everything into the kiss, feeling her respond to him in the same way. Feeling not just passion, but love, true love, enveloping them in its warm cloak.

Slightly breathless, he pulled back. 'I can't explain it, but I can feel it, and I know you feel it too. I know I love you because I just do. I know I'll never leave you because I know I'll never want anyone else. You're the other part of me, what I've been looking for all my life, and you make me whole when I didn't even know I was missing something. But I've found you now, my darling, and I won't—I can't—let you go again.'

'Oh, Kit, I've never heard anything so lovely.' Once more, Clarissa dissolved into tears, but this time they were of joy, for she believed him. He was right, and she felt it herself after all, this illogical certainty, this completeness, this simple and over-whelming love. 'Kiss me, Kit, for I love you so much.' Without waiting, she reached up and pulled him to her. This time their passion held no restraint. On the hard floor in front of the fire in a remote inn, Kit and Clarrie consummated their love.

* * *

Later, dishevelled, tired and glowing, they righted their clothing. Looking in the mirror at her face, Clarrie laughed. 'I'm afraid you've left your mark all too clearly on me, Kit. The landlady will have no doubt what we've been up to.'

Looking at her heavy lids and flushed cheeks, Kit felt a familiar stirring. He smiled lazily, his own satisfaction reflected as clearly in his disordered hair, a necktie past recovery, the sated curl to his sculpted mouth. 'I'll gladly have you branded as my property, my beautiful Clarrie, for I can't resist you. With a ring, I think, and quickly. A special licence. Tomorrow, the next day at the latest. We can shop for your trousseau later—I don't intend for you to have much need of clothes for a while.'

'Just so that we're absolutely clear this time, Kit.' Clarissa was laughing up at him, unable to believe it. 'What *exactly* am I saying yes to?'

'Just so that we're absolutely clear...' the answering smile in his eyes took her breath away '...you're saying yes to a lifetime of me, me and no one else but me. You're saying yes to being loved more than anyone has been loved before. You're saying yes to me beside you always. I'll be the first thing you see every day, and the last thing you see every night. You're saying yes to a passion that will light up the sky. To sharing every part of my life. To being my better half. And on top of all that, you're saying yes to being my wife.'

'Yes. Oh, Kit, yes.' There was nothing more that needed to be said and nothing else that mattered. Their kiss said it all, a kiss that had a new tenderness, a breathtaking prelude to a lifetime of passion and fulfilment, a promise that would never be broken.

HISTORICAL

LARGE PRINT

THE RAKE'S WICKED PROPOSAL

Carole Mortimer

Lucian St Claire, one of the wickedest rakes around,
needs an heir – so it's time to choose a wife! Opinionated
Grace Hetherington is definitely not the wife he wants.
Yet there's something irresistible about her – and, when
they're caught in a rather compromising situation, he has
no choice but to make her his convenient bride!

THE TRANSFORMATION OF MISS ASHWORTH

Anne Ashley

Tomboy Bethany Ashworth's innocent dreams were
destroyed by Philip Stavely's betrothal to her cousin.
Years later, Bethany has grown into a beautiful woman,
tragedy has left Philip knowing exactly what he wants –
he's now determined to marry the woman he should
have swept up the aisle six years ago!

MISTRESS BELOW DECK

Helen Dickson

Wilful Rowena Golding needs Tobias Searle's ship to chase
her kidnapped sister, but the boarding price he's asking is
one night in his bed! Rowena is determinedly immune to
Tobias' lethal charm and so, dressed as a cabin boy, she's
prepared for the dangers of the high seas…but is she
prepared for the notorious Tobias Searle?

MILLS & BOON®
Pure reading pleasure™

HIST120

APL	CP	CCS	
Cen		Ear	
Mob		Cou	
ALL		Jub	
WH		CHE	
Ald		Bel	
Fin		Fol	
Can		STO	
Til		HCL	